Date Due

MAR 31 '67		
JUN 30 '67		
NO 27 '07		
DE 20 68		
JY 20 73		
NY		
FE 17 03		
DE 1 03		
NO 16 05		

The Heat of the Sun

STORIES AND TALES

By Sean O'Faolain

Novels
A NEST OF SIMPLE FOLK
BIRD ALONE
COME BACK TO ERIN

Short Stories
MIDSUMMER NIGHT MADNESS
A PURSE OF COPPERS
THE MAN WHO INVENTED SIN
THE FINEST STORIES OF SEAN O'FAOLAIN
I REMEMBER! I REMEMBER!
THE HEAT OF THE SUN

Biography
CONSTANCE MARKIEVICZ
KING OF THE BEGGARS
THE GREAT O'NEILL
NEWMAN'S WAY

Autobiography
VIVE MOI!

Travel
AN IRISH JOURNEY
A SUMMER IN ITALY
AN AUTUMN IN ITALY

Criticism
THE SHORT STORY
THE VANISHING HERO

Play
SHE HAD TO DO SOMETHING

Translations
THE SILVER BRANCH

Miscellaneous
THE IRISH

The Heat of the Sun

STORIES AND TALES

by Sean O'Faolain

An Atlantic Monthly Press Book

LITTLE, BROWN AND COMPANY · BOSTON · TORONTO

The author wishes to thank the following for permission to reprint stories which first appeared in their pages: The *Atlantic, Ladies Home Journal, McCall's, Redbook, Saturday Evening Post, The Critic.*

"Passion" is from *The Man Who Invented Sin* by Sean O'Faolain; Copyright 1948 by The Devin-Adair Co., New York, N. Y.

ATLANTIC—LITTLE, BROWN BOOKS
ARE PUBLISHED BY
LITTLE, BROWN AND COMPANY
IN ASSOCIATION WITH
THE ATLANTIC MONTHLY PRESS

*Published simultaneously in Canada
by Little, Brown & Company (Canada) Limited*

PRINTED IN THE UNITED STATES OF AMERICA

Author's Note

I have included one story, "Passion," from a previously published book, because it fits the general theme, was not published in the collected volume of my stories, and I am rather fond of it.

These Tales

To these offerings I have given the subtitle *Stories and Tales* to point a distinction that has been in my mind when writing them, and which I think may be worth explaining.

As I see it a Short Story, if it is a good story, is like a child's kite, a small wonder, a brief, bright moment. It has its limitations; there are things it can do and cannot do but, if it is good, it moves in the same element as the largest work of art — up there, airborne. The main thing a writer of a short story wants to do is to get it off the ground as quickly as possible, hold it up there, taut and tense, playing it like a fish. The reader will never know how much time was spent on getting it airborne, how often it flopped, stumbled and dragged along the ground in all those first efforts, those discarded first drafts, those false beginnings that were cut out once it was up — so much dismissed, forgotten but necessary labor. The limits of the Short Story are apparent. It may not wander far; it has to keep close to its base point, within the bounds of place, time and character; it will only carry a few characters, three at least, at best not more than three; there is not time, or space, for elaborate characterization — we are flying a kite, not a passenger balloon or an airplane; and there is often no plot, nothing much more than a situation, and only just enough of that to release a moment or two of drama, enough to let the willful kite swirl, change color, catching the winds of mood. A short story is concentrated stuff. It is called a short story because it is short. An essentialist art. Maupassant and Chekhov invented it between them.

A Tale is quite different. Like a small plane it is much more free, carries a bit more cargo, roves farther, has time and space for more complex characterization, more changes of mood, more incidents and scenes, even more plot. Because it is more relaxed the reader may find the Tale easier reading, and he may even take more pleasure in it, but it is likely to give the writer-craftsman rather less pleasure, since what he always most enjoys is the fascination of what is most difficult. It has its own problems, however, for the writer, whose toughest task is to orchestrate his Tale into a single, satisfying shape of flight. For me, the greatest master of the Tale was Prosper Mérimée, even though he did not bother much about shape or form, not because he lacked the skill but because he nourished a certain, coy horror of seeming too much of an artist. Hemingway was something of an American-style Mérimée, though never quite so tough, and not good with women. Compare any of his women with the Carmen of Mérimée.

The possibilities of both the Short Story and the Tale become evident when we compare them with that plane carrier, the Novel, which can carry as heavy a load as the writer wishes, for as long and over as many seas. Yet the Novel, too, justifies itself only in the same moments of packed crisis as the Story and the Tale. These are the key chapters of its long voyage, when its planes go swoosh into the air. After they have returned to roost, the slow, majestic pace begins again — until the next moment of dramatic crisis. It is such moments that the writer of the Short Story isolates.

I set out to write Tales in "A Sweet Colleen," "£1000 for Rosebud," and "In the Bosom of the Country." I was writing Short Stories when I wrote "The Heat of the Sun" and "Charlie's Greek." Whichever is which, and the reader will easily distinguish, all I hope is that, now and again, the Story or the Tale "levitates a little," like that endearing character the Flying Monk in Norman Douglas's *Old Calabria.* Any story, tale or novel that does not levitate a little is, as far as I am concerned, a grounded albatross. A prince of the air, all he can do on the earth is waddle, because of his wings.

Contents

The Heat of the Sun

STORIES AND TALES

In the Bosom of the Country

THEN, suddenly, after all their years of love, ten of them, five a-growing and five a-dying, death came. They were lying side by side in the big, bridal bed under its looped-up canopy of pink silk on whose slope the sunset gently laid the twig pattern of the elms in her drive. She had tossed aside her fair hair so that it lay in a heavy tangle on her left shoulder, and was pensively watching him brushing up his graying, military moustaches with the knuckle of his forefinger. She started to scratch his shoulder with her nails, gently at first, then a little more wickedly until he turned to look at her. The sunset revealed the dark roots at the parting of her hair and caught a wrinkle at the corner of her eye. Recognizing a familiar mood he smiled nervously at her curl-at-the-corner smile, slightly mocking, shy, minxish, naughty. A prelude to another pretty quarrel? He soon stopped smiling; this time there was substance to her fret.

"Well, my dashing Major? Are you betraying me with one of your great galumphing horsey wenches from the Hunt? Account for yourself. Two months all but a week? And before that how long was it? Keene by name but not so keen by nature? Is this your idea of devotion? Are you getting tired of me?"

"Anna!" he protested.

He wanted to glance at his watch but his left arm still lay

under her waist. He glanced at the ruddy sun behind the elm boles. Half-past four? With a sudden blare the telephone rang. "Botheration!" she snapped, and reached out her long, bare arm for the receiver. He noticed the little purse of skin hanging from her elbow. Poor dear! He really did love her, but, dammit, they weren't either of them as young as they . . . She sat straight up, crying out, "No! Oh, no!" He heard a few more squawkings from the receiver and her "I'll be right over!" She hung up and leaped out of bed, scrambling all over the floor for her clothes.

"It's the hospital. Arty's dead. I've lost my poor husband."

Something there had kept bothering him for days, something out of tune that alerted him, something that did not seem right. It was not the time and the place. Although, dammit, if, instead of the telephone ringing to say that Arty had gone, Arty had opened the door and peeped in he could not have chosen a more awkward moment to impose himself. Nor could it have been guilt — not after all these years. It could not have been anything they said — so little had been said in their haste to dress. It could only be something tiny, like an eye glancing over a bare shoulder or some single word or gesture that was not meant to mean anything but did. Not that he ever got down to thinking it out properly. "Am I," he wondered, "shying off it for fear of finding out?"

A modest man, he knew his worth. She was not the only person who joked about his name. He did it himself. It was inevitable — F. L. Keene. In the army they used to call him old Festina Lente and kept him to the rank of Major. A good old dobbin. Sure and steady. But, at least, he tried to be honest, and he had flashes, dammit! Once, long ago, Anna had asked him how many women he had loved, and he had truly replied, "Only you." "You seem very adept?" she had said skeptically, at which he had asked her the same question about herself and she had answered, "Only you! Oh, of course, I thought I loved Arty when I married him. But I was

very young. I soon found out." Considering him she had said,
"We get on well for a pair of ignoramuses." He had thought
about this for a while and then, to his own suprise, came up
with, "Love is like jungle warfare at night, it keys you up,
you feel things you can't see." (Like now, when that indefinable something passed in the air between them.)

For her part, when he said that about love and the jungle,
she had laughed merrily, sensitive enough to respond to his
doleful humor, not intelligent enough to define it. It was his
great attraction, of which he was quite unaware, always to
expect the worst — it made him infinitely tender and pitiful
towards everybody. "I am a dull dog," he used to say to her
sometimes and it used to make her throw her arms around
him. Her big, stupid, dull, loyal dog would look at her in
astonishment and love. She was his opposite, endlessly hoping for the best, and better. Had she been smarter she would
have realized that pessimists are usually kind. The gay, bub-
bling over, have no time for the pitiful. Love lives in sealed
bottles of regret.

He went to the funeral, hoping to have a chat with Mabel
Tallant, the only person, he hoped, who knew all about the
pair of them. There were so many people there that he decided to keep discreetly to the rear of the crowd. He was surprised at the size of the turnout but supposed that a man
cannot be a District Justice without making a pack of friends.
Anyway, the Irish have a great gift for death, wakes and fu-
nerals. They are really at their best in misfortune. Used to it,
I suppose? And sport. Quid pro quo, what? The thing that
surprised him most, as he stood watching the mourners file in
and out of the church was that while he knew many of them
by sight, and perhaps a dozen by name — the vet, the
Guards' Inspector, a couple of doctors, shopkeepers from the
town, two or three fellows he had hunted with, and those
well enough to nod to — he did not know one of them intimately, apart from Mabel Tallant. With her he just managed

to get a word: she said she was taking Anna home with her for a couple of days after the relatives left. "Give her my love," he whispered hastily. Mabel had smiled sadly and whispered back, "Everybody can sleep in peace now."

He drove away, unaccosted by anybody, wondering what the devil she meant, wondering also why the devil it was that ever since he came to live in Ireland he was always wondering what somebody meant about some damn thing or another. He decided yet once more that they had to talk roundabout because they never had anything to say that was worth saying directly. The yews of his drive were dripping as he drove up to his empty house: nothing would do old Mrs. Mac but to go to the funeral. The fire was out. Why had he ever come here? But he had been over all that, too. If his uncle had not left him this place he might never have come back from Kenya; and he might have left after the first year if he had not met Anna Mohan. But now? With Africa gone to hell? Package safaris all over the place. You might as well think of living in Piccadilly Circus.

The week after the funeral, as he was hacking home from the hunt, Mabel rode up beside him. She was red as a turnip from the wind, mud-spattered to her stock, a gray lock drooping from under her hat, and on her right jaw a streak of dried blood.

"Hello, Mabel! Fall? No bones broken, I hope? You know, you are looking younger every day. But, then, we all know you are a marvel!"

"My dear Frank," she laughed in her jolly, mannish way; she always laughed at everything, "if you're referring to my great age I assure you I'm not giving up for a long time yet. Even if I am fifty I'm not decrepit. And I don't think you can give me many years, can you? I wasn't tossed, I'm more wet than muddy. I stayed behind with the Master to put back a few poles that we knocked at the Stameen. I've got half the stream in my boots this minute."

They ambled along for a quarter of a mile with no more than a few tired words about the hunt. They had had three good runs. The Master was digging out the last fox. You have to give the farmers some satisfaction. After another silence he said, "How is Anna?"

"You ask me?"

"I suppose I should call on her soon. I don't want to be indiscreet, you know."

"You could be a bit too discreet."

"I was always discreet about Anna. I owed it to her. Nobody but you ever knew about Anna and me."

"Knew? Knows? Maybe not, but you've lived long enough in these parts to know that there's damn little goes on here that everybody doesn't suspect." She hooted gaily, "Sometimes a lot more than they've any reason to suspect. It fills their lives, I suppose."

"Anna and I used always to say that they might suspect but they couldn't be sure, and that was what really counted."

"Past history?"

She laughed. He frowned. Not because her laugh suggested some unspoken blame of him but that it echoed certain spoken, and unspoken prophecies about Anna: her unbridled tongue, as of a woman who had been spoiled as a too-pretty girl, her temper, her tears, her enthusiasms, her wanting always to be smarter than she was, her melancholy days that went on and on, her warm days that were too warm to last, like a hot day in summer, her sudden bursts of generosity towards some women and her sudden bursts of jealousy towards other women — always young, pretty women. One by one Mabel had shaken her head over Anna's "ways," and he had liked her all the more for it because in spite of everything she seemed to love her. Or was it that she, too, felt sorry for her?

It was growing dusk when they got to Bardy Hill. Fumes of fog were lying over the reedy plain. The tired horses slowed to a walk. She tapped his thigh with her crop.

"Frank! You're fooling yourself. I heard a bit of gossip at the meet this morning."

"What did you hear?"

"Not much. Somebody said, 'I wonder is Major Keene going to marry her now.' "

He suddenly realized what that "something" had been. She had said, "Arty's dead, I've lost my poor husband." Lost? Or was that the word they said to her on the phone? Dammit, she had lost him ten years ago.

"Mabel! If Arty had died ten years ago, even five, even three, I'd have married her like a shot. We dreamed of it. We lived on the dream of it. Not on the hope, dammit, no! We never said 'die,' we said, 'if anything happened to him.' Always talking about how happy we could be together. Just the two of us. Morning, noon and night. Lovers' talk! But, ye know, hope deferred maketh the heart sick. Anna being a Catholic there was no chance of a divorce. And, anyway, she was fond of him. In the end I gave up hope. I'll tell ye something else, Mabel. I was with her the day Arty died. I hadn't been with her for two months before that. And before that I dunno when. That day, I knew it was all over."

He frowned again when Mabel said nothing. Venus shone, alone, in a green sky above a low spear of clouds. The horses, smelling home, began to trot downhill. They pulled up at Ballymeen Cross — they had each about half a mile to go.

"Do you think she really expects me to marry her?" he asked unhappily.

"I can only give you the woman's point of view. I'd think it damn cheap of you if you didn't make an honest woman of her. It will be pretty lonely for her in that old house at Culadrum. To put it at its lowest a husband is a handy thing to have about a house." She laughed sourly. "I should know."

She jerked the head of her horse, and cantered away. He did the same. Once, and he regretted it, he took out his anger on the animal with his crop. Twice he uttered the word "Damnation!" A pool of water gleamed coldly on his drive. A blank window held the last of the day. Culadrum would not be much of a home for Anna from now on. He should know.

He ate little, drank too much wine, slept badly, and immediately after breakfast he drove over to Culadrum. He found her in her drawing room reading the *Irish Times* before the fire, slim-looking in proper black, very becoming, with a tiny white ruff under her chin, and hanging beneath it one of those little pendants called a lavallière, a small, colored miniature of Arty as a young man. With her tight-busted dress, and her fair hair done in a coil on the top of her head she had a Victorian look, like a queen in mourning. His heart went out to her. He kissed her and said gallantly, "Now, my darling, before the whole world you can be all mine!" To his delight she blushed, a thing he had not seen her do for years. They sat in armchairs on either side of the fire.

"Frank! We have waited so long you won't mind waiting another while, will you?"

"As long as you like, Anna."

"There is a special reason why we must wait a bit. It has to do with local opinion. I want to be married in a Catholic church."

So, she *had* been thinking about it!

"By all means. I'm not bigoted. In for a penny in for a pound."

"I want everything to be done regularly. I want to clear up everything. We will live here. In this house our life is before us. All my friends and all Arty's old friends are Catholics. They move in their own circle, just as people do everywhere. I'm not one of the hunting set, as they aren't either, except for one or two maybe. So it is frightfully important that they should all become your friends too. Oh, my darling, it would make all the difference in the world if you were a Catholic!"

He sat back slowly.

"Well, unfortunately, I'm not."

"Frank! For me? It would make all the difference for me if you became a Catholic. Oh, if you could only become a Catholic, Frank! Won't you? We'd be all together then. And I'd be so happy!"

"But, dammit, Anna, you're not seriously suggesting that they'd look down on you in some way if you married a Protestant?"

"A mixed marriage? They won't have it in this diocese. Anyway we never did it in our family. Even where they do allow it it's a hole-and-corner affair. It's not the same thing at all. Documents. Guarantees. Back-door stuff. Ugh!"

"It's beyond me."

She laughed her little curl-at-the-corners Anna-laugh.

"You've lived in Ireland, Frank, for ten years, and I honestly don't believe you still understand the Irish."

"Is there anything to understand?"

"Besides, there is something else we have to face."

"Something else? What else, for God's sake?"

"We always said they didn't know. But in our hearts we always knew that they did know. They always do know. Bother them! Oh, they mightn't have known *exactly,* but they must have known that there was *something* between us. Of course, there is one way out of it. If you don't marry me now they will say they were wrong."

"But I don't want a way out of it. I want you!"

"But, Frank, if we do marry, you see, then they will know for certain that they were right all along. They'd never feel happy about us. They'd always be whispering about our past. We'd see it in their eyes. They might never visit us at all! And you couldn't blame them, could you? But if you became a Catholic, Frank, they'd be so happy about it that they'd forget and forgive everything. Besides, it was always the one thing — I mean if there ever was any teeny, little thing at all — that stood between us now and again. Now when we can be married, if we do marry, at last, at long last — Oh, my darling! — I want us to be one in everything before the world!"

"It never seemed to bother you before?"

"Of course it bothered me. I often cried about it when you left me."

"Why did you never speak to me about it?"

"I was afraid of losing you," she said somberly.

He stood up, went to the window and looked glumly out through the frosty leaf tracery on the glass. Accustomed to his ways she kept looking at his back under her eyebrows, waiting on his digestion. Presently he did a smart right about-turn.

"This," he declared, "is a bombshell. Dammit, it's an absolute bombshell. When we couldn't marry you were so afraid to lose me that you never uttered a word about religion, and now, when we can marry, you give me the choice of being a cad if I don't and a Catholic if I do."

"Darling, if you can't I shan't blame you. And if you can't I am not going to lose you. No matter what it costs me. Unless you were to ditch me, of course?"

"That I shall never do."

She joined him at the window, and with one coaxing, pussy-cat finger she stroked his mustaches right and left, and kissed his lips.

"Think about it, darling."

He stared at her, snatched his cap and left abruptly. After driving in circles for an hour he found himself outside Mabel Tallant's house at Bunahown. She was in the stables watching her groom combing her gray hunter. When he told her she laughed so loudly that he saw her gold-tipped molars.

"You're stuck, my boy!"

"But she might just as well ask me to become a Muslim or a Parsee! It isn't fair!"

She laughed gleefully again, then became solemn.

"Frank?"

"Well?"

"Suppose this happened ten years ago when you first fell in love with Anna? Suppose she wasn't married then? Suppose she asked you then to do this for her, would you have done it? Would you have said it wasn't fair?"

He glared at her, shuffled a bit, strode away.

After a week of torture, sitting for hours alone over his fire, or stalking alone about the leafless roads, he drove into town, stiffened himself with a glass of whiskey at the Royal Hotel and asked the waitress where the Catholic presbytery was. She directed him to Pearse Square with an enthusiasm that he found nauseating. The presbytery looked like a home for orphans, tall, Victorian, red brick, with imitation stone quoins in gray plaster, pointed in black. Every window looked up at the wet February sky over brass-tipped half screens. He hauled stoutly at the brass bell handle and stood to attention glaring at the door. He asked the scrubby boy who opened it for the parish priest and was shown into a chilly front room. Drawing? Waiting? Committee? Dining? He found himself faced by a life-size statue of Christ pointedly exhibiting His rosy heart. He turned his back to it. He did not sit down. This was a thing a man met on his two feet.

The door opened, very slowly. The priest who entered was an old man of at least sixty-five or more. He wore a monsignor's russet vest beneath a celluloid Roman collar that brushed the cincture of white hair about his roped neck. His voice was as mild as milk, his manner as courteous as a glass of port. When he told his visitor that he had been a chaplain with the Royal Inniskillings towards the end of the 1914 war, they were both only too happy to sit, smoke and chat about Chateau Thierry, the Sambre, the Somme, places known to the younger warrior of the two with the reverence proper to ancient history. Then they retired upstairs to the Monsignor's sitting room, the fireside and a whiskey bottle. An old Alsatian bitch lay strewn on the hearth rug between them.

By the time they got down to business the Major felt as relaxed in his armchair, prickly with horsehair, as if they had just met in a club. All went well until he uttered the name, Mrs. Anna Mohan. The Monsignor's eyelids fell.

"Mrs. Mohan? Ah, yes! Lives over at Culadrum House. I knew her father and mother very well. I wouldn't say they were exactly zealous Catholics. But they were good people. Hm! Well, well! Anna Carty, that was. A handsome girl when she was a child. I remember now, they sent her to some convent school in Kent. And after that to some place in Switzerland — Lausanne, I believe — to a finishing school. Rather a mistake that. Risky."

"Risky?"

The word could have connotations.

"Oh, I am not criticizing them. It is simply that I always feel that if a girl is going to live in Ireland it's wiser to bring her up here. She must have been very young when she married Mohan. Why, we buried him only two weeks ago. Hm! I see!"

He looked at the Major without expression, but it was plain enough that he did see.

"Well, Major? Tell me this. Would I be wrong in surmising that you are doing this chiefly, if not wholly, to please Mrs. Mohan?"

"A fair question, Padre. Yes, you've got it. That's about the run of it."

"I mean, you are not being drawn to the Catholic Church entirely for its own sake, are you?"

"I'll be perfectly straight with you, Padre, I don't know anything at all about the Catholic Church. I'll go farther. I'm not going to become a Catholic, or anything like it, until I know a lot more about the whole thing."

"Very wise. In other words, you are not asking me to give you a course of instruction. You are just asking me for some preliminary information."

"Yes! Yes, that's about the run of it."

"Is there, then, something that particularly interests you, or, shall I say, that bothers you, about our Church?"

"Why, dammit, everything about the Catholic Church bothers me. Not that I ever thought about it. But I suppose if you ask me a straight question I might say, well, for example, I might say what's all this about the infallibility of the Pope? It's a tall order, ye know, if somebody comes out every day of the week about something and says 'That's it! You've got to take it because I'm infallible!' I mean, supposing the Pope came out tomorrow and said Napoleon was a woman, or that a line isn't the shortest distance between two points, or that the Law of Gravitation is all nonsense, you can't deny it, Padre, that that'd be a hell of a tall order. You don't mind my being frank about this, I hope?"

The Monsignor patted down the glowing tobacco in his pipe with an asbestos finger and said mildly that no, he did not mind at all.

"Not, of course, that what you suggest bears any relation to reality. But I don't mind. I mean, the examples you have chosen are not the very best in the world." Here he waved his mottled hand. "Since Mr. Einstein, as the old song says, fings ain't wot they used ter be." He wandered off a bit about Tycho Brahe and the mathematics of planetary attraction until he saw a glaze gathering over his visitor's eyes. "In fact, His Holiness hardly ever speaks infallibly. The Doctrine of Infallibility was pronounced in 1870." He halted, thinking of such names as Newman and Lord Acton, and went on hastily. "Since then I don't think the Pope has spoken *ex cathedra* more than . . . Is it twice, or three times? And if I may say so, quite enough, too! Though some people might think even that much was excessive. Things change." He fell into a private thought. "Change and expand."

"Only twice or three times? Is this a fact? Dammit, I never knew this! But," he pounced, "when he does we have to believe him, eh?"

"Major Keene, I think all this would seem much simpler to us if we were to think of the whole matter as one of obedience rather than of conviction. You are a soldier. You know about obedience. During the war if your colonel told you to advance on Hill 22 with three men and that old Alsatian there and take Objective 46, which you knew quite well was held by a thousand men, what would you do about it?"

"I'd obey at once."

"Yes. You would obey. Somebody's got to give the orders."

Keene stared at him out of his two great, blue eyes like a horse facing a jump.

"By George, you're a hundred per cent right, Padre! Somebody's got to be boss. Not like all this damned, modern Whiggery we've got now. When everybody wants to be the boss. All those trade unions . . . But, mind you, you've touched on another question there. Only last Sunday my housekeeper, Mrs. MacCarthy, told me that, when she was at Mass, right here in town, one of your curates . . . You won't mind my saying this?"

"Fire away, Major. Fire away."

"She told me . . . Mind you, she's a bit of an old exaggerator, but I wouldn't say she's a liar, just Irish ye know, she told me that one of your curates said from the pulpit that any girl going around this town in tight jeans was walking straight on the road to hell. Now, that's a bit of a tall order, Padre! What do you say to that?"

The Monsignor sighed wheezily.

"Yes. Well. We do seem to have wandered a bit from papal infallibility. But, since you raise the question . . . You, again as an old soldier, must know what happens to orders by the time they pass down to the lower ranks. It's a case of the sergeants' mess, my dear Major. The sergeants' mess in every sense of the word, and you know what I'm talking about."

"By George! Don't I? Ye know, Padre, it's a downright pleasure to talk to a man like you who knows the ways of the big world. You make me feel quite homesick for it."

"So? Obedience! And order. And authority. You revere your Queen. The proud symbol of the power of your Empire. We Catholics revere the Pope. The proud symbol of our Empire. The Roman Empire. You and I, each in his own way, respect authority, desire order and uphold power."

"Splendid! I can see that. In fact I begin to see a lot of daylight. Ye know, if we had a couple of chats I shouldn't be at all surprised if we found we had a good deal of ground in common. Mind you, I'm not going to be rushed into this. I'm sure that when I start thinking about it I'll come up with a lot of things that bother me. Mixed marriages for instance. There's another tall order. And, let me see, hasn't there been some difficulty about the Virgin? And then, of course, there's contraception — I ran into that a lot in India. I need hardly say my interest in that matter is purely academic."

"So is mine."

He rose.

"Why don't you come to dinner next week, Major, when as you say you will have thought some more about it, and we can combine business, if I may so call it, with pleasure. I've got quite a sound port."

"Aha! I know something about port."

The Monsignor warmed.

"Do you now? Tell me, did you ever take port for breakfast?"

The Major guffawed.

"Oh dammit no! No! Not for breakfast, Padre!"

The Monsignor chuckled.

"Then I am afraid you don't know anything at all about port. Wait until you taste mine. But I'm afraid if you are a connoisseur in wine you had better bring your own. Ah! The great wines of France. 1917. Spoiled my palate. I can't afford vintage wine any longer."

"I've got a dozen Forty-nine Beaunes-Villages at home. I'll bring a couple of bottles with me. By God, this is a splendid idea! I beg your pardon, Monsignor, here I am cursing like a trooper in the presence of Your Reverence."

"Pshaw! I'm inured to it. I remember one morning outside Ypres. Just before we went into battle. Two dragoons fighting, one of them an Orangeman and the other a Catholic, shouting like troopers. They had to to be heard — the barrage going right over our heads, hell open to Christians, the captain staring at his wristwatch waiting for the second to go over the top. Do you remember — Ah, no, you're too young! — those old wristwatches with little metal grilles over them? I never heard such language in all my life as that Orangeman was giving out of him. In the end the other fellow, he was a Corkman, shoved his bayonet up within an inch of the other fellow's throat and he shouts, 'Look Sammy! I'm in the state of grace now before the battle, but with the help of God I won't be so handicapped before the day is out, and I tell you if I meet you then I'll shove this blank blank . . .'"

He clasped Keene by the arm for support as he bent over and laughed at the memory of it. Then he straightened and sighed.

"Poor chaps, neither of 'em came back. And I'm sure the good Lord was equally kind to the pair of them. Next Thursday, Major. At nineteen hours. Goodness me, I haven't used that phrase for it must be forty years. We'll be talking of old times together."

Keene clasped his hand. He left the presbytery, glancing in respectfully at the impassive eyes of the Sacred Heart.

Those Thursday dinners became such a solemn, as well as delightful, opening of hearts that within two months the Monsignor was straining hard to hold his neophyte from declaring himself a Catholic on the spot. Indeed, one silent April night, during their third month, as he was showing his guest out into the moist emptiness of Pearse Square he said, "I shall bless the day, Frank, when you become, if you do become, a Catholic, but I confess I shall have one small regret. The end of our little dinners."

"Nonense! Why should they end?"

"They will end."

By the end of April the Major was coming up against the hard stuff: the one sector of the battlefield to whose ground he returned obstinately, uncomfortably, scarred a little, sometimes approaching it as quietly as if he were on a lone night raid. They might be talking about books — say, *Adam Bede* or *The Three Musketeers* and he might slip in:

"Padre! Can one never, simply never, say that there are times when love conquers all? I mean, is that kind of love always, simply always, a sin?"

"I'm afraid, Frank, it is. Always a sin. I'm afraid there just isn't any way around that one. Nor, I fear, could any clergyman of any persuasion say anything else." He allowed himself a slim smile. "You remind me of old Professor Mahaffy of Trinity College in Dublin. He was a great wag, you know. One time he confided, or pretended to confide to a fashionable Dublin Jesuit, a close friend of his, that he felt drawn to the Catholic Church. Very naturally his Jesuit friend was only too eager to pluck the plum. Another glass? 'Not a drop is sold till it's seven years old.' Well, it appeared that there was just one small obstacle. Just one tiny, little problem. 'If you can only allow me,' Mahaffy said, and I am sure he said it with a poker face, 'to believe that Christ was not God I will join your Church tomorrow morning.' His Jesuit friend is said to have paused for a long time. And at last he said, very regretfully, as I say to you now about adultery, 'I'm afraid there isn't any way around that one.' There are some things nobody can get around. Not even the Pope. Let alone me."

Finally, one night, Frank said, plump out:

"Padre! When, and if, you consider me worthy to be received into the Church shall I have to go to Confession?"

"We will, naturally, have to clear up your past. Not that I think it will bother you very much. There are so few sins, and they repeat themselves endlessly. Even boringly. It is only the circumstances that change."

"I was coming to exactly that. There is a bit of my past that I would like to clear up right away. I want to tell you that I have been in love with Anna Mohan for some ten years. I mean, we have been lovers in the full sense of the word. And I have never felt guilty about it. My fault, no doubt, but there it is. After all, she was only married to him in theory as you might say. He's gone now and words cannot harm him, everybody knows that he was a roaring alcoholic. Don't those circumstances you speak of alter such cases as mine?"

"He was addicted," the Monsignor agreed sadly. "As for your case, that he was addicted is sad but it is not relevant to the law. Hard cases make bad laws. Nor is it relevant that you did not feel a sense of guilt. A stern moralist might speak to you of an atrophied conscience. I think it is enough for me to remind you that many men, known to history, men like Hitler or Stalin, committed the greatest crimes without feeling any sense of guilt. I can only repeat to you that adultery is a very grave sin. It is even two sins, for it also sins against the law that thou shalt not steal. She was his wife. I do not wish to overstress the point, but it does arise. Furthermore, chastity is not only of the body. In what is commonly called sex the body and the soul are one. You simply have to accept what I say."

"She did lose something when he died. I have realized that."

"I think," the Monsignor added, gravely, "that this is something that it is your duty to clarify." He paused, and then added, pointedly, "All round."

"I accept what you say," his neophyte sighed. "It is most troubling."

The Monsignor quietly refilled his glass, wondering a little whether his pupil had some extra reason to be troubled.

He had. By now he was also receiving intermittent instruction from Anna, and on those occasions the tender feelings that she aroused in him were at times more than he could control. On one such occasion, looking up at her pink canopy, he said to her, "Poor Anna! I can see now why you used sometimes to cry. It was a sin." She smiled her curl smile and whispered, "But, sure, it no longer is!"

"Anna! We must not deceive ourselves. We're not married yet, ye know."

"We are married in the sight of God," she said and scratched him a little. "The Church will bless us."

"The Church must bless us first."

"Ah, but sure," she wheedled, "it's so much nicer before."

"It will be much, much nicer when you will lawfully be mine before man and God."

"Darling!" she cried, and scratched wickedly. "Don't be a bore! Are you a lawyer or a lover?"

"But the Monsignor says . . ."

At this she flew into a rage.

"For Heaven's sake, who are you marrying? Me or the Monsignor?"

He forbore to reply. He was troubled, and not for the first time, by the thought, Is she in more need of instruction than me? This, however, was something that, in delicacy, he could not broach to her, or, in loyalty, to the Monsignor — unless he might, perhaps, act as a go-between?

"Monsignor! I have one last question. To revert once more to my old problem, I do see, now, that I have indeed been guilty of a grave sin. I no longer contest it. It is undeniable. I cannot understand how I ever doubted it. But, supposing I had lain not with a married woman but with an unmarried woman, may I ask, is it in that case permissible for either party to feel just a little bit less guilty?"

"In such a hypothetical case," his friend said dryly, "either party would merely have been breaking one commandment at a time."

"How stupid of me! How is it that everything becomes so simple when you explain it?"

The occasion to relay the consequences of his question was not long in coming. Under the canopy, he gently pointed out to Anna that they would both have to confess all this sooner or later, as one sin on her part, as two on his. She declared at once, and with passion, that she had no intention of doing anything of the sort.

"Do you think," she cried, drawing blood from him this time, "that I am going to spoil all our years and years of love by saying now that they were beastly and horrible?" Then seeing in his terrified horse eyes how deeply she had shocked him, she added, easily, "One could of course go through the *formality.*"

"Of course!" he agreed, profoundly relieved to find that she really was, after all, a Catholic. She went on:

"Why not? One will say that one has transgressed. That's it. Transgressed. To pass over. To step beyond. Beyond the red line. A little."

"Indeed," he agreed happily. "So we will! I'm so relieved! I'm so glad!"

She chuckled happily.

"But, sure, Frank, we'll know in our hearts, of course, that we didn't really do anything very bad at all!"

"But, my dear Anna, there is the law! *Thou shalt not commit adultery.*"

At this she sat up, seized him by the hair and shook him like a dog.

"Are you calling me an adulteress?"

He sat up, waved his arms despairingly, and wailed at her.

"My darling! I sit in judgment on nobody. But I!" he said miserably. "I *have* been an adulterer."

She stroked his moustaches and kissed him cajolingly.

"Not really, darling. That's just an old afterthought you are having now. You were as innocent as a child at the time."

He sank back and rolled his tousled head sadly on the pillow.

"I'm such a simple sort of chap, Anna, and it's all such a simple thing, and I understand it so simply, and I do wish that you didn't make it all so damned complicated."

She laughed and laughed.

"I make it complicated? It is I who am simple about it — your new friends who are tying everything up in knots with their laws, and rules, and regulations, and definitions, and sub-definitions that nobody can make head or tail of. I was brought up on all that stuff. I know it. You don't. They are at it all the time. So many ounces you may eat during Lent in France, so many in Spain. You can't eat meat on Fridays but it's no harm to eat frogs, and snakes and snails. I suppose you could even eat tripe! How much profit may one business-man draw on this deal. How much may another draw on another. Do you think anybody can really measure things like that? A baby who dies without being baptized must go to some place called Limbo that nobody ever knew what it is or in what corner of creation to put it. All that stuff has nothing to do with religion. How could it? Do you know that Saint

Augustine said that all unbaptized children are condemned to suffer in eternal fire? Is *that* religion?"

"Are you sure Saint Augustine said this?"

"I was educated in Lausanne," she said proudly. "It's the home of Saint Augustine. All those stinking Calvinists." She began to sob into the pillow. "I wish I'd never asked you to become a Catholic. I wouldn't have if I knew you were going to take it as seriously as all this."

In his unhappy arms she became happy again.

For six days and six nights he kept away from the Monsignor, thinking of all those millions of babies burning in eternal fire, until his whole soul felt beaten by devils armed with sticks, and shovels, and red-hot tongs. On the seventh night he invited the Monsignor to dinner. Like a good host he kept from his troubles until the port passed. Then, unsteadily, he said, "Monsignor, I have another question, a small, tiny little problem. Tell me, where is Limbo?"

The old man paused in the act of raising his glass to his lips and looked at him apprehensively. He had dealt with Transubstantiation, Miracles, the Resurrection, Indulgences, Galileo, the Virgin Birth, the Immaculate Conception, Grace, Predestination, the Will, Mixed Marriages, even Adultery. These great mysteries and problems had presented no lasting difficulty either to him or to his dear friend. But Limbo? He knew from long experience how easily the small things, rather than the big ones, can shatter a man's faith.

"Why did you ask me that question?" he said sadly.

"It just occurred to me," the Major said loyally, and curled a little at his lack of frankness to his friend.

"I see!"

"Is it true, Monsignor, as I have read, that Saint Augustine said that all babies who have not been baptized must burn in eternal fire?"

With a whole movement of his arm the Monsignor pushed his glass slowly to one side. His night was in ruins.

"I believe so," he said, and thrust gallantly on. "Still, there are other and more benignant views. It all arose, I presume, out of the problem of where to place those unbaptized souls who died before Christ, and those others who died after Him without ever hearing of Him. I believe it was the Council of Florence that decreed it." He faltered. "It was a rather confused Council. So confused that I gather that its Acts have perished. It laid down, it was in the fifteenth century, that nobody who is unbaptized may enter Heaven. Since then many thinkers have, in their mercy, felt a repugnance to the idea. Many theologians have sought out ways of accepting the doctrine while, as you might say, circumventing, or anyway softening its melancholy implications. Major! Do you really want me to go into this matter of Limbo? It is not a primal question."

"It bothers me, Monsignor."

"I see. Well. I do know that one Italian theologian, whose name escapes me at the moment, felt that God might instruct the angels to confer baptism on those children — who might otherwise perish without it. Another theologian felt that the sincere wish of the parent that the child might have been baptized could be a fair equivalent. Saint Thomas felt, humanely, that those children suffer no pain of the body, although they must, indeed, always grieve that they can never see God. Just as a bird or a mouse might grieve that it can never be a man, or speak to an emperor or king."

"How sad!"

"Of course, Major," the Monsignor whispered, "we have to recognize that we have no purely human right to Heaven. Heaven is a gift. God could, without injustice, deny it to us. I suggest it was originally a rabbinical idea."

The priest looked into the glowing ashes of the fire. The Major looked out at the darkness of the night. Through the open window the invisible fields sent in the sweetness of the May blossom. After a long while the Monsignor said, "There are many mysteries in life that we have to accept in humility without understanding them. Indeed, it is because we do not understand the mystery that we do accept it — and live with it."

As he drove away the Major watched the beams of his car until they touched the last of his yews, and stood there until the smell of his petrol faded in the pure air. He walked up and down his avenue many times. Afterwards he sat before his dying fire until sleep came to him where he slouched by its ashes.

It was quite early, a bird-singing May morning gleaming after a light shower of rain, when he faced her, fresh and handsome, breakfasting beside her cheerful morning fire. He said firmly, "Anna, I can never become a Catholic."

Her cup clattered into its saucer.

"But Frank, you must! Do you expect me to marry you like a Protestant in a registry office? Or to live with you for the rest of my life in what you now think of as a cesspool of sin?"

"I am proposing nothing. I can think of nothing. It is just that I am too old, or too stupid, to be able to follow you both."

"You just want to be shut of me." She raised her tear-filled eyes. "Or is it that it is I who am too old and too stupid? Why can't you be as I am? After all, I am a Catholic!"

"I have sometime wondered, Anna, what you are."

Her fury burst about him like shrapnel. She dashed down the *Irish Times*.

"How dare you? Of course I am a Catholic! What's wrong with you is that you want everything to be perfect. As clean, and bare and tidy as a barrack square. That's it! All you are is a bloody English major who wants everybody's buttons to be polished and everybody's cap to be as straight as a plate."

"But it wasn't I who raised the question of Limbo!"

"To hell with Limbo! If there is a hell! Or a Limbo! What's wrong with you is you're too conceited. You want to cross every I and dot every T. Why do you want to understand everything? Why can't you just accept things the way I do?"

"Do you accept Limbo?"

"I never think about Limbo. I never think about stupid things like that. I think only of God, and the stars, and of Heaven, and of love, and of you."

"You put me to a great test, Anna. As the Monsignor says I must also think of the cross and the nails. Just as he says that in love the soul and the body are one."

"You're a liar! All this is just a cute device to get out of marrying me. I see through you. I see through your cheap trickery. I see through your dirty Saxon guile. If you were the last man on earth this minute, Frank Keene, I wouldn't marry you now. Please don't come near me ever again!"

She swept out and crashed the door. He retrieved the *Irish Times* from the fire, beat out its flames, and went away.

He had no one left to talk to. He had pestered the Monsignor beyond endurance. He had never attended the Church of Ireland. Anyway he doubted if they knew very much about Limbo or the Council of Naples. Mabel Tallant would only laugh at him. He had devoted so many years of his life to Anna that he had made no friends. And now she neither loved him nor respected him, and he did not . . . He crushed down the bleak admission.

After three weeks of the blackest misery, he dashed off a letter.

MONSEIGNEUR, MON GENERAL, MON AMI,

If I may be allowed to declare my belief in things that I do not understand and to accept in humility things that I do not approve I am ready, at your command, to take Mount

Sion, even unaccompanied by your Alsatian bitch. Give me
your order. I will obey.

> *Your obedient servant,*
> Francis Lancelot Keene,
> *Major,*
> *L.R.C.P.E. and L.M.,*
> *Late R.A.M.C.,*
> *Dunkirk, Tunisia, Libya, Egypt, Italy.*
> *Despatches, medal and clasp, D.S.O.*
> *1940-1945*
> *Retired.*

The reply came by telegram the next day. At the sight of
the single word of command a sudden rage boiled up in him.
Who did he think he was? A bloody general? One man? And
no dog? Against an army of doubts . . .

He chose July ninth for it, the feast day of two English
saints, John Fisher, Bishop, and Thomas More, Chancellor,
both martyrs.

It was raining as he entered the presbytery. In the Monsignor's parlor the old Alsatian half looked up at him and sank
back into its doze. The two men walked silently across to the
church where the Monsignor invested himself in his surplice
and stole, and the Major knelt by the rails of a side chapel,
feeling nothing whatsoever as he repeated the words of recan-
tation and of belief. They then retired to the presbytery where
the Major knelt by the Monsignor's chair for his first confession. During the previous days he had been girding himself
for his complete life story. The Monsignor truncated even
that piece of the ceremony, saying, "I imagine I know it all.
Women, and drink, and I suppose swearing like a trooper.
Unless there is some special sin of your past life that you
want to mention?"

Humbly, the Major said, "Sloth," and got a faint satisfaction from the painful admission.

Then sunshine flooded his heart when the Monsignor told

him that his penance would be to say, that night, three Ave Marias.

"So little? After so long?"

"God loves you," the Monsignor said, and bade him to say his Act of Contrition.

The Major's eyes filled with tears as he heard the murmuring words of absolution mingle with his own. The Monsignor then raised him to his feet and warmly shook both his hands.

"My dear friend in Christ. Now you are one of us. Do your best. In the bosom of the Church. And," briskly removing his vestments, "let's go back now and have a good dollop of malt."

Over the glass the Major said happily, "I was afraid I was going to feel nothing at all. Wouldn't that have been awful?"

"My dear Frank, we are strange cattle. Often, even when I say Mass, I don't feel that it is doing me a bit of good. But I know it is, so I do not worry. The heart may be the center of all things but in the end it's not our feelings that matter but our good works. As you and I know well, more men go weak in battle from feeling too much than from feeling too little." He chuckled. "I remember one time we had a Colonel Home-Crean in the Inniskillings who was always carrying on about the martial spirit. He meant well. But the troops called him Old Carry On. It wasn't a bad pun, because whenever he finished one of his speeches he always said, 'Carry on, sergeant.' "

The Major laughed wryly.

"Pass the buck."

"I say it still. I say it now, Frank, to you."

He tore back at sixty miles an hour to Culadrum to meet her, singing all the way at the top of his voice "When the Saints Go Marching In." There was a shower, the sun ebbed and flowed, and "Blow me," he cheered, "if they haven't sent me a rainbow!" He hooted his horn along her drive, and there she was running down the steps onto the gravel to embrace him.

" 'Tis done," he laughed, and she said, "You look about seventeen!"

"God loves me!" he said.

"Did you fix up about the marriage?"

"Good Lord! I forgot all about it!"

"You immense dope!" she laughed. "That was the whole point. Go back tonight and fix it. And do remember — the tenth of August. We've got all the tickets, darling! Promise?"

"You're still sure it's not a bit too soon? I mean that people may think that . . ."

She laughed triumphantly.

"I want them to think! I'll blame it all on my impetuous lover. And, now, you must come and see my new dresses and hats, a whole crateful of them came this morning from Dublin."

She took him by the hand, and galloped him upstairs to her room's litter of hillocked tissue and colored cardboard boxes.

"Sit there. And don't dare stir." She tore off her frock; he sat and beamed at her, in her panties and bra, circling, preening, glaring in the long mirror at herself in pale toques, straw hats in white, in mauve, in liver-pink, and he was so happy at her childish happiness that for a moment he was terrified that she would next want him to go to bed with her. Thank Heaven, she was too excited to think about it. Once as she poised a pale blue pillbox on the back of her poll, saying, "Or this one?" he wondered whether she had gone, or when she would go to Confession, and decided that he would not press her about it just now. Perhaps never at all.

They were married before a large congregation in the cathedral. He recognized many whom he had seen six months before at the funeral. He felt a bit self-conscious about his age, and hers, and several times, when it was over, he had to stop himself from interpreting their broad smiles and their hearty congratulations. Still, whether confetti-speckled in his gray topper and tails outside the church door, or mingling with the crowd in his new pinstripe at the champagne reception in the Royal Hotel, he felt he had carried it all off like a soldier and a gentleman, talking now with the Inspector about tinkers, now with a very serious young librarian about the publications of the Irish Manuscripts Commission, now with Mulcahy the chemist about the "extra-ordinary" number of women in the town who took barbiturates for "the narves," or listening in polite astonishment to a curate whom he had never met before weighing the comparative merits of President Salazar and General Franco. Then they were in his car driving off amid huzzas and laughter, down along the Main Street, out into the country for Dublin, for London and Lausanne. They were both tipsy. She was weeping softly. He filled with pity and love.

"You're not upset, darling?"

"It's just my nerves," she smiled bravely, took a pill from her bag, and was soon chortling once more.

Everything turned out afterwards just as she had foretold. They set up house together in Culadrum. All her old friends and her late husband's friends came regularly to visit them. They played bridge with them at least twice a week. In the season he hunted three times a week. He took complete charge of her garden. He developed an interest in local archaeology. She was entirely happy, scratched him no longer, and wept no more. He enjoyed all the quiet self-satisfaction of a man who, at some cost to himself, has done the right thing and found everything turning out splendidly. As he marched the roads, erect, chest out, with his stick and his dog, he was admired, liked and envied by all.

Winter came. The rains and the barometer fell. She began

to make excuses about going to Mass on account of the awful weather and her health. At first he found, to his regret, that he was often going to Mass alone. Then he found that he was always going alone. He began to wonder at this, ask questions about it, become testy about it, and at last they argued crossly over it every Sunday morning. There were long silences because of it. Once a whole week passed without a word spoken. He finally realized that she had no interest at all in religion, and had never had. Then he felt a great hole opening in his belly, crawling like fear, recurrent as a fever, painful as betrayal, until he could no longer bear his misery alone.

"But, Monsignor," he wailed, "why did the woman insist on my becoming a Catholic if she doesn't believe in it herself? Why in God's name did she do this to me?"

His friend did not hesitate — he never had hesitated.

"Superstition. Fear perhaps? She has memories of childhood. Of the dark. The thin red line that may not be crossed."

"But we crossed it over and over again, for years!"

"That was not forever."

"Could we not have had a mixed marriage?"

"It could have been managed. Somehow. Somewhere. She wanted the Real Thing. The laying on of hands. The propitiation. The magic touch. I suspect, Frank, that your wife is a very simple woman. We have millions of them in the Church. Full of what I call ignorant innocence. They don't do much harm to anybody, except to themselves. Or if they become vain, or proud, or we press them too hard, then they turn on us like a knife. Don't force her. You have a problem. You took a chance and now you must find some way of living with it, in faith, and courage and trust. Just remember that your wife is a little vain, rather spoiled I imagine, possibly a trifle conceited, too. And, or so I feel, very unsure of herself. Hence her superstition. African missionaries tell me that they are very familiar with it."

The Major stared at him, containing the urge to say, "Why the hell didn't you tell me all this before?"

"And what is my superstition?" he asked curtly.

"You are different. You worked your passage. Only . . ." Here he did hesitate.

"Only?"

"Only do not expect miracles. You may, of course, pray for one. I suppose it is what we all pray for really."

He took to going to early Mass every morning, much to her annoyance because no matter how quietly he stole out of her bed she always woke up, turning over and muttering things like, "For God's sake isn't Sunday enough for you?" or, "My nerves are shot to bits with you and your blooming piety!" By Christmas he had taken to sleeping alone. By February he was praying for the gift of silence and drinking like a fish. In spite of that he had lost eleven pounds' weight by March and was thinking of running away to Malaysia. By April he could no longer keep his food down. And then their war suddenly ended, in an explosion of light. He had gone out one morning into her walled garden to jab, stoically, at the grass and the pearlwort between the cracks of her crazy pavement. The night had been a blur of wet trees; now a skyload of sun warmed his stooped back. He smelled the cossetted earth, glanced at her ancient espaliers, became aware of a thrush's throat, blackbirds skirling, the chaffinches' in-and-out, the powerful robin, two loving finches that flicked into the gleaming cloud of an old cherry tree propped over his head. As he picked on and on, patiently and humbly, his memory slowly expanded in widening circles out to the covert of Easter Hill, out beyond the furze-yellow slopes of the Stameen River, away out after that great wheeling run of a month ago across the reedy plain, past its fallen dolmen and its ruined abbey, losing the scent, finding it again, five, glorious nonstop hammering miles of it. As he shifted the kneeler he noticed the first tiny bells of her white rhododendron. Christ was risen. Steaming roads stretched like wet rulers across the bog, past a pub, a garage, a gray National School, under a procession of elms against a foam bath of clouds. At his toe he saw a blue eggshell.

At that moment a window in the house was lifted. Looking up, he saw her, in her pink morning dress, leaning on the sill with both hands, staring over the countryside. He had a vision. In a flash it burst on him that everything she saw and he remembered came out of one eggshell. She waved to him, casually. He waved back wildly with his weeder. She retired.

"Monsignor! It was something that could only happen in Lourdes! How right you were! Never force things. Change and expand. Move slowly. Live with your problems. There are no laws for hard cases. Trust and courage solves everything. And, as you say, most of those laws are just so many old-fashioned rabbinical ideas. And the decrees of the Councils all lost! Heaven is a gift. The heart is the center. Carry on. We can only all do our best. God loves us. Not a single cross word for two weeks! Everything absolutely ticketyboo. Monsignor, you should be a cardinal!"

They had met in the street. The old man had heard him impassively. Leaning forward on his umbrella he lifted his head from his toes for one quick glance, almost it occurred to the Major in his excitement, as if he were not a cardinal but an African missionary.

"You say nothing?" he asked anxiously.

"I was just thinking, Frank. An odd thing! When we were in the Connaught Rangers we never said 'Ticketyboo!' What we used to say was 'All kiff!' Hindustani, do you suppose? That's good news." He shook hands limply, turned to go, turned back, said, "Carry on, Frank," and went on his slow way down the street, followed by his friend's wide-eyed stare of puzzlement, annoyance, affection and undiminished admiration. Two days later he attended his funeral. It was a damp day, and it did not do his rheumatism any good.

The next morning was a Sunday. The storm woke him. Through the corner of his blind he saw spilling rain, waving treetops and Noreen the maid, wrapped up in yellow cellophane like a lifeboat captain, wobbling on her bicycle down the avenue to Mass. He felt a twinge in his shoulder. He said, "Well, I was at Mass yesterday," lay back and dozed for an hour. He heard the soft boom of the breakfast gong, and Anna's door open and close. As he went downstairs in his dressing gown he smelled bacon and coffee. She was sitting by the breakfast table in her morning gown. The fire blazed cozily. "Good morning, love," he said, and kissed her forehead.

"Are you going out?" she asked and looked at the overspilling gutters dropping great glass beads of water past the window.

"Arthritis," he said sheepishly.

"Why, in God's name," she groaned, "do we live in this climate?"

"We live where we are fated to live, in the bosom of the country," and he lifted the chased lid of the breakfast dish.

She frowned. They munched silently. To cheer her he suggested that they might go in May to Italy, to Venice, to Rome, and he began to plan how they could go and what they could see there together. Far away a church bell tolled, on the wet wind, like a bell for the dead. He went on talking very gaily, very rapidly, very loudly. She smiled her curl smile and said, "Why not Lausanne?"

"Indeed, indeed! Anywhere! Anywhere! To get away!"

Dividends

A S FAR AS Mel Meldrum was concerned *l'affaire Anna,* as he was to call it, began one wet and windy April morning in 1944 when his chief clerk, Mooney, knocked at the door of his sanctum, handed him my letter, marked *Personal* and *By Hand,* and said that the bearer was an old lady in a black bonnet sitting outside in the main office "shaking her blooming umbrella all over your new Turkish carpet." I can see Mel glancing at my signature, smiling at his memories of our college days together twenty years before, rapidly taking the point of the letter and ordering Miss Whelan to be shown in to him at once. He rises courteously, begs her to be seated, watches amusedly while she fumbles in her woven shopping bag, and produces, proudly I have no doubt, a fat, wrinkled envelope containing the £350 in thirty-five white Bank of England notes. He receives it from her with a small bow. It was why I sent her to him; he was always affable, almost unctuous, with old ladies.

My Aunty Anna Maria was my mother's sister. Until she got this small legacy from another sister, who had recently died in a place called Toogong in New South Wales, she had never before possessed such a lump sum. She had existed for thirty-odd years on a modest salary as cook-housekeeper to a highly successful horse trainer in County Kildare; and then on the small pension he kindly gave her, supplemented occasionally by minute subventions from a nephew here and a niece there whenever we had the decency to remember how she used to stuff us with cakes and lemonade during our summer holidays on the edge of the Curragh where we loved to visit her in the staff quarters of the trainer's house. My father died, in Cork, so she came down there, when she was about fifty-five, to live with my mother; and when my mother died she had stayed on, alone, in the city, living in a single room in a battered old fabric of a tenement overlooking one of Cork's many abandoned quaysides — silent except for the poor kids from the lanes around playing and screaming in the street, or the gulls swooping over the bits of floating orange skin, bread crusts, or potato peelings backing slowly upriver on the high tide. When Mel saw her she was turned seventy. To my shame I had not seen her for twelve years. I had left Cork before she came there, and returned only once, for my mother's funeral. I was now married and living in Dublin.

It had taken me weeks of letter writing, back and forth, to persuade her to invest her legacy, and I was delighted when she agreed, because I knew that if she did not she would either scatter it in dribs and drabs, or lose it in the street some day, or hide it in some corner of her room and not remember where before the mice had eaten it into confetti.

Mel described in a long, amusing letter, how he had accepted the envelope "with measured ceremony." He had given her his best advice "like a pontiff." He explained to her that the sum was too small for an annuity, and she was too old for growth shares, so he must advise her to buy 8% preference shares in Sunbeam-Wolsey. He refused to charge her his usual stockbroker's fee, and, kindest act of all, told her that instead of waiting from one six-month period to the next for her modest dividends (twenty-eight pounds a year) she might, if she so wished, come into the office on the first of every month, and his chief clerk would there pay her the

equivalent of her twenty-eight pounds per annum in twelve
equal portions. She accepted his offer "like a queen." I could
henceforth be happy to think of her toddling on the first of
every month into Meldrum, Guy and Meldrum, smiling and
bobbing under her black, spangled bonnet, and departing,
amid the pleased smiles of everybody in the office, with her
six shillings and eight pennies wrapped in two single pound
notes clasped in the heel of her gloved fist.

I sent him my cordial thanks and thought no more about
her until exactly one year later when he wrote to me that she
had ordered him to sell her shares. It appeared that she had
become smitten by a sudden longing to possess a blue, brocaded, saddle-back armchair that she had seen one morning
in the window of Cash's in Patrick Street. It appeared further
that for months past "a certain Mrs. Bastable and a certain
Mrs. Sealy," two cronies as doddering as herself, also in her
tenement on Lavitt's Quay, had been telling her that nobody
but "a born foolah" would leave "all that lovely money" lying
idle in Mister Meldrum's fine office on the South Mall.

It was easy enough to hear these two tempters at work on
her:

"Sure, Miss Whelan, you could buy all the armchairs in
Cork with that much money! And look at your poor ould
room with the paint falling off the ceiling like snow! And your
poor ould curtains in tatthers on yer winda! Why don't you
buy an electric fire that would keep you warm all the winter?
And two grand, soft Blarney blankets for your bed? And a
pink, quilted eiderdown? And, anyway, sure that measley
ould two quid that Meldrum gives you wouldn't buy a dead
cat! And supposing yeh die? What'll happen it then? Get a
hold of your money, girl, and *spend it!*"

Mel counterargued and counterpleaded. I pleaded. I got
her parish priest to plead with her. I even offered to buy her

the brocaded armchair as a present. It was no use. Mel sold her shares, gave her a check for £350, wished her well, and we both washed our hands of her.

I next got a long and slightly testy letter from Mel, written on the first day of the following month of May. It began, "Your good Aunty Anna has this morning turned up again in my office, bright as a new-born smile, bowing and bobbing as usual, calmly asking my chief clerk Mooney for what she calls, if you please, *her* little divvies . . ."

In dismay he had come out to her.

"But, Miss Whelan, you've sold your shares! Don't you remember?"

Aunt Anna Maria smiled cunningly at him.

"Ah, yes!" she agreed. "But I didn't sell my little divvies!"

"But," Mel laughed, "your dividends accrued from the capital sum you invested. Once a client sells his shares he withdraws the capital and there can be no more dividends. Surely you understand that?"

At once Aunty Anna's smile vanished. A dark fright started at the bottom of her chin and climbed slowly up to her eyes.

"Mister Meldrum, you know well that I didn't sell me little divvies. I want me little divvies. You always gave me them. They belong to me. Why can't you give them to me now the way you always gave me them at the first of every month? Why are you keeping them back from me now?"

"Miss Whelan, when a client sells his shares they are gone. And when they are gone the dividends naturally cease forthwith. You instructed me to sell. I did so. I gave you back your money in a lump sum. If you now wish to give me back that lump sum I shall be most happy to buy you more shares and your dividends will begin again. Otherwise we have nothing for you."

Aunty Anna had burst into floods of tears, and begun to wail, with the whole office staring at the the pair of them.

"What do I want with shares? I don't want any more ould shares. I gave you back me shares. Keep 'em! I don't want 'em. All I want is me little divvies. And anyway I haven't the money you gave me, I bought an armchair with it, and an electric fire from the E.S.B., and a costume from Dowden's, and I gave fifty pounds to the Canon to say masses for my poor soul when I'm dead, and I loaned ten quid to Mrs. Bastable on the ground floor, and ten quid to Mrs. Sealy on the third floor back, and what with this and that and the other all I have left is a few quid, and I don't know where I put 'em. I'd lay down me life I put 'em in the brown teapot on the top shelf but when I went looking for them yesterday I couldn't find them high nor low. Mrs. Sealy says I must have made tea with them, but I tell you, Mister Meldrum, I wouldn't trust that one as far as I'd throw her. Mister Meldrum, give me me little divvies. They're all I have to live on bar that mangy old pension. I want me divvies here and now, if you please, or I'll go out there in the street and call a policeman!"

Mel led her gently into his inner sanctum, together with his bookkeeper, and the two of them spent an hour explaining to her, in every way they could think of, the difference between shares and dividends. They showed her the receipt for the purchase of the shares, for the dividends they had earned over the year, the notation of the resale of the shares, and the red line drawn clearly at the end of her account to show that it was now closed forever. They might as well have been talking to the carpet. Aunty Anna just could not understand that he who does not speculate cannot accumulate. The upshot of it was that she became so upset, and Mel became so angry with her, and then so upset because he had upset her that, to comfort her, he took £2.6.8. out of his pocket, the equivalent of what she had hitherto lawfully drawn every month, told her that this was the end, the very end, and that she must now reconcile herself, firmly and finally, if she would be so very kind, to the plain fact that she was no longer in the market for anything. And so he showed her out, bobbing, and smiling, and happy, and (he hoped), convinced. He was most forbearing about it all. Three pages he wrote about it to me. All I could do was to write him a properly apologetic and deeply grateful reply, enclosing my check for £2.6.8., which, I noted, in some surprise, he duly cashed.

On the morning of the first of the following month of June he was on the telephone. His voice over the wire sounded rather strangled.

"Your good aunt is back here in my office again. She is sitting directly opposite me. She seems to be in very good health. And in good spirits to boot. In fact she is beaming at me. Nevertheless she is once more demanding dividends on shares which she does not possess. Will you kindly tell me at once what you wish me to do with, for, or to her?"

"Oh, Lord, Mel! This is too bad! I'm very sorry! I'm awfully sorry. Look, Mel, couldn't you just explain firmly to the old lady that . . ."

At this his voice rose to a squeak of utter exasperation.

"Miss Whelan has been in my private office for the past three-quarters of a bloody hour with my bookkeeper, my assistant bookkeeper, my chief clerk . . ."

"Mel! I'll tell you what to do. Just give her the two quid six and eight and I'll send you a check for it this minute, and then tell her never, just simply never to darken your doors again."

Mel's voice became precise, piercing, priggish and prim in a way that suddenly recalled to me a familiar side of his nature that I had completely forgotten until that moment.

"I have no hope what-so-ever of achieve-ing the entire-ly de-sirable state of affairs that you so blandly de-pict. I am afraid the time has arrived for you to come down to Cork in person and talk in person to your good aunt. Furthermore, I must tell you that your proposal about a check is totally contrary to my principles as a man and as a stockbroker. It is contrary to the whole ethics, the whole philosophy, the whole morality of stockbroking. It is inconsistent, unrealistic, unprofessional and absurd. As I have explained to Miss Whelan, he who saves may invest, he who invests may accumulate, he who does not save may not . . ."

"Mel, for God's sake come off it! How the hell can she save anything at all on that measley old pension of hers? Who do you think she is? Bernard Baruch? Henry Ford? John D. Rockefeller? Gulbenkian?"

"In that case," he retorted, "it is as absurd for her to expect as it would be unrealistic for me to pretend that she is entitled to returns on nonexistent capital. In the name of justice, equity and realism, above all in the name of realism, I will not and I cannot pretend to pay to any client dividends that simply do not exist . . . Excuse me one moment."

Here I could hear a confused babble of voices as of four or five people engaged in passionate argument, a hundred and sixty-one blessed miles away from my study in Dublin.

"Hello!" he roared. "How soon, for God Almighty's sake, can you come down to Cork and settle this matter with your aunt?"

I saw that there was no way out of it. It was a Friday. I said that I would take the morning train on Saturday.

"I will meet you at the station."

"Is this an order?" I asked wryly.

His answer was clipped. He recovered himself sufficiently to add "Please!" and even to mention that I could get some sort of ragtime lunch on the train. When I said I would be there, he calmed down. He expanded. He even became amiable. When he broke into French I remembered how, in his student days, he used to go to France every summer and Easter with his widowed mother.

"Bon! Nous causerons de beaucoup de choses. Et nous donnerons le coup-de-grace à l'affaire Anna, et à ses actions imaginaires," — and hung up.

Actions? My dictionary told me that the word means *acts,*

actions, performances, battles, postures, stocks, shares. As I
put back the volume on its shelf I remembered how good he
always used to be at social work among the poor of Cork. I
also wondered a little how such a man could see nothing
wrong with giving charity outside his office in the name of
Saint Vincent de Paul but everything wrong with the idea of
bestowing largesse inside it in the name of pity. I also realized
that I had not met him for some twenty years.

2

It was a perfect June morning. All the way down from
Dublin to Cork the country looked so soft and fresh, so green
and young, and I lunched so well that my heart gradually
warmed both to Aunty Anna and to Mel, the dual cause of
this pleasant excursion back to my home ground. As the fields
floated past and the waves of the telegraph wires rolled and
sank I started to recall the Mel I used to know. Indeed if
anybody had at that moment asked me about him — say,
that old priest half-dozing on the seat opposite me — I would
have launched on a eulogy as long as an elegy.

Stout fellow! Salt of the earth! As fine a chap as you could
hope to meet in a day's march! Honest, kind and absolutely
reliable. The sort of man who would never, simply never, let
you down. A worthy inheritor of his father's and his grandfa-
ther's business. Handsome, strong, tall, always well dressed
— in the old days, we all thought him a bit of a dandy. And so
easy! As smooth and easy as that bog stream outside there.
Oh, now and again he could be gruff if you rubbed him the
wrong way, and he was sometimes given a bit to playing the
big shot. And by that same token he always boasted that he
was a first-class shot. A real, clean-living, open-air man. What
else? Well informed about music. And the opera. Spoke
French well — those visits abroad with his mother. A strong
civic sense, always proud of his native city. Who was it that
told me a few years ago that he is up to his neck nowadays in

all sorts of worthy societies in Cork? The Old Folks Association, the Safety First Association, Saint Vincent de Paul, the Archaeological Society, the Society for the Prevention of Cruelty to Animals, the African Missions Brotherhood . . .

I glanced across at my old priest. He was looking at me as if I had been talking aloud to myself. I turned to the fields.

Well . . . Not exactly very sociable, I suppose. Unless a committee meeting in a hotel room can be called a jolly sociable occasion.

Come to think of it, he always did keep a bit to himself. Not standoffishly, more of a class thing, being so much richer than the rest of us. Or was he a little shy? And I did hear recently that he has given up shooting and taken to bird-watching — from a weekend cottage he has outside Cork, some place along the valley of the Lee beyond Inniscarra. His private hideout where he can "get away from it all."

The old priest was still looking at me. I turned to watch a racing horse.

"All"? I suppose he means the roaring traffic of Cork, which, when I was a student, chiefly meant jarvey cars, bullocks, drayhorses and bicycles. It is a quiet place. Not really a city at all. And, then, of course, we mustn't forget Cork's famous social whirl. Bridge every night, golf every Saturday, and, for the happy few, a spot of sailing in the harbor over the weekend. And tubs of secret drinking in hotel lounges for the happy many, stealing in discreetly by the back door. Or were they the unhappy many? Cork can be a pretty grim place in the winter. As I well know! Lord! don't I know!

A sunshot shower of rain flecked the windows of the train.

We may as well face it. Cork is a place where it rains, and rains, and rains, with an implacable and persistent slowness. A frightful place, really, in the winter! Of course, if you have enough piasters you can knock out a good time even in Cork. But you have to have the piasters. And I never did. Mel did. And lots of 'em. Rich? Very. At least by Cork standards. A tight, bloody hole, full to the butt of the lugs with old family businesses that keep a firm grip on their miserly homesteads.

Was that priest raising his eyebrows at me?

Naturally, he's a Catholic! A most devoted Catholic. No! A baptized, confirmed, and unmarried bachelor. That is odd — because he always had a great eye for the girls. Funny I never thought of it before. In Ireland you don't, somehow. You get so used to the widowed mother in the background, or the uncle who is a bishop, or the two brothers who are priests, or the three sisters who are nuns. The tradition of celibacy. But, by God, he did have that roving eye! Why didn't he marry? And he was quite good-looking. Even if he has slightly prominent teeth, and a rather silly, affected way of shaving that leaves a tuft of hair on each cheekbone.

I closed my eyes to see him better. I wondered why the hell I was coming down here at all.

He must be forty-six or forty-seven by now. If his taste in clothes is what it used to be he will be wearing a check sports coat with two splits behind and a check cap slightly yawed over his gamesome eye. The country squire's weekend costume.

"Is there," I asked the old priest, "a train back out of Cork tonight?"

He smiled crookedly.

"There is. A slow one. You're not staying long with us, I see?"

"I have to get back tonight."

I felt my face flushing. My wife not well. My youngest daughter has a fever. I am in a bad shape myself, Mel. In fact I am running a temperature of 102°. My brother is arriving from London on Sunday morning. My best friend is dying. My uncle died yesterday. I simply have to go to his funeral.

"Are you sure, Father, there is a train out of Cork tonight?"

"There is. One of these days they say we are going to have our own airport. With airplanes."

The rain stopped and the sun burst out, but I did not trust it one inch. I recognized familiar fields. Poor-looking fields. The rain. The cold. My poverty-stricken youth in Cork. We passed Blarney. Then we were in the tunnel, and though I knew there is this long tunnel into Cork I had forgotten how long it was, how smelly, and how dark.

He was the first person I saw on the platform, in his tweeds and his sporty cap. The wings of his hair were turning white. His teeth were much too white to be his own. He wore spectacles. We greeted one another warmly. People talk of well-remembered voices. I recognized his slightly hectoring Oxford-cum-Cork accent only when he said, "So we got Your Highness down to Cork at last?" I laughed, "Why do Cork people always say 'up to Dublin' and 'down to Cork'? Here I am, like Orpheus." He sniffed by way of reply, and we went out of the station yard teasing one another amiably about our advancing years, got into his white sports Jaguar and shot across the station yard like a bullet.

3

"Well?" I said. "And how did you finish up yesterday with my dear old Aunty Anna?"

He pretended to be coping with the traffic — at that point a dozen bullocks lurching wild-eyed all over the street before the howls and waving arms of two equally wild-eyed drovers. Then, with a sheepish side glance and a grin that was clearly meant to involve me in his illogicality, he said:

"I gave her the odd two quid again. She will obviously be back in a month. And every month for the rest of her life. Unless we do something drastic about her."

"I see. Are we going to beard her now?"

"No! I don't work on Saturdays. And I'm not going to

break my rule of life for that accursed old hairpin. I'm driving you out to my Sabine farm. We've got the whole weekend. We'll talk about her tonight after dinner. And not one minute before!"

I bridled. After all, I was very fond of my Aunty Anna, even if I had not visited her for the last twelve years, and I objected to being shanghaied like this without as much as a "If you'd like it," or "If you can spare the time," or "By your leave." Was he at his old game of playing the big shot? The bossy businessman? At close quarters, over a whole weekend, was he going to turn out to be an awful bore? However, he had been very kind to Aunt Anna, and I had got him into this mess, and I was under an obligation to him, so I said, as pleasantly as I could, "That's very kind of you, Mel. I can see my aunt tomorrow morning, and I'm sure there must be an afternoon train home."

"If that's what you want," he said, rather huffily. Then he said, cheerfully, "If there is a train to Dublin on Sundays I'm sure it takes about ten hours." Then he said, so smugly that anybody who did not know him could well have taken an immediate dislike to him, "You're going to like my cottage — it's a real beauty. Nobody in Cork has anything like it!"

I did not talk much during the drive into and out of the city. It reminded me too much of my father and mother, of my lost youth. He blathered on and on about its great future, its economic development, the airport they were sure to have some day, as if he were the Lord Mayor of the damn place. Then we were out of it and in the country again, and presently — it cannot have been more than twenty minutes at his mad speed — he said, "Behold my Sabine farm!"

At first glance, through the trees, it looked like the sort of cottage that would make any estate agent start pouring out words like "rustic," "picturesque," "antique," "venerable," "traditional," "old-world," and every other kind of pin-headed euphemism for damp, dirty, crumbling, phoney, half-ruined, fourth-hand and thoroughly uncomfortable. When we drew up by its little wooden gate, it turned out to be the sort of dream cottage you meet in English detective stories, or on the travel posters of British Railways. It stood under its trim roof of thatch on a sunbathed side road, in about two acres of orchard, kitchen garden and lawn, facing a small, old church with a not ungraceful spire in brownstone, directly above the Lee murmuring far below in a valley scooped eons ago out of the surrounding hills and covered now with young pine woods. It was long, low and pink-washed, with diamond panes in its small windows, and its walls were covered by a thick curtain of Albertine roses that would be a mellow blaze within a week or two. The door, painted in William Morris blue, was opened by a brown-eyed young woman whom he introduced as, "My housekeeper. My invaluable Sheila." The living room was long and low-ceilinged, furnished in elegant Adams and Chippendale, carpeted in pale green from wall to wall, with an unnecessary but welcoming wood fire sizzling softly in an old brick fireplace. Later, I found that he had put in central heating, electric light and an American-style kitchen. His Sheila brought us Scotch, water and ice cubes, and we sank into two deep armchairs beside the fire.

"You seem to live pretty well, my friend," I admitted, grudgingly.

"I like the simple life," he breezed. "But I'm not simple-minded about it. I'm a realist."

I humphed internally. I recognized the common illusion of most businessmen that writers are all mental defectives, dreamy romancers with about as much common sense as would fit in one of their small toes. Really, I thought again, all this is going to be a frightful bore.

I became aware that his housekeeper was still standing beside us. Her brown eyes reminded me of two shining chestnuts. If her chin had not been a shadow overshot she would have been a beauty. What struck me most about her was not, however, her face, her trim figure or her straight back, but her air of calm self-possession. He gave her a quick, all-over glance.

"Well, my dear? What are you giving us for dinner to-night?"

"Two roast chickens. Parsley potatoes. New. Your own. And fresh peas from the garden."

"And for sweet? Apart from yourself?" he asked, with that kind of gawky smile with which elderly men try to curry favor with scowling children, and that celibates overdo for handsome young women.

"Apart from myself," she replied calmly, "there will be an apple pie. They are the last apples left in your loft."

"With cream?"

"Naturally."

"And the wine?"

She nodded to two bottles standing at a discreet distance from the brickwork of the fireplace. Gevray-Chambertin, 1947.

"Excellent. We will dine at seven-thirty." He turned away from her. "Drink up! I saw two kingfishers flashing along the river last week and I want to check whether they are still there. They've just got married," he added, with a raise-your-eyebrows grin at Sheila, who tossed her head and went off about her business.

"And where did that treasure come from?" I asked, carefully keeping the note of suspicion out of my voice, and noting inwardly that twenty years ago I would have started to pull his leg about her.

"Pure luck. She is a typist in my office. I used to have a dreadful old hairpin, as old and almost as doddery as your mad aunt. Then I suddenly found out that Sheila lives half-way between here and Cork, in a laborer's cottage on the side of the road. When I suggested to her that she might lend a hand and make some extra cash she jumped at it. Every Friday night I drive her home from the office on my way here, collect her on Saturday morning, and Bob's-your-uncle."

He gathered up his binoculars, notebook and camera, and we went off after the kingfishers. I enjoyed every minute of it, tramping for about three hours up and down the river bed. He found his kingfishers, a nesting heron, and became madly excited when he picked out through his binoculars, and let me also see, a buff-colored bird about the size of a thrush but with a long beak, a crest, and black and white stripes on its wings, perched on a tall beech tree.

"Can it," he kept saying in a shouting whisper, "but it can't be, can it *possibly* be a hoopoe?'

He entered every detail in his field notebook, date, hour, temperature, compass bearings and heaven only knows what else, and he became so boyish about it all that my earlier annoyance with him vanished completely. When, on the way home, I asked him casually how old he was, and he said forty-seven, my earlier suspicions also vanished. He was at least twice her age. By the time we got back to his cottage I felt not only so pleasantly tired but so pleasantly relaxed that I told him I had decided not to return home until the Monday morning.

The wood fire, now that the evening chill had come, was welcoming. I found that there were two baths, and lots of hot water. I wallowed in mine for twenty minutes. When we both emerged his Sheila made us a shaker of martinis, and through them we moved leisurely into a perfect dinner. She had not roasted the chickens, she had broiled them *en papillotes*. She must have spent an hour on the apple pie alone — my wife, who is a first-rate cook, could not have improved on its delicate crust.

"Did you teach her all this cooking, Mel?"

"I confess I have tried to play Professor Higgins to her Pygmalion. But only," he winked, "as to her cooking. So far."

By the time we had finished off the two bottles of Burgundy and retired to our armchairs before the fire we were the old — that is the young — Mel and Sean. She lit two shaded lamps, brought us Italian coffee, a bottle of Hine, two warmed glasses, the cigar box and our slippers.

"Wonderful woman!" I murmured. "I hope you never lose her."

"She is useful," he agreed shortly, poured the brandy and, like me, stretched out his long legs to the fire.

For a while there was not a sound except the sizzle of the logs and an occasional slight tinkle from the direction of the kitchen. The deep, darkening country closed around us in such utter silence that when I strained my ears to listen I could hear, deep in the valley, the whisper of the river. Did I hear a pheasant coughing? Drowsily I remembered that he had said that we would talk tonight of Aunty Anna. I had no wish to talk about Aunty Anna, and by the sleepy way he was regarding the fire through his brandy glass I hoped he felt the same. Then I heard his voice, and with something sharper than regret I gathered that he had begun to talk about himself.

4.

"Sean, I'm very glad you came. For a long time now I've been working out a certain idea, something rather important, and I want to try it out on you, just as a sort of test."

Just barely holding off the sleep of bliss, I nodded easily.

"Did it ever strike you that every man — which includes every woman — is his own potter? I mean, that sooner or later every man takes up what you might call the clay, or the plasticene, or the mud, call it what you like, of his experience of life, and throws it down on his potter's wheel, and starts the pedal going, and rounds it up into a shape? Into what I call his idea of the shape of his whole life? Are you following me?"

I nodded myself awake.

"Good! Now for the big snag. It is, why do we do this? I can't say we do it to please ourselves, because we can *have* no selves — can we? We can't *see* ourselves — can we? — or *know* ourselves — can we? — and therefore we cannot *be* ourselves — can we? — until we have made this shape, and looked at it, as one would look in a mirror, and said to ourselves, 'That's me! That's my vocation. My ambition. My politics. My faith. My whole life.' I mean," he pounded on, with a force of energy that made me even more tired and sleepy than before, "I cannot say 'That's me' until I have made my shape, because there is no *me* until I have made my shape. Therefore I can get no real pleasure of it all until the job is actually done. That's a pretty disturbing thought, what-what?"

I pulled myself awake. What had I walked into? Two nights of this twaddle? There simply had to be an afternoon train tomorrow!

"And when the job is done, Mel?"

He gave me a powerful slap on the thigh.

"Then I begin to live. When I at last know exactly what I am, I at last know exactly what I want to do, because my shape, my image, now tells me what I do want to do."

I sighed and stretched.

"And, then, Mel, some other fellow comes along and he looks at your portrait of the artist as a young dog, and he says, 'No! This may be some crazy dream Mel has of himself, or some crazy dream he has of the world as he would like it to be, but it's not our Mel, and it's not our world.' "

"Ha ha, and I might say the same to him, and to his world?"

"You certainly might. But, of course, I hope you're not so daft as to deny that all the time there must be a real objective world outside there? Made up of stockbrokers and tax collectors, and physicists, and isoprene, and polymerization . . ."

"By the way, rubber is going up."

". . . . and gravitation, electricity, atomic weight, blood pressure, measles, kids getting sick, old people dying, kingfishers mating and so on and so on. And a real, objective you, me, and Tom, Dick and Harry inside in each one of us, and no fancies and no fooling." I laughed. "Mel, you're a joy! I'm glad to inform you that you haven't changed one iota since the days when we used to come out from old Father Abstractibus's philosophy lectures, long ago in University College, Cork, and lie on the grass of the quadrangle, and talk for hours about the Object and the Subject and 'What is Reality?' and 'What is the stars?' and never get one inch beyond chasing our own tails. And here you are, still at it! It's a pointless pursuit, and I'm in no mood for it. Mel! If we have to talk about anything at all on top of that wonderful dinner, and that marvelous Gevray-Chambertin, and this perfect brandy, let's talk about a painfully real subject. Let's talk about my Aunty Anna."

"That," he said calmly, "is what I am talking about. About people who live in imaginations, and fantasies, and illusions about themselves. What, so far as I can see, the whole blessed world is doing all the time. Including your dear Auntie Anna Maria Whelan." He stretched out his foot and touched my ankle with the toe of his slipper. "Do you know what your dear Auntie Anna did with that three hundred and fifty quid?"

"You told me. She bought an armchair, and an electric fire, and an eiderdown, and curtains, and masses for her soul, and she gave loans to . . ."

"Rubbish! That's what she said. She bought a fur coat with the three-fifty quid."

"You're a liar!"

"She is the liar."

"Then you're joking."

"It's no joke, my friend. The old divil had the cheek to

have it on her back when she came into my office yesterday. When she went out I had a brain wave. I rang up a friend of mine who works with the Saint Vincent de Pauls in her part of the city and I asked him to drop around and have a look at her place. No armchair, no electric fire, no eiderdown, no new curtains, no nothing. And as for those loans that she invented, as he pointed out to me, the poor don't give anybody loans of ten quid a time. Ten shillings would be more like it. If that! You talk very glibly about the 'real, objective world outside there.' You don't seem to know so very much about it, after all, do you?"

His air of condescension infuriated me.

"It was probably a cheap, secondhand coat!"

"I checked up on that too. Cork is a small place, and there aren't many shops where you can buy new fur coats for a sum as large as that. I rang up Bob Rohu and I told him the whole yarn. I hit a bull's eye at once. He sold it to her himself. He remembered the transaction very well — as you might expect. A poor old woman like her doesn't come in every day to buy a bang-up fur coat. She paid him two hundred and seventy-five pounds for that fur coat. In notes." He paused. He concluded with sardonic formality, "You perceive my trend?"

I was furious, chastened, and filled with pity for my Aunty Anna. I saw, also, that whatever picture Mel had made of himself it would not show him as anybody's fool. I could have choked him. Here was I, who had known Aunty Anna all my life, a man who was supposed to know something about human nature, and here was this fellow who had only met Aunty Anna three or four times in his life, pitilessly exposing her to me as a woman perched out there for thirty years on that big grassy, empty plain of the Curragh of Kildare, working, since she was twenty, for a wealthy trainer, seeing his rich, horsey clients coming and going in all their finery, and thinking, as she grew older and older, with no man ever asking her to marry him — Why the hell had I never realized that she would think it? — that she would never possess anything even dimly like what they possessed. Until, by pure chance, at the age of seventy-odd, she finds herself drawing dividends like the rest of them, trading in the stock market just like the best of them, being received like a lady by the best stockbroker in Cork — and sees that fur coat gleaming in a shop window.

Mel was slowly rolling his brandy around in his brandy glass, and watching me slyly.

"Interesting, isn't it?" he said.

"Very," I said bitterly. After a while of silence I said, "And this is why she won't get any more of what she thinks are her little divvies? Even if I agreed to pay you for them?"

He answered with anger, almost with passion:

"It is. The woman is fooling herself, and I refuse to encourage her. She is trying to make nonsense of everything I believe in. And I won't let her do it. Would you, as a writer, write something you didn't believe to be true?"

"Don't be silly! I'm pleased and proud any time I think I'm able to tell even one tenth of the truth."

"Would you, if you were a doctor, tell lies to a patient?"

"Doctors have to do it all the time. To help them to live. To make it easier for them to die."

"Well, I don't and won't tell lies. Facts are facts in my profession, and I have to live by them."

"You gamble."

"I do not."

"You encourage your clients to gamble."

"I do not."

"Then what do you do for a living?"

"I hope."

We laughed. We calmed down.

"What about charity, Mel?"

"I would have no objection to giving your aunt charity. I

like the old thing. She is a nice poor soul. And my friend in
the Vincent de Pauls assures me that she is a very worthy
creature. In fact I'd be quite happy to pay the old hairpin . . ." Here the chill caution of the trained businessman
entered his voice. "I'd be quite happy to go halves with you in
paying her the equivalent of her blasted divvies every year.
But not as dividends! Strictly as a gift from the pair of us."

"Mel, that's kind of you! Our whole problem is solved.
Let's give her the twenty-eight pounds a year as a present.
What are you looking at me like that for?"

"She won't take it."

"Why won't she take it?"

"Because it's charity. And she doesn't want charity. The
poor never want charity. They hate it because it makes them
feel their poverty. Any of them that have any pride left in
them. And that old lady is stiff with pride. You could take a
gift from me, I could take a gift from you, Queen Victoria
would have taken all India and hung it on her charm bracelet
without as much as a thank you. But not the poor! However,
try her. Take the Jaguar tomorrow morning and drive into
town and take her out to lunch. I bet you a tenner to a bob
she'll refuse." He rose. "Ah! Here we are!"

This was for our housekeeper, waiting, ready to be driven
home. She was wearing a small fur hat and a neat, belted
tweed coat. From under her hat her dark hair crooked around
each cheek. Now that she was wearing high-heeled shoes I
noticed how long and elegant her legs were.

"That," said Mel, surveying her, "is a darling little hat you
have."

"I had it on this morning," she said quietly. "But men
never notice anything."

"Where did you get it?"

"I bought it of course. It's wild mink. I've been saving up
for it for years. I got it at Rohu's."

"Good girl!" he said enthusiastically, and winked at me in

approval of his pupil, while I wondered if he knew how much even that little dream of wild mink cost her. She might well have been saving up for it for years. "I'll bring around the car. I won't be long," he said to me. "Play yourself some music while we're away. I've got some good records."

When he had gone out I said to her, "Won't you sit down while you are waiting?" She sat sedately on the arm of his vacated chair and crossed her pretty heron's legs.

"Do you like music, Sheila?"

"I used to like only jazz. Recently I've come to prefer classical music. Mr. Meldrum has been introducing me to it. Shall I show you how to work the machine? It's new and he is very particular about it. It has two extensions. They give you the impression that you are surrounded by an orchestra. Oh!" lifting the lid and looking in. "There's a record on it. Yes, here is the jacket — it's the *Siegfried Idyll*. Would you like to play this one. Or would you perhaps prefer something more modern?"

(I thought, you may only be a typist in his office but you have the manners of a woman of the world.)

"Yes, I'd like to hear that again. It's years since I heard any Wagner. Do *you* like it?"

"We've played it so often now that I'm just beginning to understand what it's all about."

"And what is it all about?" I smiled.

She switched on the machine and closed the lid.

"I suppose it's about happiness through love. It takes a little time to warm up. Then it works automatically."

I glanced at her. Was she a deep one? His horn hooted from the road. For the first time she smiled. She had perfect teeth.

"I must be off. Don't let the fire die down. He sometimes sits up late. There are plenty of logs. And I've fixed the electric blankets at number two heat, so they will be nice and cozy before you have finished your last nightcaps. Good night."

When she was gone I walked to the window to look after her and saw that a vast moon had risen over the dark hills surrounding the valley, touching their round breasts as softly as a kiss. He and she stood arm in arm looking at it, he leaning a little over her, pointing up to the moon as if he were showing it to an infant, and saying something that, for once, must have not been off the mark, because she swiftly turned her face up to him and laughed gloriously. Just as he touched her furry cap with his finger the record behind me fell into place and a score of violins began whispering, pulsing and swelling around me as powerfully as the immense moon. In that second I had no more doubts about the pair of them. He released her arm, opened the door of the car for her so that its carriage light fell for a second on her radiant smile. He banged her door, got in on his side and shot away. I returned slowly to my armchair, my brandy and cigar, and stared into the flickering fire.

Gradually the idyll rose in wave after wave to its first crescendo until the bows of the violins were so many lashing whips of passionate sound. The lunatic! Sitting here, of nights, in this silent valley, with her opposite him, listening to music like this Christmas morning music, composed by a lover for his sleeping beloved. If it made me wish to God I was at home in bed with my wife what, in Heaven's name, must it do to him? I suddenly remembered something that made me snatch up the jacket of the record. I was right. Wagner wrote that love idyll when he was fifty-seven, having fallen in love with Cosima Liszt when he was in his forties and she in her twenties, and I began to think of other elderly men who had married young women, finding them even in that tight little city a few miles away. Wintering men plucking their budding roses. Old Robert Cottrell, the shipowner, who

married a barmaid out of the Victoria Hotel. Frank Lane, the
distiller, who at sixty picked a pretty waitress out of the
Golden Tavern. And who was that miller who, after being a
widower for twenty-five years, fell in love with one of his mill
girls and had children by her, younger than his grandchil-
dren? It is the sort of thing that can easily happen to men who
have lived all their lives by the most rigid disciplines, and
then suddenly get sick of it all and throw their hats over the
moon.

I became more calm as the music slowly died in exhaustion
of its own surfeit. He was as open as a book — all that talk
of his about men taking the clay of life and making a self-
shape of it. Of her I knew nothing except that he had said she
lived in a roadside cottage and, as he must know well — and
he would be the first to say it — that a rich stockbroker
would be a wonderful catch for her. I started to walk restlessly
about the house. By error I entered his bedroom. I shut the
door quickly, feeling that I was floundering in deep and dan-
gerous tides. The covers of his bed had been neatly turned
down at an angle of forty-five degrees and on his pillow there
lay a red rosebud. I went to bed and fell into such a sound
sleep that I did not hear him return.

When I woke up it was blazing sun outside and the cottage
was empty: he had presumably gone to Mass and to collect
her. When they came in he was wearing the rosebud in his
lapel. After breakfast I took the Jaguar and drove into town
to meet my Aunty Anna.

5

The city was full of the sound of church bells but there was
hardly a soul out along the quay where she lived. Even the
gulls were silent, floating on the river or perched along the
quayside walls. I drew up outside her old fabric of a house, its
railings crooked, its fanlight cracked, its traditional eight-
paneled door clotted with years of paint asking only for a

blowlamp and a week's scraping to reveal chiseled moldings and fine mahogany. I sat for a while in the car thinking of the Aunty Anna I knew, and the best way to handle her.

She had always been a soft, slack, complaining creature with, so far as I knew, no keener interests in life than backing horses, telling fortunes on the cups and cards, eating boiled sweets and reading violet-colored penny novelettes. I should have brought her a box of chocolates. I drove off and managed to find a shop open that sold them. It may have been, it occurred to me, this love of boiled sweets that used to give her so much trouble with her teeth; they used to pain her a great deal and several of them were decayed in the front of her mouth. At that time there was some kind of pulp, paste or malleable wafer that poor country folk used as a dental stopgap to hide these marks of decay on special occasions. Or perhaps it was only white paper chewed-up? She used it constantly and it made her teeth look like putty. The poor woman had also had an operation performed, unskillfully, on her left elbow, which had a moist hollow, like a navel, where the point of the ulna ought to have been; she used to nurse it all the time with her fondling right hand, especially on cold or windy days. Would the poor old thing respond to the idea of going to a good surgeon? Or I could, perhaps, tempt her with some good, stout, comfortable dresses: my wife could easily get those for her. Not that I feared, looking up at the crumbling bricks of her tenement, that I would have any difficulty in persuading her to accept an annual gift, and I thought back to those days on the rolling, green Curragh when she had at least had every comfort, the best of food, and healthy, country air, and I realized that she should never have left her base, and that the ideal, but now impossible, thing for her to do would be to go back and live in the country where she belonged.

A few minutes later I was holding her weeping in my arms, in her one room where she had cooked, slept, and sat day after day, for so many years, and as I smelled the familiar, indefinable musk of urban poverty, suggestive mainly of sour clothes, bad sewage and fried onions, I was overcome with shame that I had not visited her once during the twelve years since I left Cork to be married. I kissed her, and she kissed me, as maternally as if I were still a small boy. Then I stood back, looked at her and got a shock of memory. She had a face like an old turtle, she was humped like a heron, and she was rouged. Long ago, my mother had laughed one day and said she did it with geranium petals rubbed lightly in pale brown boot polish. I noted, too, that all her decayed teeth were replaced by a good denture, and that her hair was tinted and blued. Like a boy I endured the reproaches that she poured over me, and then, eager to be out of that jumbled, stuffy room, I bustled her to get ready and come out to lunch at the Victoria Hotel.

She put on her fur coat, and a small, ancient straw hat, gay with white daisies. Once she was dressed she became rigid with what Cork calls grandeur, as when she said: "This is quite a nice little car," and started talking about all the much grander cars she used to drive in at the Curragh Races. At lunch she held her knife and fork at right angles to her plate, sipped her wine like a bird, drank her coffee with the little finger crooked, hem-hemmed into her napkin like a nun, and small talked as if she were royalty giving me an audience, all of it gossip and chit-chat about the gentry of the Curragh and their fine ladies and great houses. At the end of the lunch she produced a compact, powdered her nose, examined her face intently all over, and delicately applied a pink lipstick. She evaded all my efforts to talk of old times until we moved into the empty lounge where I had a stout brandy. She preferred a gin-and-lime. At last I did lure her out of her glorious past to my proposal that I should give her twenty-eight pounds a year (I carefully left Mel out of it) as a little gesture, "For old times' sake, *Aunty?*" — trying to make her stop being Her Majesty, and become my Aunty Anna again. She made short work of me.

"No! Thank you very much. Now that I have my divvies I don't need it."

From there we went back and forth over the whole thing, over more brandy and gin, for two fruitless hours. Gifts she would ("of course") not accept. Her divvies she would ("of course") not renounce. By the end of it I had gained only one point. She said, coldly but with spirit, that if "that man" denied her her rights she would never darken his door again.

"I will have nothing more to do with this so-called Mister Meldrum. I am finished with all fraudulent stockbrokers forever."

It was four o'clock before I surrendered, furious, rejected, humiliated and exhausted. I drove her around the city, slowly at her queenly request, in my white Jaguar (in which, I told her, I had arrived from Dublin that morning), and ended up at her door amid a crowd of lane kids oohing and aahing at what one of them called Snow White's car. I promised faithfully to visit her again next summer, kissed her goodbye, excused my haste by saying that I had to be back in Dublin before nightfall, and drove away amid the huzzas of the tiny mob. As soon as I got around a corner I paused to rub off her lipstick. I felt very proud of her, I despised myself, and I hated Mel and all that he and his kind stood for — by which I do not now know what I meant then, unless it had something to do with the corrupting power of money over us all.

I was in no mood to face his guffaws of triumph. I parked the Jaguar on the empty South Mall and went wandering through the silent, Sunday streets of this city of my youth, seeing little of it. I was too angry, and too absorbed in trying to devise some means of helping her, and at every turn bothered by unhappy thoughts about Mel and myself, and about whatever it was that the years had done to us both. Was he right in saying that I knew nothing about poor people like Aunty Anna? His Sheila was a young, pretty Aunty Anna, poor like her, being drawn now, as she had been, close to the world of wealth. What did he really know about her? The question brought me to the point — I was then leaning over the old South Gate Bridge, looking down into the River Lee, far from sweet-smelling at low tide — of thinking again not of him alone but of myself and him, as we were when we were here, at college together, years ago. What did I really ever know about him? My Aunty Anna was dead, replaced by what would have been described in one of her violet-covered novelettes as "Miss Anna Whelan, a country lady in reduced circumstances," with nothing left to her from her better days but her memories and her fur coat, defrauded and impoverished of thousands of pounds — her lost fortune would be at least that much within a matter of weeks — by a slick stockbroker. Had my Mel ever existed?

We are not one person. We pass through several lives of faith, ambition, sometimes love, often friendship. We change, die and live again. In that cozy cottage of his I had been the guest of a ghost. Myself a ghost? If he was a new man his Sheila might know him. I did not. For all I knew, she was creating him. All I knew, as I rose from the parapet and walked back to the car, was that I must return to his cottage, as I must leave it, in the most careful silence.

I got back in time to join him and the local curate in another of Sheila's cool five-to-one martinis. Over the dinner, which was just as good as the one the night before, I left the talk to Mel and his guest, all about archaeology, birds, the proposed airport, Cork's current political gossip. I envied the pair of them. Nobody in any capital city can ever be so intimately and intensely absorbed about local matters as provincials always are about the doings and the characters of their city-states. The curate left early. Mel drove Sheila home immediately after. He returned, within twenty minutes.

I was standing with my hand on the high mantelpiece of the fireplace listening to the verso of the *Siegfried Idyll,* the end of the last act of *Die Walküre.* As he came in I raised a silencing hand, excited as I was by the heroic loveliness of this music that lays Brunhilde on the mountainside in Valhalla, at the center of encircling fires through which a young man, who will be Siegfried, will one day break to deliver her with a kiss. Mel threw himself into his armchair, his hands behind his head, and we both listened until the music ended and the silence and the dark of the country began to hum again in our ears. For a while we said nothing. Then I did what I had promised not to do.

"Well?" I asked, looking down at him.

"Well?" he said, looking up at me.

"Do I congratulate you?"

"On what?"

"On your Brunhilde."

Lazily he rolled his head on the back of his chair.

"Meaning no? Or that you don't know?"

Again he slowly rolled his head.

"Giving nothing away? Mel, you didn't used to be so damn cautious. What has happened to you? Come on, Mel, take a chance on life. Begin by giving Aunty Anna her divvies."

"Aha? So she refused our gift?"

"She refused. Also she will trouble you no more. She is now convinced that you are a fraudulent stockbroker who has robbed her of a fortune. Come on, man! Gamble for once in your cautious life. Stop being a fraudulent broker."

"Are you suggesting that I should let your aunt blackmail me?"

"I'm suggesting that you forget the idol you have made outside in the woodshed. It's not you. It can't be you. The Mel I knew can't be that fancy portrait of an unbreakable, incorruptible, crusty, self-absorbed old man, stiff-necked with principles and pride and priggishness. It is a false god. Kick it out on the rubbish heap. When you have made yourself a real image of yourself you'll find there is nothing so terribly frightening about giving Aunty Anna her divvies — or marrying Sheila."

I had said "frightening" because immediately I started suggesting that he was different to whatever he wanted to be I had seen his eyes under his blond eyelashes contract, a blush appear on his cheekbones under their gray outcrops of hair, his mouth begin to melt. With a flick he threw away the sudden fear.

"I haven't changed. I am what I am, always was and intend always to be. And if I am a prig, as you so kindly call me, I'm content to be a prig. It's better than being a cock-eyed dreamer like you and your mad aunt."

"Then why are you playing with the girl?"

"I am not."

"In that case you might wipe that lipstick off your cheek."

"You know nothing about her." He paused. "She has a boy friend. He was waiting for her again at her cottage tonight."

"I shouldn't be surprised if she had a dozen boy friends. A girl as pretty as that! You have seen him often?"

"I have. He comes around here on his motorcycle whenever she stays a bit later than usual. Just to offer her a lift home. Just by way of no harm. Each time, she goes off with him at once. I followed them one night. I saw them kissing and mugging under a tree. If she can deceive him she could deceive me. If I married her I might be unhappy all my life, I'd be jealous and suspicious of her all my life."

"You make me sick! *You* might not be happy? Why don't you say she might not be happy? What sort of a thing do you think marriage is? One long honeymoon? Happiness is a bonus. You smuggle it. You work for it. It comes and goes. You have to be in the market to snatch it. Where's your realism? He who does not speculate cannot accumulate. Stop being such a coward! Live, man, live!"

"I prefer to be logical."

"Then you certainly will not give Aunty Anna her imaginary divvies, and you will have to sack your imaginary Sheila, and then you will be very unhappy indeed."

"I may be. It will wear off. And, anyway, it's none of your damn business."

For a couple of moments we looked at one another hatefully. Then I turned and without saying good-night went to my room. Almost immediately I heard the front door slam. Parting the curtains I saw him stride down the path, out into the moonlit road, and around the corner under the deep shadows of the trees towards where we had gone yesterday to watch the kingfishers, the nesting heron and that unlikely, crested, exotic bird. For a second my heart went out to him. Then I shrugged him off in despair. I was awakened — my watch said it was two o'clock — by the sound of the Brunhildian flames wavering, leaping, pulsing from their mountaintop among the gods. I, in bed, he, by the ashen fire, listened to it together. After it died away I heard his door click.

In the morning I rose to find him already up and in his spotless yellow and white kitchen making coffee and toast.

"Morning, Mel!"

"Hello! Sleep well? I'm the cook on Monday mornings. She leaves everything ready, as you see," nodding to the napery, china and silverware on the table.

She had even left a tiny bouquet of polyanthuses, alyssum, and cowslips in a vase.

He was dressed for the city in his black jacket, with black and gray striped pants, gray suede waistcoat, stiff white collar and striped shirt, a small pearl tiepin in his gray tie. Over the coffee he talked about birds, and for that while, as on the Saturday, he was again his old attractive, youthful, zestful self. He talked of the hoopoe, saying, "It cannot have been one — they pass us by in the spring." He talked about nightjars. He sounded knowledgeable about owls. When we were ready to go he saw to it that every curtain was drawn ("the sun fades the mahogany") and every window carefully fastened, took down his bowler hat and umbrella, double-locked the door, felt it twice, looked all over the front of the cottage, and we drove off into another sunbathed morning.

On the way into town we picked up Sheila outside her roadside cottage, and after that we did not speak at all until he dropped her at his office. There I tried to insist on his not seeing me off at the station — he was a busy man, Monday morning and all that, he must have lots to attend to — and he insisted against my insisting, and we almost squabbled again before he gave in so far as to go into his office to ask if there was anything urgent. He brought me in with him, and formally introduced me to his chief accountant and his book-keeper. While he ruffled through his mail, I chatted with them, and noted the Turkish carpet, and all his modern gadgets, and thought that this was the place where Aunty Anna began to change. At the station he insisted on buying me the morning papers, and on waiting by my carriage door until the train should carry me away. I thanked him for our enjoyable weekend, assured him I meant it, praised his cottage, remembered the food and the wine, promised that we would meet again, to which he nodded, and exchanged a few polite, parting words. As the porters started to slam the last doors, and pull up the windows against the rank smells of the tunnel at the platform's end he said, his pointed face lifted below my window, his eyes sullen above the two little tufts of graying hair on his cheekbones:

"You will be pleased to hear, by the way, that I have decided to give your aunt her dividends, as usual. Naturally, we go halves in that."

I leaned down and grasped his shoulder.

"And marry Sheila?"

"I know when I'm licked. I'm going to give her the sack

this morning. I'll have to get a new housekeeper. I am going to ask your Aunty Anna."

"But she's seventy! And a lady in reduced circumstances. She will refuse."

"Not when she sees my cottage," he said arrogantly. "I'm only there on weekends. She can imagine she is a real lady for five days in the week. Not bad! And she has been a cook. And she won't tempt my flesh. Hail! And Farewell!"

The train started to puff and chug and he and the platform slid slowly away.

Seconds later I was in the tunnel. My window went opaque. I got the rancid smell of the underworld. "And Farewell?" Evidently I was not, it was a just judgment on my presumption, to meet him ever again. I had probed, I had interfered, I had uncovered his most secret dream and destroyed it by forcing him to bring it to the test of reality. I had been tiresome in every way. I had counted on finding the Mel I had thought I had always known, felt affronted at finding him rather different, tried to make him more different, and yet at the same time have my old Mel, and was furious when he insisted on remaining whatever he thought he always had been. In such irreducibly plenary moments of total mess, shame and embarrassment the truth can only be trite, though none the less the truth for that. Youth only knows embryos. Life is equivocal. Life is a gamble. Friendship is frail. Love is a risk. All any man can do when fate sends some shining dream his way is to embrace it and fight for it without rest or reason because we do all the important things of life for reasons (It *has* been said!) of which reason knows nothing — until about twenty years after.

For that mile of tunnel I had them all there together with me in that dark carriage, with the cold smell of steam, and an occasional splash of water on the roof from the ventilation shafts to the upper air. Abruptly, the tunnel shot away, and I felt like a skin diver soaring from the sea to the light of day. Green country exploded around me on all sides in universal sunlight. Small, pink carts went ambling below me along dusty side roads to the creamery. Black and white cows munched. Everywhere in the fields men were at their morning work. I opened the window to let in the fresh air. Then, with only occasional glances out at the fields floating away behind me, and at certain images and thoughts that became fainter and fewer with the passing miles, I settled down to my newspapers and gathering thoughts of my home and my work.

I have never seen him since, although we are both now aging men, but, perhaps three times, it could be four, as if a little switch went click in my memory he has revisited me — a dubious shadow, with two gray tufts on his cheeks and a long nose like Sherlock Holmes . . . No more. He did write to me once, after — not, I observed, *when* — Aunty Anna died, in his service, aged eighty-one. Piously, he had attended to everything. He enclosed some snapshots that he had found in her bag: myself as a young boy, herself as a young woman, horses in the green sunlight of the Curragh. In her will, he mentioned, she had bequeathed her dividends to him.

The Heat of the Sun

THEY never said, "Let's go down to Rodgers's," although it was old Rodgers who owned the pub; they said, "Let's go down to Uncle Alfie." A good pub is like that, it is the barman who makes it, not the boss. They gave their custom to Rodgers, they gave their confidence to Alfie. He knew them all, some of them ever since they were old enough to drink their first pint in a pub. He knew their fathers, mothers, brothers, sisters, girls, prospects, wages, hopes, fears and what they were always calling their ideas and their ideals and that he called their ould guff. Always their friend, sometimes their philosopher, he was rarely their guide. Your da gave you money (sometimes) and you hardly thanked him for it. Alfie loaned it. Your da gave you advice and you resented it. Alfie could give you a rap as sharp as lightning, and you accepted it because he gave it as your equal. Your da never had any news. Alfie knew everything. He was your postman, passing on bits of paper with messages in pencil: "Deirdre was asking after you, try 803222, Hughesy." Or, "For Jay's sake leave a half-note for me, Paddywhack." He might hand you out a colored postcard with a foreign stamp, taken from the little sheaf stuck behind the cash register. The sheeting around the register was as wallpapered as a Travel Bureau with colored postcards from all over the world. Best of all, he was there always: his coat off, his shirt-sleeves rolled up, his bowler hat always on his balding red head, a monument in a white apron, with a brogue like an echo in an empty barrel.

You pushed the two glass doors in like a king.

"Hi, Alfie!"

"Jakus, Johnny, is that yourself?" With a slap on the shoulder and your drink slid in front of you unasked. "Fwhere were you this time? Did yoo have a good voyage?"

"Not bad. Same old thing — Black Sea, the Piraeus, Palermo, Naples, Genoa. Crumby dumps!" Your half-pint aloft. "What's the best port in all creation, Alfie?"

"As if yoo needed to ask me!"

"Here's to it, and God bless it. *'Dublin town, O Dublin town| That's where I long to be,| With the friends so dear to me,| Grafton Street where it's all so gay,| And the lights of Scotsman's Bay.'* Theme song of every poor bloody exile of Erin. Up the rebels. Long live the Queen of Sheba. How's Tommy? How's Angela? How's Casey, Joanna, Hughesy, Paddywhack? Does my little black-eyed Deirdre still love me?"

"Paddy was in on Chuesday night. He's working with the Gas Company now."

"Poor old Paddywhack! Has he the gold wristlet still? And the signet ring? Will the poor bugger never get a decent job?"

(He noticed that Deirdre was being passed over.)

"His wife had another child. That's six he has now."

"Sacred Heart!"

"Hughesy is going strong with Flossie."

"Sure that line is four years old. When is the bastard going to make an honest woman of her?"

"Is it a busman? She's aiming higher than that. The trouble with yoo young fellows is ye pick gurls beyond yeer means. Yeer eyes are bigger than yeer balls. Leave them their youth. Wedded, bedded and deaded, the world knows it."

Alfie was anti-woman. Everybody knew he had a wife some-

where, and three kids, separated five years ago. She was before their time — none of them had ever seen her. Poor old
Alfie! In hope and in dreams and in insecurity is life. In home
and in safety is . . .

It would make you sick the way they always want to corral
you into the blooming home. Like tonight:

"Oh, no! Johnny! You're not going out from us on your
first night home? We haven't seen you for four months! And
your father and me looking forward to a nice bit of a chat.
About your future, Johnny. About your plans, Johnny. About
your prospects. Sit down there now and be talking to us."

You sat back. They talked. You mumbled. The end of it
was always the same. After another half-hour of twitching
you said it again.

"I think I'll drop down to Uncle Alfie for an hour to see
the boys. I won't be late, Mum. But leave the key under the
mat. Don't wait up for me, I'll creep in like a mouse."

Hating the way they looked at one another, knowing well
that you wouldn't be in before one in the morning — if then
— shoes in hand, head cocked for the slightest tweak of a
bedspring upstairs, feeling a right bastard or, if, with God's
help, you were tight enough, feeling nothing but your way.
Hell roast 'em! Why couldn't they understand that when you
cabled "COMING HOME THURSDAY STOP LOVE STOP JOHNNY,"
it meant you wanted to see them okay, and you were bringing
presents for them, okay, and it would be nice to have your
own old room, okay, but what you were really seeing was the
gleam of the bottles, and the wet mahogany, and the slow,
floating layers of smoke, shoulders pushing, hands shooting,
everybody talking at the top of his voice to be heard and old
Alfie grinning at ye all like an ape. God Almighty! When a
fellow has only seven lousy days' shore leave . . .

It was dry October, the softest twinge of faintest fog, the
streets empty, a halo around every light, a right night for a

landfall. Tramping downhill, peaked cap slanted, whistling, he foresaw it all. A dollar to a dime on it — Alfie would resume exactly where they left off four months ago:

"Johnny! It is high time yoo thought of settling down."

"Gimme a chance, Alfie. I'm only twenty-three. I'll settle down some day. Why don't you say that to Loftus or Casey?"

"Loftus will find it hard. With that short leg. Anyway I mean settle down ashore. That wandering life you're leading! It's no life!"

"I'm not ready, Alfie. I want to meet the right girl. I'm mad about Deirdre, but she's always talking about motorcars, and houses in Foxrock, and Sunday morning sherry parties. I'm not sure of her. The right girl is damn hard to find. It's a funny thing, Alfie, all the nice women I meet are married women."

"An ould shtory. And the ladies tell me all the nice men are married men. I think the truth is that no wan is ready until they know by heart the music that tames the wild bashte — know it and are beginning to forget it. I don't think Deirdre is the right sawrt for you at all, Johnny. She's too expensive for you. She's too ambitious. She's like Flossie — playing with Hughesy, trying to learn the chune on the cheap, as you might say. Johnny! If I were you, I'd choose a woman of experience. What'd suit you, now, down to the ground would be a nice, soft, cozy, widow woman that knows every chune in the piper's bag."

"Oh, for God's sake, Alfie! With a wooden leg? And a yellow wig? And a blue bankbook? I'm young, Alfie. What I dream about, in the middle watch, looking up at the stars, is a young, beautiful, exquisite, lovely, fond, right-dimensional Irish girl of eighteen. Like my little Deirdre. Pure as the driven snow. Loyal and true. Gentle as the dawn. Deirdre, without the motorcar!"

Alfie would draw up from the counter and make a face as if he was sucking alum.

"Yoo could sing it if yoo had the voice for it. *'She was luvely and fair, as the roase of the Summer,/ But it was not her beauutye aloane tha-at won me'—"*

He would snatch it from him tonight:

" 'Oh, no! 'Twas the truth in her eyes ever dawning,/ That made me love Mary, the Rose of Tra-a-leee.' A hundred per cent right, Alfie. Lead me to her."

"I wouldn't give you two pinnies for a gurl of eighteen — she couldn't cook an egg for you. And dimensions are all very fine and dandy, but they don't lasht, boy. They don't lasht! Did I ever tell yoo about the fellow that married the opera singer? She was like an angel out of heaven on the stage. In the bed she was no better to him than an ould shweeping brush. He used to wake her up in the middle of the night and say, 'Sing, damn yoor sowl!' "

Aboard ship he had told them that one many times. Always the old deckhands would nod solemnly and say, "And 'e's dead right, chum! Feed me and love me, what more can a man ask for?" Well, if he said it tonight he would be ready for him; drawing himself up, with one hand flat on his top left brass button:

"Alfie! In this rotten, cheating, stinking, lousy, modern world my generation is going to *fight* for our ideals!"

Four miles out over the shadowy sea the light on the Kish bank winked drowsily. Fog? It was so quiet along the promenade that he could hear the small waves below him sucking into the rocks. Wind soft from the south. The only person he passed was a Civic Guard in a cape. He turned right, then left, passed the Coal Harbour, wheeled right again, left, and there were the lights flowing out on the pavement. He pushed the two glass doors in like a king.

"Hi! . . ."

He stopped. The young barman was staring at him with uplifted eyebrows. He looked around. The place was like a morgue. He recognized old Molly Goosegog, her fat legs spread, soaking it up as usual with the one-armed colonel. Three business types, their hats on, hunched over a table, talking low. In the farthest corner two middle-aged women were drinking gins and bitters. Dyed, dried, skewered and skivered, two old boiling hens, cigarettes dangled from their red beaks. He moved slowly to the counter.

"Where's Alfie?" he asked quietly.

"On leave."

"Alfie never took leave in his life unless he took leave of his senses."

"Well, he's on leave now. What can I get you, sir?"

Sir! Sullenly he said, "A large whiskey," although he had been planning a night of draught porter. Alfie would have said, "Johnny! There is no such thing on earth as a *large* whiskey." Or he might have said nothing but come back with a half-pint of draught and said, "That'll be better for you."

Was it because it was Thursday night? Nobody much ever came on Thursday night: less even than came on Friday night. Everyone stony. Behold my beeves and fatlings are all killed, and nobody cometh to eat them. Seven lousy nights and the first a flop? Go forth into the highways and byways. From pub to pub? The whiskey appeared before him. The barman stood waiting. He looked up.

"Four and sixpence, sir."

With Alfie, you let it run for a week, for two, for three, for as long as you liked. Then you asked, "What's on the slate, Alfie?" and, if you were flush, you paid a half-note over and above for future credit. Man knoweth not the hour nor the night. He paid out four shillings and a sixpenny bit. The barman rang it up and retired down the counter to lean over his *Herald*.

"How long is Alfie going to be on leave?"

The fellow barely glanced up.

"I don't know, I'm only here this past two weeks."

"Is the boss in?"

"He's gone down to the chapel. The October Devotions."

Thinking of his latter end. *Dies irae, dies illa.* Back in Newbridge with the Dominicans. All Souls' Night. He glanced at the door. Would there be anyone down at The Blue Peter? Or in Mooney's? Maybe in The Purty Kitchen?

"Any message for me there behind the old cashbox?"

"Name?"

"Kendrick."

The barman, his back to him, went through the light sheaf. Without turning he said, "Nothing," shoved it back and returned to his *Herald*. Out of sight out of mind. Bugger the whole lousy lot of them! And Deirdre along with them! The glass doors swished open and there were Paddywhack and Loftus. He leaped from his stool.

"Hi, scouts!"

"Johnny!"

Handshakes all around. Paddy was as hungry looking as a displaced Arab. His shirt-sleeves too long. The gold wristlet. The signet ring. Loftus, as always, as lean and yellow as a Dane. Hoppity Loftus with his short leg. He never worked. He was a Prod and had an English accent, and he lived off his mother. All he did was to get her breakfast in the morning and have her supper ready for her at night. She worked in the Sweep.

"Name it, boys! I'm standing!"

Paddy looked thirstily at the glass of whiskey.

"Are you on the hard tack?"

"Naw! Just this bloody place gave me the willies. The usual?" He commanded the barman. "Two half-pints. Make it three and I'll use this as a chaser. God, it's marvelous to see ye! Come on, come on! Give! Give! Gimme all the dirt. Tell me more, tell me all. Are you still with the Gas Company, Paddy?"

"I'm with a house agent now. Looney and Cassidy. In Dame Street." He made a fish face. "N.B.G. Paid on commission. Just to tide me over a bad patch." He laughed cheerfully. "The wife is preggers again."

"Paddy! I dunno how you do it."

"I'm told," said Loftus lightly, "that it's a very simple matter, really."

"How's your mother, Loftus?"

A rude question. Loftus shrugged it away. They took their drinks to one of the round tables. Paddy lifted his glass.

"Johnny! You don't know how lucky you are. A steady job, cash in your pocket, a girl in every port."

"And as brown," said Loftus, lifting his glass, "and as round as a football."

"Me round?" he shouted, ripped open the jacket of his uniform and banged his narrow waist. "Feel that, go on, feel it! Hard as iron, boy! Eight stone ten. You," he said condescendingly, rebuttoning, "must be about ten stone eight." He paused. Then he had to say it: "Does Deirdre still love me?"

Loftus's eyes glinted as he proffered the sponge on the spear.

"I saw her two weeks ago in a red Triumph. A medical student from Trinity, I believe. She looked smashing."

His heart curdled, his throat tightened, he laughed loudly.

"So the little bitch is betraying me, eh?"

He could see her, with her dark hair curled down on one shoulder as if she had a monkey on her head. The red lips. The high bosoms.

"It's just because you're not around much," Paddy said comfortingly. "Wait until she hears you're home!"

"How are all those girls of yours?" Loftus smiled. "In foreign parts."

Paddy poured sad oil.

"Too bad about poor Alfie?"

"I heard nothing," he said sourly. "Nobody writes to me. Where *is* the ould divil?"

"You didn't know! Hospice for the Dying. Cancer. These last three months. It'll be any day now."

It gagged him. There was a long silence. His first death. The double doors let in Hughesy and Flossie; their oldest and youngest — a blonde mop, black lashes, a good looker, but not a patch on his D. Their welcomes were muted. They sat down stiffly like people who did not mean to stay.

" 'Here,' " he chanted mournfully, " 'here, the gang's all here.' "

"Not all of us," Paddy said.

"This is a committee meeting, really," Hughesy said, taking charge of it at once. "Well?" he asked Paddywhack and Loftus. "How much can we raise?"

"We're gathering for Mrs. Alfie," Paddywhack explained. "She hasn't a sou."

"I managed to borrow five bob," Flossie said, taking two halfcrowns from inside her glove and laying them on the table.

"That," said Hughesy, putting down half a crown, "is all I can manage."

Paddywhack squirmed and said, "Six kids and another coming, and Thursday night."

Loftus showed empty palms. "Unless I could pop something?"

He felt worse than a wanderer — a stranger.

"Mrs. Alfie? How in God's name did ye meet *her?*" he asked Hughesy.

"It was Alfie asked us to keep an eye on her and the kids. I saw him again today," he told the others.

"How is he?" he asked.

Hughesy looked away.

"Alas, poor Yorick," Loftus said. "A skull!"

Flossie began to cry.

"But where's the rest of the gang? Joanna, and Tommy, and Angela and Casey."

He stopped short of Deirdre. Paddywhack shook his head and made faint gestures.

"I nearly didn't come myself. Can you manage anything, Johnny?"

He took out his pocketbook and planked down a pound note.

"Good man!" said Hughesy, and looked up at the barman standing over them, and down at the pound note. He smiled apologetically at Johnny. "Any more of that nice stuff?"

"Come on, scouts, I'm standing. If it's to be a wake, for Christ's sake let it be a wake. What's yours, Flossie? Still sticking to the dry sherry? Hughesy? The old pint?" He nodded to the barman, who departed silently. "Let me in on this. Tell me all about Alfie."

As the drinks warmed them they talked. A man, by God! A true friend if there ever was one. They don't often come like that nowadays. True from his bald head to the soles of his feet. Tried and true. A son of the soil. A bit of old Ireland. Vanishing down the drain. Not one bit of cod about him. His jokes . . . We shall not look upon his life again. The pound note melted. Paddywhack said, "Life is a mystery all right. She looks such a nice woman, and she *is* a nice woman, and full of guts, not one word of complaint, and three kids. What in God's name happened to them?" They told him, asking how she lived, that she used to work as a dressmaker. "Yes, he did!" Loftus answered him. "After a fashion, he did. He supported her. After a fashion." Flossie said she would never come to this pub again. They agreed with Hughesy that Dublin wouldn't be the same without him. She said the fact was he had nothing to do with all those . . . They followed her eyes down to Molly Goosegog and the one-armed colonel, and the three business types, and the two boiled hakes with the gins and bitters. Hughesy slapped the table. "And that's a true bill, Flossie! He was one of us. Old in body but young in heart. You agree, Johnny?" He agreed that Alfie was the only man he ever met who understood them. "He fought for his ideals." They talked of understanding, and ideals, and truth, and true love, and how well Alfie understood what it means to be young, and to believe in things, that was it — to believe in things. A second pound was melting, and it was after ten when Flossie said to Hughesy that she must go home soon.

"Mind your few quid, Johnny," Hughesy said. "What's left there will be enough. A dozen bottles of stout, say a dozen and a half. Just to cheer her up. We'll drop around for a minute, Flossie. Just to cheer her up."

"One for the road," he insisted, and held them. They leaned back.

It was nearly eleven when they left in a bunch, carrying the three brown paper bags of stout, out into the dry streets, the nebulous night, under the dim stars and the gathering clouds that were lit by the city's glow. Loftus said it was a fine night for a ramble. Hughesy laughed and said, "Or for courting." Two by two, hooting merrily backwards and forwards at one another, they wound up among shaggy, dim-lit squares with names like Albert Gardens, Aldershot Place or Portland Square, all marked on green and white tablets in Irish and English, until they came to a basement door and, stepping down to it, rang and waited in a bunch under a stone arch. In the dark they were suddenly silent, listening. A light went on over the door. She opened it.

Alfie's youth. She was soft and welcoming. All the parts of her face seemed to be running into one another, dissolving like ice cream in the sun, her mouth melting, her blue-blue eyes swimming. A loose tress of her gray-fair hair flowed over a high forehead. Her voice was as timid as butter. She was not a bad-looking woman, and for a moment a little flame of youth flared up in her when they introduced him to her, and she laughed softly and said, "So this is Johnny! He said you were the baby of the lot." She held his hand in her two hands,

moist and warm as if she had been washing something, and
he remembered a line from a poem they used to read at
school, long forgotten, never understood. *"Fear no more the
heat of the sun . . ."*

"Glad to meet you, Mrs. Alfie," he said and realized for
the first time that he did not know Alfie's name.

"We brought a few drinks," Hughesy explained. "Just to
brighten the night."

"Come in, boys, come in. Talk low," she begged. "Jenny is
only just gone to sleep."

The low room was small and untidy, and smelled of soap.
The fire was ashen. She had only two glasses. They sat in a
circle and drank out of cups, or from the bottle necks. Moist
cloths hung drooping and wet on a line; the stuffing of the
chairs tufted out, he saw a toy horse with three legs, torn
green paperbacks, a house of cards half-collapsed on a tray.
Staring at her, he heard nothing of their whispering; both surprised and pleased to hear her laugh so often. He became
aware that Hughesy and Flossie were fading out, for the last
bus. Around midnight Paddywhack said he must give the
wife a hand with the kids, and slid away. She put a few bits
of sticks in the grate and tried ineffectually to remake the fire.
Then Loftus clumped off home to his mother and there were
only the two of them in the room, stooping over one flicker in
the ashes, whispering, heads together.

Only once again did she mention Alfie; when she said,
"They're a grand bunch. Ye are all good boys. Decent young
men. It was what he always said about ye."

"Did you see him often?"

"Hardly at all. He might drop in after he shut the pub. To
see the children. He told me he was always at ye to settle
down. Hughesy, and Flossie, and Casey, and Loftus and you.
Do you like Loftus?"

"He's cold. And bitter."

"Is Deirdre your girl?"

"Yes. But I think she's letting me down. Did you meet her? She's a smasher."

"She is a beautiful girl. I don't want to interfere in your life, Johnny, but I would be inclined to think that I would nearly say that she might have a hard streak in her."

"Not like you?" he smiled.

"I'm not faulting her. A woman must think of her own good."

There he was off, full-cock, about youth, ideals, loyalty, truth, honesty, love, things that only the gang understood, everybody else talking to you about your future, and good jobs, and making money. "Ireland is the last fortress. The Noah's Ark of the world. No place like it." And he should know, an exile! She agreed, she agreed. She said, "The people here are warm and natural still in spite of all." He was with her, all the way with her. "We are not materialists. Not the best of us." At that they were both off, whispering, breaking into louder talk, hushing, glancing fearfully at the door of the bedroom.

The last flicker of the fire died away. They drank the last bottle of stout between them, passing it from mouth to mouth. Her voice grew softer, her hand when she held his was padded like a cat's. The night became a fugitive. Faintly a foghorn in the bay moaned through a muffled blanket. He looked out and up through the window and saw a yellow blur of street light, and the mist that clung wetly to a fogged tree. She got up to make tea. He followed her into the messy kitchen to help and talk. They came back and she put a few more futile chips of sticks on the warm ashes. She laughed at the slightest thing — when the toy horse toppled, or when he told her about the dog, kicked, and beaten, and mangy, that he bought in Palermo, and how it swam ashore back to its Moorish slum. Or that night in Odessa in the Y.M.C.A. when he got into a fight by pretending that the C stood for Communist.

When it was two o'clock he said, "You must send me away." She said, "Listen to the dripping outside. Oh, don't go away, Johnny!" He said, "You must sleep." She said, "I don't know what sleep is," and held him by his wrist, frightened to be left alone. "Listen to the dripdrop," she wheedled. "And look! It's yellow as mustard outside. Sleep here. Sleep in my bed. We're friends, aren't we? Just lie and sleep. You're a good boy. I know you. Go in there and lie down." She led him into the bedroom with its unmade bed. He barely made out the child asleep on a campbed, one arm hooped around its head. She took her nightgown from a chair and went out.

He hung up his jacket, removed his shoes and lay down, gazing out the door at the yellow blur of the street lamp. It was as cold as the grave in the bed. She came back in her rumpled nightdress, her hair about her shoulders, got in under the clothes beside him and put out the light. The yellow street lamp bleared in through the bedroom door.

"It's bloody cold," he said.

"We'll soon warm up. You should have taken your clothes off and got under the blankets, sure what does it matter?"

He undressed to his underpants, and got under the blankets beside her warmth.

They lay in silence for a while, hearing nothing but their breathing and the faint, far fog horn. He moved closer and began to whisper into her ear about what it means to be homeless, and she whispered to him about the time she came up to Dublin for the first time from County Cavan, for her honeymoon. She never once went back there. He whispered to her, "You are a heroine." She said, "You're a good lad, Johnny."

After a while more she said, "We must sleep," and he lay on his back, his hands clasped behind his head. After a long while he said, "Deirdre is a bitch," and she said, "She is very young." After another while he whispered, "Try to sleep," and she whispered, "Yes." After another long time he said,

"You're not sleeping. You are thinking of him. When will you know?" She said, "It might be any minute. Then I'll sleep. And sleep. And sleep."

Sleep stole on him. He woke abruptly, at five o'clock. She was no longer in the bed. He saw her in the front room, a man's overcoat on her shoulders, leaning her elbows on the windowsill staring out. In his stockinged feet he went to her and put his arm around her shoulder.

"You can't sleep?"

She did not stir. Her face had melted completely, her two cheeks were wet. He did not know what to say to her. By the cleansed lamplight outside he saw that the fog had lifted. She whispered, "It's all over."

"You can't tell!"

"I know it. I'll go out and ring the hospital at six o'clock. But I know it." Her face screwed up and more tears oozed from her closed eyes. "You'd better go, Johnny. Your people may be worrying."

He dressed, shivering, among the empty bottles of stout on the floor, some of them standing to attention, some of them rolled on their sides. He put on his peaked cap with the white top, patted her hooped back, said, "God help you," and went out up the steps to the street level. It was black as night. From the pavement he looked down at the shadow of her face behind the misty glass, lifted a hand and walked away.

When he came to the Coal Harbour he halted on the center of the railway bridge and leaned his hands on the wet parapet. Six miles across the level bay a string of orange lights flickered along the shoreline, and farther west the city's night glow underlit its mirror of cloud. The harbor water, dark as oil, held the riding light of a coal tub. He drew in deep breaths of the raw air and blinked his sanded eyes. He said quietly, "I still love you, you bitch." Then he lifted his head, put his two palms about his mouth like a megaphone, and howled in a long, wild howl across the bay, "Do you love me?"

The city lay remote under its mirror.

He rubbed the stone and remembered, *"Quiet consummation have: and renowned be thy grave!"* — and marched homewards, arms swinging, chin up, white cap slanted. The water of the main harbor was inscribed by a slow wheel of light. Far out from the Kish bank a flight of light beamed and died at regular intervals. The whole way home the only sound he heard was a faint, faraway humming like a bee, a dawn flight out of Dublin across the sea.

The Human Thing

IT is not always cold in the Basses-Alpes — but on that late September evening (was it as long as ten years ago?) when I rang his presbytery bell it was very cold. The only answer to my call was the wind funneling down that tiny, flagged street of his, narrow as a bedspread and smelly as a bedpan. It was like aerial gunnery aimed over thirty miles of forests and ravines to strike the sea five miles out beyond the warm beaches of Nice where I had toasted myself that morning in the Riviera sun. Was I to have to spend the night alone up here in Argons? And, if so, was there even a half-decent hotel in Argons? It would be dusk within an hour. I rang again and pressed, for shelter, against his studded door. Suddenly it opened and a woman passed hastily out into the narrow street. All I saw was a snapshot glimpse of a brightly made-up mouth in a dark face, a stocky figure, well dressed, a bit overblown in the Italian way that you so often see along this border. Afterwards I wondered if she had been wearing a long black veil like a war widow. The old housekeeper all but closed the door after her, glared at me with two sooty eyes from under a topknot like the ace of spades, accepted my card and my tiny letter of introduction, closed the door within an inch of its jamb and backed into the house. This meant at least that he was at home, and I straightway forgot everything except what the Abbé de Saint Laurent had told me about him a few days before in his sunbathed little study in Nice.

"Argons?" he had said. "In that case I know the very man for you. You must call on my good confrère the Abbé Morfé. He will tell you everything you want to know about the traditional life of the Basses-Alpes."

And straightway sat to his desk and began to write on a small sheet of paper, murmuring over one sunlit shoulder as he wrote:

"He is not French, of course. Although you would never suspect it he has been with us so long — for at least twenty years. He is an Irishman. One of several who volunteered for the French mission after the war, when we were badly in need of priests. As we still are! You may talk to him freely. Not," he smiled back at me around the corner of his glasses, "that you will need to. He will do the talking. How do you spell your name? Thank you. A very outspoken man. Sometimes, I think, a little too outspoken. But," and here he turned right around to me, "zealous! Beyond my vocabulary. A downright man. And absolutely fearless." He turned back to his desk to inscribe the tiny envelope. "The perfect priest for the mountains. Ireland, as you must know, was never Romanized. So you, as an Englishman . . ." (He did not observe my sigh; I am always being mistaken for an Englishman.) ". . . will understand readily what I mean when I say that he represents the best, the very best of *l'église des barbares.*"

He folded his small letter into its small envelope, handed it to me courteously, and wafted me upwards and onwards toward nether Gaul.

As if under another wild blast of wind the door was flung open. I saw a powerful-looking countryman. His face was the color of raw bacon cured by the sun and the wind. In his left hand he held my card, in his right a fat claw hammer which he flung behind the door with such a clatter that for a second

I was taken aback by the violence of the gesture; all the more
so because he was shouting back into the house, "Mais, je
vous ai dis que je ne la connais pas!" He turned back to me
warmly welcoming, cried, "Come in, Sean! Come in!" and I
was straightway back in the County Mayo; though in Ireland
only a Protestant clergyman would have looked so indigent.
His soutane was old and dusty, his boots were unlaced, he
wore an old, fraying straw hat on the back of his balding poll,
he was smoking a pipe mended with twine.

"I was making a coop for the hens!" he said.

"I'm interrupting you?"

"The most pleasant interruption in the world!" he laughed,
and with one big hand on my shoulder he drew me in and
invited me to stay not only for the night but for as long as I
pleased: to which I cautiously replied that it could, alas, only
be for one night. When we were in his living room — oh! the
joy of that sizzling log fire! — he at once produced a full bottle of Tullamore Dew, which, I noticed, was not only dusty
but had never been opened. He sank as slowly as an elephant
into his leather-covered armchair and began to talk nonstop
about Ireland.

Everything in the room was of the region, and it was all as
darkly impersonal as a convent: the hand-wrought firedogs,
the heavy furniture that had obviously been made on the spot
a long time ago, the graying, pious prints, the brown tiles, the
adze-marked beams under a ceiling that had once been white
plaster and was now tea-colored from years of wood smoke
and nicotine. As my feet thawed my heart rose — all this was
exactly the sort of thing I needed for my article. But for well
over an hour he did not give me a chance to ask him any of
the questions that had brought me to his door — he asked all
the questions, and rarely waited for my answers. I could see
only three tokens of our common country: the until-now un-
opened bottle of whiskey; the corner of the *Sunday Independ-
ent,* still in its folder, still bearing its green Irish stamp, edging

out from under the papers of the *midi;* and a small cushion embroidered with green and red leprechauns bulging from under his fat elbow. I could imagine it coming to him, with a "Merry Christmas," from some distant Deirdre or Mary. At long last he let Ireland drop. Touching the Abbé's note (a little frigidly?) he said:

"Well, so you are going to write about us? And what have you discovered so far, pray?"

"More or less what you'd expect."

"And," a little guardedly, "what would I expect?"

"What every traveler in a strange place expects, that the truth about every place is the sum of everybody's contradictions."

"Such as?"

"Well, for example, everybody I meet east of the Var tells me that the old, traditional life now exists nowhere except west of the Var, and everybody west of the Var tells me that if I want to see the old ways I must come up here into the mountains. What would you say to that?"

He sniffed, and at once struck the chord that dominated everything else that was to follow.

"Do you know phwat it is?" he said in a buttermilk brogue, with a buttermilk smile, "I'm not sure that I'm fit to tawlk about this ould counthry at all, at all. 'Tis a quare counthry. To tell you the honesht truth, Sean, I'm gettin' a bit fed up with the Frinch. I have to live with them you know."

Meaning that I was just a tourist? The jab and the brogue delighted and alerted me. A false brogue, as every Irishman knows, is a sure sign that the speaker is about to say something so true that he wants to blunt the edge of it by presenting it as a kind of family joke. I said, adopting the same sword-in-the-scabbard technique:

"Shure and all, isn't it a bit late in the day for you to be feeling that way now, Father? After all your thirty-odd years shepherding thim?"

He looked at me unamiably. A point apiece. We were playing that ancient Irish game known as conversational poker, a game which nobody can win and nobody can lose because nobody may utter the open truth but everybody must give and take a few sharp little smacks of it or the game is no good at all.

"Better late than never," he said sourly. "As is the way with most of us?"

He began to talk slowly. Was he feeling his way into my mind? Or into his own? He casually refreshed my glass. But as we progressed I thought I noticed a difference in his way of playing the Game: if we were playing the Game. After all he was a priest, and a French priest, and a French priest of the mountains — a man, that is, for whom the stakes in every game are infinite.

"The Basses-Alpes? Mind you Sean, the Basses-Alpes aren't such a bad counthry. Not rich, of course. Anyway not rich the way the coast is rich. But it has things the coast never had and never will have. There are people who like to bask on the Riviera, who like to have Nice sunny apartments and Nice sunny congregations. But, sure, the Riviera isn't country at all! What is the Riviera but one blooming esplanade forty miles long? A string of international resorts without a stem of local character? Without any character! Without any values except cold, commercial cash values. But we aren't poor either. The land down there, you've seen it, is all ravined and gorged. Hard, stony uplands. With their olive-groves abandoned, and their villages crumbling, or turned into tourist traps, and their farmhouses for sale to foreigners. And all the young people going. Gone! Lured away down to the bright lights along the coast. All of them wanting to be croupiers, or traffic cops in white helmets, or factory workers in white overalls. When I think of places like St. Paul! A sink of iniquity I call it. For all I know it may be a place that you like to visit. And for good reasons, comfortable hotels, good food.

But fifty years ago that was a decent, little country hill village. What is it today? Packed to the last corner with what, with who? The *haut monde!* Paahrisians! In bikinis and beach pajamas! Do you know who the organist in that little church is today? A Protestant! And glad to have him. And now don't start talking to me about arty-arty chapels like that one by Matisse up in Vence. A chapel? It's a bathroom designed by a freethinker."

"Was Matisse a freethinker?"

"You can have him! Listen! There's one thing on earth that I can't stand and that's milk-and-water Catholics."

His eyes glinted. If this was, by any chance, a jab at me, maybe we were still playing the Game. He went on:

"Up here it is different. Up here the forests mean — well, you might call it comparative wealth for some and a good living for all. So our people have stayed on. The bright lights are farther away." His voice slowed. "Yes, our people have stayed on."

"And," I leaned forward eagerly, "kept the old life-ways?"

He knocked his pipe out with slow, careful taps on the head of a firedog. I had the feeling that the Game was over.

"I'll explain to you what I mean by milk-and-water religion. I know of instances of women in these parts deliberately going off and having affairs — and I mean respectable, married women with families — for no reason but because it is the modern fashion. Women born and reared in these parts, copying, that's all it is, the ways of places they think better than their own. To be as smart as the best. To be in the fashion. I find that utterly contemptible."

He was so passionate about it that I demurred, though cautiously since he felt so strongly about it.

"Surely," I proposed gently, "one must go by cases? I mean a woman might be terribly unhappy. Her husband might be a boor, or a bore, or even a drunk. She might have met with some man whom she wished she had married, some man she loved or thought she loved . . ."

"That has nothing whatever to do with it! I could understand it if there was a bit of real passion in it. I could make allowances. I could even forgive it. It is my job to forgive. But they do it for the most vulgar of all reasons, just to be up to the minute. To be *à la page*. They do it simply to have something to boast about at the tea table."

"And the men?"

"The same! People like that have no religion, no character. They have nothing. That's what I mean by milk-and-water religion."

"And for this you blame the gentry?"

"I never mentioned the gentry."

"You said they want to be as smart as the best. To be in the fashion. Which best? Whose fashion? The nobs'?"

"You never get this sort of thing among the gentry, certainly not among the real noblesse. Oh, of course, you will find sinners among them, as you will everywhere. The flesh is the flesh, high or low. We are all creatures of the flesh. But this thing doesn't come from the flesh. It isn't even honest sensuality. It comes from the corruption of the mind. It comes from meanness of the mind. It's plain, vulgar, bloody tomfoolery. It is indifference. It is spiritual death. It is apostasy."

He slapped the side of his armchair. An uncomfortable silence fell on us. Was he always as irascible as this?

"Maybe I'm in a pessimistic mood," he grumbled. "Gimme your glass. I'm a bad host. Maybe what I need is a week after the grouse in County Mayo."

"Aye," I said, more than willing to return to the Game. "They say there's nothing like a good grouse for a bad theologian."

"Why is it bad theology, pray?"

"Well, after all 'the greatest of these is charity.' "

"Oho! There is always charity."

(He sounded as if he was a bit sick of Charity.)

"This couldn't be a long backwash from the French Revolution? I notice your little street here is called the Rue Carnot."

"There is also," he parried back, "a Rue Saint Roch. That's San Rocco. The good Italian influence. The bond with Rome."

"Yes!" I said dryly. "I noticed that Italian influence. In the Place Garibaldi."

He snarled it:

"That crew!"

We both laughed. (There really is a lot to be said for the urbanity of the Game.) Just then old Ace of Spades came in to say in her sullen voice:

"Dinner is served, Father. And that lady telephoned to say the funeral will be tomorrow at nine o'clock."

He looked hard at her.

"Anastasia, do you know this Madame Bailly?"

"She has been living in Alberon this five years."

"Funny that I can't remember her. I'll just ring Father Benoit." He turned to me. "He is one of my curates. We have a big parish. We divide it among the three of us."

I had driven up through Alberon: one of those small places with a couple of sawmills, and with more garages than hotels, which means that everything goes stone dead after October when the big passes get clogged with snow.

"Let's eat!"

We went into his dining room. As he flung out his serviette and tucked it under his jaw and began to pour the wine he said:

"The poor woman's husband was killed this afternoon in

an accident. A tree fell right across his back. He owned a hotel, a garage and a sawmill in Alberon. She came about the funeral." He paused in the act of filling his own glass. "Bailly? I know a couple of Baillys around Grasse. And," he growled, "nothing much good about any of them."

"Liberals?" I teased.

"Puh! You mentioned Garibaldi. And Carnot. It would be very interesting study for you to find out at what date these names came in . . . and at what date a lot of other things began to come in."

We talked at random. Presently he said:

"I don't want you to misunderstand me about the gentry. When all is said and done they are still the best people in France. They're on the way out, of course. They have no political gumption. And no money. And no influence. Your Liberals, as you choose to call them, are pushing them over the last edge of the ravines. What's left of them." He sipped his wine and frowned. "Bailly? Somehow or other that name keeps ringing a bell somewhere in what's left of my poor old head."

"Haven't you the Liber Animarum?" I asked, meaning the thick, black notebook I had been shown once in an Irish presbytery by an old priest who had once been a dear friend of mine. These stubby books have a page to every parishioner: name, business, address, married or single, whether he practices his religion or not, and sometimes, though rarely, a more intimate comment if the priest considers it necessary to probe more deeply. He snorted.

"Ha! Liber Animarum, how are you? 'Tis easy seen that you come from Holy Ireland. Themselves and their card-indexes. What I call IBM Catholicism. It's as much as my two curates and myself can do to get around to visiting our parishioners once every two years. If that! And sometimes none too welcome at that! Have you any idea at all of the size of our parishes? If it wasn't for our housekeepers . . ." He stopped dead. He sighed. "I must be getting old. I'm losing my grip."

He rang the little brass bell on the table and waited for her to appear at the door.

"Tell me," he said. "Do you really know this Madame Bailly?"

"Everybody in Alberon knows her."

"Yes, yes, you told me she is from Alberon."

"I said she lives in Alberon."

He pushed his chair back and faced her.

"Anastasia! What are you trying to say exactly? Where did she come from?"

"Cannes."

"And Bailly married her and brought her to Alberon five years ago?"

"Monsieur Bailly's wife and four children are living in Grasse with his mother."

There was a long silence. He said, "Bailly sent them away?"

Her sooty eyes stared at him. Her shoulders barely moved. He thanked her and nodded her out. He pushed his dinner away and his face was pale about his tightly clenched lips — the only part of that ruddy face that could grow pale.

"Five years! What sort of a priest am I? What sort of a parish do I run? Under my very nose! And now this person has the insolence to come here and ask me to give him a Christian burial! I'll soon put a stop to that!"

"My God! You can't refuse to bury the man? You can't let him be put into a hole in the ground like an animal?"

"And do you think that after leading this kind of life, giving public scandal for five years, openly and brazenly, that I am going to give him public burial now as a good Catholic? What would my parishioners say? What would they think?

Do you think that it's for this I came here thirty-three years ago, to bless scandalmongers like those two apostates?"

"Isn't that a bit extreme? Sinners, yes. Call them that if you like. That, of course. But in mere charity . . ."

"Charity! Everybody always talks to me about charity! What is charity?"

"Love, I suppose. I suppose those two unfortunate people loved one another."

"And his wife? And his four children? Did he love *them?*"

"But he may, even at the last minute, have hoped for forgiveness. If you had been there when that tree fell on him would you not have given him Extreme Unction? Anointed his eyes, and hands, and mouth and prayed for his forgiveness?"

Outside, a wild rush of wind rattled leaves against the pane like a million clamoring fingers.

"Well, I was *not* there," he said heavily. "He died as he lived, struck down by the hand of God. I'm going to phone Father Benoit."

Alone in the room I tried to visualize that stocky Italianate woman I had seen hurrying away from his door. I tried to see her and her dead lover in their hotel in Alberon, and I realized that this was one life story that I would never know. All I could imagine was a hundred spade heads like old Anastasia in that little hill town besieging her with their cruel silence and their bitter eyes. He came back and slumped into his chair.

"He is out."

I sat opposite him and I thought: "And here is another life story that I will never know!" After a few moments he said, quietly:

"Charity, Sean, is a virtue. It is, as you say, love — the love of all things through God, the love of God in all things.

As for your love, human love? It is that, too. As Saint Bonaventure said, it is the life that couples the lover to the beloved. *Vita copulans amantem cum amato.* But it is that in the name of God, for God and by God. One act of love in a lifetime is an immensity. But one mortal sin can of itself destroy all love, and all life, as that man destroyed two lives over and over again before the eyes of the world." He stopped and got up again. "This thing must be ended publicly! As it was begun publicly. I must go down there at once."

"Tonight?"

"Yes! At once!"

We both looked at the window. The mistral was at its full force. A wild sheaf of leaves whirled horizontally past the window.

"Let me drive you," I offered, miserably.

"I'd be glad if you did. I'm in no fit state to drive."

We buttoned ourselves up in our overcoats, pulled on our berets, and crushed into my little Dauphine. He directed me on the long, winding road where the woods on each side waved in one solid mass like a turbulent sea. I was too busy watching the road to talk. All the way he never spoke except to say "Fork left," or "Right here." I felt like a man driving an executioner to the place of execution and I did not know which of the two of us I disliked the more at that moment. When we entered Alberon the streets were empty and dark. Two cafés were lighted, their windows opaque with condensed moisture. He suddenly said, revealing that he had been thinking in that language:

"C'est dans la Place. Il s'appelle Le Chamois."

It was a three-story house with the usual Alpine roof pitched to a peak and smoothing out at the base to let the great weight of snow slide down and melt on the gutters. On the ground floor there was a café, all dark and buttoned-up. Two windows on the story above it were lighted. When he got out and was ringing at the door I withdrew to the center of the little Place to park and wait. It took a couple of rings to produce an answer. When the door opened I saw, against the light inside, the dark outline of the woman who called herself Madame Bailly. He stepped inside at once. The door closed. I was alone with the mistral, the darkness and the empty Place.

The perfect priest for the mountains. Getting a bit fed-up with the Frinch. Nice people and Nice apartments. Absolutely fearless. Downright. A finger on a switch lit up two more windows upstairs. *Vita copulans amantem cum amato.* Would he be laid out in there on his bed of love? Zealous beyond my vocabulary. The mistral blew around and around me in moaning circles. Two men, an older and a younger, came, heads down, into the square from the left. I saw them pause at the closed-up Café le Chamois, look at its dark window, making some gestures that could only mean, "Ah yes! I heard that . . ." Then one of them stretched his arm forward and they went on again, heads down, to, I presumed, one of the other two cafés, where no doubt as in every house in the town . . . I started the engine and turned on the heat.

After another long wait those two extra windows went dark. Still he did not come out. One mortal act of love in a lifetime is an immensity. One mortal sin can destroy the whole of that love and of that life for ever. Damn it, why doesn't he finish her off quickly? That, at least, would be a small act of charity! A big truck and trailer laden with long balks of timber trundled into the square and out at the other end. Then only the wind and the darkness again.

At last a flood of light beamed out on the pavement as the door opened and I saw his great bulky outline. He was shaking hands with the woman in black. As I peered forward I saw that it was not the same woman. He bowed to her and looked around for me. I drove over to meet him. She slowly closed the door, he clambered in, and silently waved me on-ward.

I could not see his face in the darkness but by the dash-board light I saw his hand, lying loosely on his thigh, shaking like a man with the palsy.

"Well?" I asked.

He spoke so softly I could barely hear him.

"I could not believe such love existed on this earth."

"Madame Bailly?"

"She came down from Grasse. With her four children. For the funeral."

"There will be a funeral?"

"Could I refuse his wife?"

"And the other?"

"The two of them are there together. Comforting one an-other."

No more was said until we were back in his living room, in his dark presbytery, in his tiny, smelly street. There, standing by the gray ash of his dying fire, still in his beret and his long overcoat, he turned on me a face twisted by agony and cried:

"Did I do right?"

"You did the human thing, Father."

"Ah! The human thing?" He shook his head, uncomforted. He laid his hand in a kindly way on my shoulder. "Sleep well, you!" — as one who himself would not. "And I never told you anything at all, at all, about the damned ould Basses-Alpes!"

I hardly slept at all. All night the wind moaned through his narrow street, down over every forest, village and black ra-vine. Were those two women awake? Comforting each other? Triumphing over each other? I wished to God I was down where the bright lights of the empty esplanades would now be glinting in the calm, the cold, the whispering, the supremely indifferent sea.

One Man, One Boat, One Girl

THE first time I met Olly Carson I was sitting on a crate with T. J. Mooney in the Despatch Yard of the factory during the lunchbreak, each of us holding a bottle of Guinness in each fist. We were celebrating two famous birthdays, my twenty-first and his thirtieth, and T.J. was giving out the score about *Man and Superman,* his favorite anti-female tract. Olly came by, stopped, looked at the two of us out of his comical, gooseberry eyes, winked, pulled another bottle of Guinness out of his lunch bag, sat up beside us without being asked, and started at once on a bawdy story about a barmaid and a champagne cork. From that moment we were a cabal. When he told us that he had only just come over from Sheffield and did not know a soul in Cork I nudged T.J., he looked at me, I raised my eyebrows, he nodded. Straightway we introduced Olly to the Rules of the River. One man, One boat, One girl.

The next Sunday, by way of initiating him, we sent him off down the Marina while we were getting out the boats from the rowing club. In those days, before cars started ruining the roads, before outboard motors, and caravans, and cinemas, and telly, and touring buses, and Teddy Boys and all this bloody modern fal-lal, the Lee used to be full of boats every Saturday and Sunday, and the Marina full of strolling couples from dawn to dark. As T.J. once said, there were as many marriages made on the Marina as were ever made in Heaven.

"Why don't we fix up with the girls beforehand?" Olly asked.

"That," T.J. explained, "is on account of Rules four, five and six. Adventure. No attachments. And no regrets."

"Suits me!" says Olly and off he went.

Within fifteen minutes he was back leading two of them by the grin. He trotted off again and he was back almost as quickly with a real dazzler for himself. After that he became the official Club Decoy. God knows what he had for the girls. He was no beauty. He had a pug nose and hobby-horse nostrils. He was strong and powerful but in a bathing dress he had stubby thighs and legs like a grown-up circus dwarf. He had no least idea how to dress — he always wore brown shoes with a dark suit, and on the river he wore his bowler hat even with his coat off. His pay packet was no fatter than T.J.'s or mine or anybody else's at the works. If it was not for his two rakehell eyes I do not know what he had for the women. Whatever he had they used to swing out of his arm, gazing adoringly and uncertainly into his two pop eyes as if he was Rudolph Valentino in person.

"What's the trick, Olly?" I once asked him. "Do you spray 'em with Secrets of Venus out of your cuff? Or drop cigarette ash into their lemonade?"

Olly was very serious, very English, no matter what you asked him.

"I ain't got no tricks, Alphonsus," he said. "I think maybe the fack o' the matter is I've got a kind heart for the girls. They trust me, see? Or maybe the fack o' the matter is I'm not afraid of 'em, like all you bloomin' Irish."

"That," said T.J., prophetically as I now see, "is where the ferry boat will leave you some day. You'd be wiser to be afraid of 'em. As Shaw says . . ."

"Oh, F. Shaw!" says Olly.

"I beg your pardon," says T.J. "G. B. Shaw."

In the end T.J. decided that it was not that they trusted him but that they thought he was a bit of a mug; but, then, as he said, regarding me pityingly: —

"You are a bit of a mug, too, Al, so the mystery remains."

Will somebody tell me what has happened to time? There were a hundred hours in every one of those long Saturdays and Sundays on the river. And is it only in memory that it never rains, and that all girls are gamesome? Inside one month of that first season with us Olly knew every creek on the river, every stream on every creek, every field on every stream where you could tie up and get down to business, as cosy as a squawl of kittens in a basket, full of peace and joy and contentment the livelong day. In the late evening — lightsome until eleven o'clock in June — we would fore-gather and row home, tail to prow, like a little musical armada, T.J. swinging his old roundy concertina, me with my trumpet and Olly had a voice that made Caruso sound like a tomtit. When we came to the lights of Montenotte we used to wake the echoes in the hills.

I will never forget one late August night, it was our second season together, when we drew up for a rest opposite the old Shandon Rowing Club on the Marina. Before you could sing *A* to a tuning-fork we had the boys and girls creeping out of the shadows of the avenue two by two down to the edge of the quay, sitting on the limestone wall, legs dangling, chiming in harmony all the songs you ever heard out of Grand Opera, Victor Herbert, G. and S., all those nice, sentimental, happy, pre-bloody-jazz-age songs like "By the Light of the Silvery Moon," or "Farewell My Own, Light of My Life, Farewell," or "Home to Our Mountains," or "The moon hath raised her

lamp above/ To light the way to thee, my love . . ." The
night came down like a curtain over the elm trees. Across the
river the engine of the last excursion train from Youghal was
blowing sparks up to the stars. The excursionists were waving
their handkerchiefs out of the windows like mad, and the
lights in the hundreds of houses up on the hill were dancing
like fireflies. It was near two in the morning before we got
home. We had to hire a sidecar and dump the girls on tiptoe,
one by one, fifty yards from their doorsteps and their frothing
fathers. We never saw them again. "No attachments. No regrets." No wonder you get all those angry young bums nowadays. They never knew how happy the world was between
the two wars. Sheer heaven!

2

We had three good summers of it — and then the inevitable *femme fatale!*

It was a Sunday morning, blue sky, wind from the southwest, boats almost ready — rugs, grub, cushions, concertina,
trumpet — and T.J. was just about to say to Olly, "Off you
go, boy, collect the flesh!" when Janey Anne Breen hove into
view. I knew her slightly through a third cousin of mine, a
very pretty girl named Fan Looney; the two of them used to
go off together once a week saving sinners with the Ladies'
Saint Vincent de Paul. Without thinking, I said:

"Hello, Janey Anne!"

"Good morning, Alphonsus," says she. "Off for a little
row? Very good. Very healthy."

I introduced the boys, we chatted for a bit, and before I
could warn Olly he did it. It must have been pure reflex action because she had, and still has, a thin hardbeak smile,
mousy hair, as dry as a Temperance Club cat and crimped
like corrugated iron, two peg legs the same width all the way
up stuck into size eight shoes, black and squat-heeled, with
big, black bowknots, and she was wearing, as she always did,

and when I saw her the other day she still was wearing it, an electric-blue frock that T.J. said always made him think of methylated spirits. If she had anything at all that you could look at it was her two goofy eyes, sweety, softy eyes, twice their natural size behind her thick, rimless spectacles, and two big front teeth lying white and wet on her lower lip as if she was always saying fuf-fuf. Whatever made him do it, Olly slips his arm around her waist and says, in his best Harry Lauder accent, "Coom on, lass, what about a kiss and a squeeze for poor old Olly, eh?" She gave him a crack across the puss that you could hear echoing down the Marina half an hour after, and off she stalked, nose and specs in the air, her heels digging holes of anger in the ground, and Olly picking up his bowler hat off the grass and gazing after her with his mouth open and T.J. in the splits of laughter.

T.J. always had a very strange way of laughing. He used to bend over as if he was trying to kiss his knees, his hands trailing to the ground, for all the world like a cow laughing at a pound of butter. That was the way he was now, and me leaning across his back, patting him like a baby with the hiccups. As soon as he could talk he explained matters to Olly.

"No, Olly! No, boy! Not with black shoes and bowties to them. Not with specs. Not with a Child of Mary medal around her neck. Not with no mother, a brother a priest, and a sister a nun."

"Nun?" he says. "You mean locked up for life in a bloomin' convent?"

"That's the idea," I said. "And if somebody doesn't pick Janey Anne up very soon she'll be locked up too in about a hundred yards of nun's veiling. She's a good girl, Olly. GOOD. One of those girls you read about in ancient books."

He stared after her, gargling.

"Pure," says T.J., "as the driven snow. Now off you go, Olly, like a good boy, and find us a couple of nice bad girls

like you always do. Young, and tender and jumping like April
lambs."

He trotted off, after her, caught up with her, and took off
his hat and began adulating in front of her.

"For God's sake," says T.J. watching him, "surely he's not
trying to persuade that stick to come on the river with him?
She must be turned thirty if she's a day."

We watched the two of them walking away from us along
the path, Olly with his hat in his hand, angled sideways towards her, bowing like a shopwalker, and her ladyship talking
down the side of her arm at him as if she was ticking-off a
bold, bad doggie. They went on, and they went on, along the
path, under the trees, around the bend of the Marina, out of
sight. We sat down to wait. After half an hour T.J. jumped up
and said, angrily, "Come on. We'll take one boat between
us."

We rowed down the river, not speaking, until we passed the
end of the Marina. I was stroke. I said over my shoulder:

"Do you see what I see?"

The two of them were sitting on the last bench of the Marina and they were laughing.

"So be it!" says T.J. "He can have his attachment. And his
regrets."

"We might have a few regrets, too."

"You're young, boy, you'll find you get over these things."

I could not see his face but I did not like his tone. He
sounded like a bitter old man.

3

They were married that July, and I had to drag T.J. to the
wedding, the usual hole-and-corner affair in the presbytery,
Olly being a Baptist and sticking to it; and after the honeymoon I had to drag him with me to visit them in their little
garden-flat on the Lower Road, a bare hundred yards from

the river. I think T.J. came only because it was a damp night and he had nowhere else to go.

"Anyway," I said, as I squeaked open the garden gate, "it's only polite. This looks like a cosy little love nest."

"Says the setter to the snipe."

He was just after buying a purebred, golden setter pup named Babs, spayed.

"I bet you tuppence we'll have to leave Babs outside," he said. "And I bet you we won't get a drink either."

She opened the door. Specs, bird's eyes, wet teeth, electric-blue dress. An old black, mongrel cocker ran out and in a second the two dogs were at it. She retrieved the mongrel.

"Come to mumsy-wumsy," she says, almost suckling him. "Poor little Charlie-Barlie. Bold, bad, foxy dog! Boo!"

"Bitch," says T.J. coldly.

Olly was behind her, grinning.

"Charlie's a present from an old admirer," he says, with a lewd wink.

"Oliver!" she upbraided. "He is not. Charlie-Barlie," she explained primly, "was left in my care a year ago by an old friend who had to go to sea."

Olly pinched her behind.

"Old friend? Ha ha!" and he winked at us again.

We had to leave Babs outside, tied to the railings.

"Won't you wipe your feet?" she begged. "I did the lino today."

We could smell it. Brand new, red roses climbing all over golden latticework. She had the Infant of Prague on the wall with an electric bulb glowing in front of it. She had a holy-water font on the wall, too. For spite T.J. dropped his cigarette ash into it. The little parlor was as neat as an altar. They sat on each side of the fire, and T.J. and me sat on a new settee against the opposite wall. Olly produced two bottles of Guinness and poured them for us. She took away the bottles and the corkscrew and we knew that was that.

"Well," I said, friendly-like, "and how did the honeymoon go?"

"Guess where we went?" Olly grinned.

"London? Isle of Man? Killarney? Southend? Brighton?" Olly grinned a No to all of them.

"We took a rowboat and set off to explore the river. Lots of nice little cosy corners down there, eh?"

He clicked his tongue and raised shocked eyebrows.

"Oliver!" said Janey Anne, and we knew that he had told her all.

If T.J.'s slow smile was a knife it would have cut his jaw off.

"Nice time?" I asked Olly, and his tone changed.

"So so!"

"It rained," she grimaced.

"A little accident," he gestured.

"Oliver rocked the boat," she said and glared at him.

"As a matter o' fack, poor little Janey fell into the river. She got a bad cold. She lost her glasses. So we came home."

T.J. made a very sad face and looked very happy. Then he slowly began to go as white as cheese because Olly had started in on the story of the blind salesman who met the deaf whore. This was always a thing about T.J. Any story you liked among men, but a single off-color word in the presence of women made him go white with anger. I looked at Janey Anne. She was chuckling. Olly finished his yarn, winked at me, and looked expectantly at Janey. Her face at once did a quick curtain and she said severely:

"Oliver!"

He guffawed. His gooseberry eyes rolled in their sockets. He said:

"Did I ever tell you the one about the barmaid and the champagne cork?"

"Yes," said T.J. like a bullet.

That did not stop Olly. Janey Anne gurgled. Olly finished,

winked, waited, got his "Oliver!" and guffawed happily. He then started in, at length and detail, on our river days. T.J. looked four times at his watch. He held his empty glass between his clasped hands as if he was trying to press it to bits. Janey listened, radiant until it was all finished with Olly singing our barcarolle, *"River girls, O river girls, How we love your dancing curls."* Then she snapped down the black curtain and said to T.J.:

"I think you have been a bunch of very bad boys, Mr. Mooney. I am really shocked at you. After all you are older than Oliver. Not to mention poor Alphonsus there, and he's only a boy."

Oliver, lolling in his armchair, beamed at us both. His beaming face said it for him:

"Did you ever in all your life see such a sweet innocent little girl as I found?"

When we at last got out of that flat T.J. untied the setter without a word, and he did not say a word until we were back in our digs, him sitting on his bed, and me on mine looking at the rain flecking the window, thinking of one wet Sunday, a couple of years back, when I was on the river with that pretty girl Fan Looney.

"Well?" he said at last. "What are you thinking about?"

"Me?" I said, looking away from the rain on the window. "Nothing!"

"Damn it," he snarled, "you must be thinking about something."

"Very well," I laughed. "In that case tell me what was I thinking?"

"How the hell do I know what you were thinking?"

"Then I don't know what I was thinking either."

"So you admit you were thinking?"

"T.J.," I pleaded. "Come off it."

"And you were looking at me!" he growled.

"I was not looking at you, I'm sick of looking at you, do you think I'm in love with you?"

"Oh! So you were thinking about love?"

"Are you going slightly daft?"

"I got over that stage years ago. But *I'll* tell *you* what *I* was thinking. I was thinking, why is it in the name of all that's holy that fellows see things in girls that simply aren't there? And that's what you were thinking, too, whether you know it or not."

"Tell me," I said, to pacify him, "why *do* we see things in girls that aren't there?"

He whispered across to me:

"Because they aren't there!"

I began to think that maybe he really was going a bit daft. I started looking again at the drops of rain on the pane.

"Well?" he said, after another while. "Why don't you say it straight out?"

"Say what straight out?"

"What you're thinking."

"I'm not thinking! Unless," I said, on an inspiration-like, "maybe I was thinking, Why do girls see things in fellows that aren't there?"

"You're a flaming liar! You were thinking no such thing! You were thinking when will I start seeing things in some girl that aren't there. And that's why you were looking at me."

I laughed very loudly at that, because it had crossed my mind that it was a funny thing that he had never married.

"And," he said, very solemn-like, "I'll tell you another thing I was thinking. It won't be long before I see you starting to see things in some girl that aren't there. If you haven't started doing it already."

At that I peeled off and went to bed. So did he. I stayed awake for hours listening to the rain, and I could tell he wasn't asleep either.

4

After that night we could not be kept away from Olly and Janey. Once a week, at least, we would tie Babs to the railings, ring the bell, wipe our feet, sit on the settee, accept our glass of stout, and, as T.J. put it, wait for Olly to start unveiling. He was right — it was just like the quick-change artist act in an old-time Music Hall. Enter Olly as Cork's Casanova, the historian of the river and all its wily ways. Loud Guffaws. Black curtains. Enter Professor Oliver Carson as the warm admirer of Little Tich, George Robey, Lord Beaverbrook, Chief Scout Baron Baden-Powell, Marie Stopes, Stanley Baldwin and Eamon de Valera. Blackout. Bright lights. Drumrolls. Enter Olly in a check suit, straw hat, white bowler and malacca: "Did I ever tell you the one about the Absentminded Professor who took his dog down to the garage to be oiled and greased?" Guffaws. Black curtains. Enter the Confirmed Pacifist: "Let me ask you a question, sir. If you was to say to me, 'What would you do if you saw your poor, dumb sister being raped by a German?' what would I answer you? I would answer you, 'I ain't got no dumb sister! That's my wife!' Ha ha ha!" Oliver! Black curtains. Enter Olly, very serious, as John Calvin announcing the doctrine of the salvation of the elect; which, so far as I could make out, included everybody in the world except the foreman of the works and the population of Germany. To that particular shebang Janey Anne could only respond with small, gasping noises.

Every night T.J. would come away either in a daze of silence, or asking the same question in a variety of ways: What did I think of *that* performance? I answered him once and only once. I said that I thought Olly was being very honest with her, that he was laying his soul open at her feet, and that it was very noble of him. I thought T.J. would strike me with the setter.

"Honest?" he roared at me. "Noble? Do you want to drive me mad? Well, that's the end of it. I'm finished with him. If that's what you think he's doing I'm never going to put my head inside that madhouse again. For the first time in my life I'm actually beginning to sympathize with that eedjut of a woman. I'm beginning to conclude that the unfortunate woman is so bewildered at finding herself married to that roaring lunatic that she'll either sink an axe in his head or end up raving in a padded cell."

The week after that Olly unveiled in a way that dumb-founded the three of us. He revealed that he was a Freema-son, that his father was a Freemason, and that not only had he been a member of a Sheffield Lodge but that the first thing he did when he landed in Cork was to join the local Lodge. I looked over at Janey Anne, and by the fright in her face I saw that, like us, this was the first she had heard of it. As if I was sitting inside in her head I could feel the rats running around in her brain. Secret society, condemned by the Church, ene-mies of the Vatican, Grand Orient, goats, devils, Carbonaries, Black Magic, passwords, handgrips, tip-the-wink, never-know-who-you're-talking-to, red fire, dark rooms, the-Lord-save-us-or-we-perish — all this time, unbeknownst to her, in her own house, from her Olly whose jokes she laughed at, whose life she thought was an open book to her, whom she had by this time seen night after night padding around on his stubby legs in his nightshirt, now looking at her as mild as milk saying:

"Very fine body of men. Very philantropophic. Philan-tropophic to everybody. Without respect to class or creed."

T.J. got me out as fast as he decently could. As we untied Babs we could hear the voices rising inside the window of the little parlor. When we taxed Olly the next day about never telling us he was a Mason he said, shortly, that he did not want to upset us.

"But what about Janey Anne?" T.J. asked.

"Well, I've told her, haven't I?"

"You didn't tell beforehand," I charged him.

"She wouldn't have had me."

At that T.J. said one of those daft things he was always saying:

"She'd have had you double-quick. A brand from the burning, Olly. A brand from the burning."

We did not go so often to the flat after that. The atmosphere, if I might make so bold as to borrow the vivid image, had changed. For one thing the Troubles were starting, and Olly was English and she was Irish. For another thing they could not talk about anything now without her dragging the Masons into it. A sign of it was that Olly had got hold of a little toy Union Jack, the sort you might put up in front of your motorcar if you were daft enough; and she had bought a little toy papal flag, yellow and white; and they had stuck the two flags into vases on each side of the mantelpiece, so that all they had to do then was to look at one flag or the other and off they were, hammer and tongs. If we walked into the middle of one of these arguments they barely took time off to greet us, and as Olly drew the two bottles of stout he would hardly look at what he was doing.

"England," he would say to her, hauling at the cork, "is my! Country! Right! Or! Wrong!"

"Then why didn't you fight for your country during the war?" from Janey Anne, never afraid to hit below the belt.

"I 'ave my convictions," he said. "And I stand by 'em."

"Ha!" she said. "Locked up in your bedroom drawer in tissue paper — your little green and gold apron, with your sash, and your trowel and your secret book of the devil's rules!"

When she talked that way, T.J. said afterwards, she looked like Bluebeard's wife talking about the locked chamber.

"Are we discussing the Empire or the Freemasons?" Olly asked politely.

"How any man," she sailed on, "can be so ignorant, so misled, so benighted, so superstitious as to be riding a goat around a room . . ."

"Janey Anne," Olly protested, "we don't go riding no goats around no rooms. You're not allowed to keep a goat in a room. The R.S.P.C.A. would be after you like a shot."

"Ye call up the devil!"

"Janey Anne! Do you really and truly think I'm the kind of man who . . ."

"Then why don't you tell me what goes on there?"

Very quietly he explained all over again that Freemasonry is a purely philantropophic society.

"Good works. Helping poor boys who are afflicted in any way. Orphans. Polios. Bastards. All the same to us. Each for all. All for each. Assisting one another in our private or commercial difficulties. Naturally these are things we don't wish to be discussed in public. You can see that, darlingkins, can't you?"

She looked at him, doubtfully, tight mouth, teeth buried, eyes big as plates, and started muttering about secret societies condemned by the Pope.

"Janey Anne! Don't you trust your own Ollykins?"

We could see her wavering. Then she cracked her beak on a hard, hempseed "No!"

"I think it's wicked, and sinful and evil. I don't know why I ever married a man who keeps secrets from his wife. A man with a double life. Not like other men I've known. Carol Costigan wouldn't have deceived me like this. Johnny Hartigan wouldn't have done it. Georgie Conlon wouldn't have done it. But you . . . Come to mumsy, my own Charlie-Barlie," she says, picking up the old mongrel and putting her nose down to his nose. "You wouldn't deceive me like that, would you?"

"No," says Olly sourly. "Not unless he went riding a goat around a room."

"Oliver!"

"Or started wearing a little green apron like a nancyboy. Go on, kiss him, do!"

"Don't you dare say one word against a woman's best friend! You Mason! You!"

T.J. would always leave the flat whistling after one of these hot nights; or saying something cheerful like, "It's on the rocks! We'll all be back on the river next June."

5

Just before Christmas Olly came up to me in the works one Monday morning red with pride and excitement.

"Know what's happened? I've been made Master of my Lodge. Elected last Friday night."

"Here?"

"Here in Cork. Wot an 'onor! My old man'll be tickled to death."

"What about Janey Anne?"

"Delighted. She'll be at the Banquet. She's gone into town to buy a frock. She's thinking of blue."

When I told T.J. he said he did not believe it. I assured him that Olly himself told me. He said he meant about Janey being delighted. After supper he said we must go down to the flat at once. Olly was not at home but she brought us in, gave us the two bottles of stout, so far forgot herself as to bring out two more, and started in to tell us all about it, as excited as a girl going to her first dance.

"Of *course* I'm going to the Banquet! It really is a great honor for Oliver. And as his wife I shall be the First Lady."

"But what about the Church?" T.J. goaded.

"Well," she said primly, "at first, when he asked me would I sit beside him in the place of honor at the Banquet I didn't know what to say. So I went around on Saturday morning to

Saint Anne's to consult Father Butts. It was he married us.
He said he would have to think about it and to come back
that night. When I went back that night he asked me why I
wanted to go to the Banquet. I said I wanted to stand by my
marriage vows to love, honor and obey. He said he must
think some more about it and to come back on Sunday afternoon. So I went back on Sunday afternoon and he said:
'Where will this Banquet be held?' I said, 'In the Imperial
Hotel.' He said, 'Very well, Mrs. Carson, you may attend the
Banquet. The place is neutral. And the intention is to avoid
domestic friction. But, after this, you must try to wean him
away from his ungodly ways.' I thought he was very understanding. Even when I asked him should I tell Oliver that I
had consulted him he said, 'It would be tactless and unnecessary.' I was thinking of blue."

"Your taste is perfect," T.J. said. "And you are very
loyal."

On our way home I told him I was surprised at his paying
her the compliment of being loyal. He explained to me that he
did not mean that she was being loyal to Olly.

6

I think it was in the end of January that Olly came over to
us one morning waving a telegram. It was a radiogram for
Janey that her father had sent down to them the night before.
It said: ARRIVING CORK THURSDAY NIGHT FOR THREE DAYS
STOP HOSPITALITY WELCOME IF AVAILABLE STOP THREE
CHEERS AND WHAT-HO CAROL.

"It's from her old boy friend Carol Costigan. A radio
officer with P. and O. Wonderful man. Salt of the earth. Janey
wants the two of you to come to supper on Thursday night
and view my defeated rival." He began to laugh like a zany.
"The joke of the whole thing is Janey's like a cat on hot

bricks. She never told him she's married. He's going to get a right land when he sees me."

We went down, we tied Babs to the railings, rang, were let in by Olly, who gave us a rather watery wink, we wiped our feet and went into the parlor. The first person I saw was Mrs. Charles Costigan, a luscious blonde. Then I saw Mr. Salt-of-the-Earth Costigan. He was about the size of a jockey, false teeth, hair going thin, and he had a bulge under each eye like a blue moon in its last quarter. Mrs. Costigan turned out to be Yorkshire, and a nonstop talker, with all of Olly's sense of humor, who roared at his roughest jokes, told a few blue ones of her own, and lowered her liquor like a man — whiskey, in honor of the double marriage. I will say this for Janey Anne, that she carried the whole thing off like a good sport: loud jokes and laughter about secret marriages, and "I-only-had-to-turn-my-back," and "We-both-seem-to-like-the-English-don't-we?" But Olly was not taking it so well. He kept looking at Costigan, and then glancing over at Janey Anne, and it was as plain as a pikestaff that he was wondering what she had ever seen in the fellow. All the same, the man was his guest, so after the supper was over he had no option when Costigan said, probably because he saw there was no more liquor coming up, "Say, chaps. Why don't we leave the girls alone for a bit to get acquainted and drop around the corner for a little bit of manly powwow and a nightcap? What-ho?"

We went down the road to the old Internationale, just where the houses stop and the river is wide open. It was a lovely calm night, with a tingle of frost in the air. The buses were like stars, and the stars were like buses. A ship went slowly chugging down the river on the high tide. For an hour it was just like the good old days, boozing there together, swapping yarns — if Olly was being a bit quiet, for him — so that I was disappointed when T.J. said it was getting late and we must push off for home. On the way I said:

"Did you remark how quiet Olly was? I think he's feeling sorry for poor Janey. That fellow Costigan was a terrible let-down."

T.J. snorted at me.

"Simple Simon," he said.

"What do you mean, Simple Simon?"

"Don't you know a Woolworth's wedding ring when you see it?"

The following morning Olly stepped into the line with us and came right out with it.

"I told that fellow this morning that if he and his floozy aren't out of my house when I come back tonight I'll throw the pair of 'em out on their necks in the middle of the road."

"How did you find out?" T.J. asked.

"He had the cool, brazen brass to tell me. He had the gall to think that I'm his kind of a man. I didn't sleep a wink. I could hear Janey crying all night. Do you know what? Her pillow was as wet this morning as if you'd thrown a bucket of water on it."

At that T.J. stopped dead, and doubled over, pawing the ground, and all the fellows passing by looking at him and smiling to see him laughing. Olly dragged him up and around by the shoulder, and I thought he was going to hit him.

"What the 'ell are you laughing at?" he bellowed, and all the fellows stopped to look.

"Jealous!" T.J. wails, between his laughs. "Jealous!"

"Janey! Of that floozy? For that rat?" he roared.

T.J. quieted. He stared at Olly as if he had been struck dumb. He shook him off.

"Did I say *she* was jealous?" he sneered, and walked away.

7

We never visited the flat again. We did not talk to Olly for the best part of two months. I did not see much of T.J. either, outside the digs, and not very much in them — I had seen a streak of cruelty in him that I did not like. Besides, that winter I was in the I.R.A. and I was doing a special night course three times a week at the Tech., and I may as well also mention that once or twice I tried courting Fan Looney. And if I must tell the whole truth of it she would have nothing to do with me. She said she had heard too much about my goings-on from Janey Anne. In the end it was Olly who talked to us. He came and sat down beside us one day in the canteen. He was his old, cheery self.

"Boys!" he said right off the reel. "My Janey Anne is one of the great women of all time. As Father Butts said to me last night when I was seeing him off at the door, 'Your wife, Mr. Carson, is a credit to Faith and Fatherland.' I never before realized wot comfort a troubled soul can get out of religion. It's made me think, let me tell you that. It made me ponder very seriously on a lot o' things."

"Coming over?" asks T.J. "And, if so, what about the Freemasons?"

"As a matter o' fack," says Olly, obviously dying to talk about it, "Father Butts is very understanding about that particular question. He opened my eyes to a lot of things I never knew about the Masons. And he opened Janey Anne's eyes too. He lent us a very interesting book on the subjeck there last month. The two of us are reading it every night over the fire. It's these bleeding Continentals that gave us a bad name. The fack is English Freemasonry is away out on its own. British to the backbone! Not that I'm entirely convinced, mind you. But historically speaking . . ."

And off he went about the Scotch Rite, and some crowd called the Knights Templar, and the French Revolution came into it, and six Papal bulls, and only the siren stopped him.

"Hooked," said T.J., as we walked back to the bench, "booked and cooked to a cinder. He'll be dripping holy medals by Easter!"

T.J. was wrong. That Easter, Olly got the flu and died as he had lived, a true-born English Baptist. T.J. and me went down to the house for the funeral and she brought us in to see him in the coffin. When I saw what I saw the tears started rolling down my face. She had him laid out in the Franciscan habit, and at his head she had laid the little Papal flag that used to stand in the vase on her side of the mantelpiece. I never saw any woman look so happy.

"He was a bad, bad boy," she smiled. "But God will forgive him. As he will forgive ye, too. Praise and glory be to His name."

That afternoon we walked away from the graveside as silent as the grave. It started to rain and we halted under a yew. The funeral was very largely attended, Catholics, Masons, Baptists, Boys' Brigade, all sorts and sizes of people, workers from the factory, every class and creed, scattered under yews all over the place sheltering from the rain.

"I suppose," says T.J., after a while, "we know what we're thinking?"

"T.J.!" says I, and I was wiping my face with my handkerchief. "I'm not thinking anything at all, no more than that pile of ould yellow bones there. And I don't want to think, because all I want to do is to forget."

"Well, I'll tell you what I'm thinking. That woman fattens on guilt like a cemetery worm."

"Guilt? What has she to feel guilty about?"

"Nothing!" he shouted at me, forgetting where we were. "That's why she loves it."

"Daft!" I said and I threw the back of my hand to him and

walked away down the path. He came raging after me, he shoved me up against a Celtic cross, he put his long nose into my face and he started haranguing me as if I was a public meeting, one hand on my chest, the other pointing like a politician's statue across the white headstones.

"Do we or do we not know what she did to that poor sucker lying there in his fancy dress under five feet of ground? Did she or did she not hypnotize him into thinking she was the incarnation of all goodness and virtue and that he was nothing but a Sheffield ourang-outang?"

"Well, Olly, certainly, had a very high opinion of his wife."

"And why? Why? Isn't this the question that's been tormenting you and me from the first day they laid eyes on one another?"

"Look," I said, "all I know is that the cold of this old cross is going in through the small of my back."

He held me gripped tighter than ever.

"I have decided," he said, and his eyes were like two gimlets, "that in what is commonly called love man creates woman after his own unlikeness. In love woman is man's image of what he is not. In love man is his own creator, midwife and gravedigger, awake, asleep, dreaming or hypnotized the way you are at this very moment into thinking what I damn well know you are thinking only you haven't the guts to say it."

I threw him off, and graveyard or no graveyard I let a roar out of me:

"I'm thinking of nothing! And I'm proud to say I'm thinking of nothing! And I'll give you a sock in your greyhound's puss if you don't stop thinking for me. Aye, and tormenting me in the middle of my sorrow for my poor dead friend Olly Carson lying over there under a ton of wet earth and a pile of glass flowers."

He leaned one hand against the Celtic cross and he sneered at me:

"You're thinking of your lousy soul and of your latter end."

I can still hear the whistling of the blackbirds. I can see the sun on the raindrops of the yews, and the mourners fluffing themselves out, and the long black cloud moving like a black pot lid away over the city. I knew somehow that this was going to be the most wonderful night of my life and I began to cry rain down into the old cross at the thought of it. At that the kindness broke out in him, and I was never more touched by anything he ever said to me as by what he said then. He put his arm around my shoulder and he said:

"Al, boy," says he, "will you wipe your face, yeh slobbering eedjut? And stop disgracing me in the public graveyard? Come on out here to The Last Post and I'll stand you a pint of the best."

The pub was full of mourners. We leaned on the counter looking down into our two pints. Someone lit the gas mantle. It was like the green sea. I started thinking to myself that no man can do without a friend. And I was thinking, wouldn't it be sort of nice, when all is said and done, to have somebody to look after me when I got old, and to lay me out when I'd be dead, with the tricolor over my coffin, and my I.R.A. gun lying on top of it, and the band after the hearse playing "The Flowers of the Forest," or the "Dead March" from *Saul*. I looked up at T.J. smoking his pipe and pondering on his pint, and I confessed it to him. I expected him to bawl me out. He looked at me a bit sadly, but kindly too, like some old priest after listening to you telling him your sins. He patted me on the shoulder, and he began at me, soft and warm, kind of pleased, I suppose, that I had confided in him:

"Al! There is no doubt whatever about it, you are a gom. And you always were a gom. And you always will be a gom. And it's a good job for you that you have somebody like me to advise you. A babe in arms, a poor, young fellow up from the country that knows nothing about the ways of the world or the wiles of women. If it wasn't for me looking after you you might have been hooked long ago by some vampire like that wan," with a jerk of his head to the cemetery. "Sucking your blood. Leeching you like a succubus. Turning you into a poppet. Let me tell you this one thing, and mark it once and for all. All every woman is waiting for is the day she can lay you out and be praying for you, and feeling good about you. They keep you out of their bed when you're alive, and they sleep with you when you're dead. The war of the sexes is declared by women on the weaker sex, and entered into by men because we are the weaker sex. And when we're beaten to the bed, that is to say when we think we have conquered our woman, what do we do but put her up on an altar and grovel before her, and work ourselves to a lather for her into an early grave?"

"But, T.J., what about love?"

"Love, my dear, poor boy, is a sedative disguised as a stimulant. It's a mirror where man sees himself as a monster, and woman as a thing of untarnished beauty. If it wasn't for that all men would, otherwise, and normally, fear all women. You fear women. I fear women. But because we need them we have to have them. And that's where they have us, in the great and final triumph of women over men, called — by them, not by us, and well called — Happy Wedlock. Love is a prison staffed by female warders. Let me tell you . . ."

It went on for an hour, nonstop, pouring into me, pint after pint, like the sea into a cave. I did not understand one-hundredth part of it. But I understood enough of it. I understood that he was advising me to look into the mirror of my own heart and there I would see Love smiling sweetly out at me. I went down to Fan Looney that night, and I told her all about it. When I was finished she said in her nice, sweet way that she always knew that T.J. Mooney was no proper com-

pany for a nice young man like me, and if I had found him
out she was very glad.

"Maybe," I said, daringly, " 'tis the way I found you? Have
I a chance, Fan?"

She looked at me, and her eyes filled and her voice broke.

"Oh, Alphonsus!" she says. "What are you after doing to
me? I was a happy girl without a thought of anything in the
world until you came talking to me and now you're after turning me into a grown woman. And," she said, sobbing into my
shoulder, "now we'll have to start planning."

"We will, Fan," I said and I felt just as miserable as herself, and she made me feel an awful brute.

"You'll have to give up the drink," she wailed.

"I will, I will," I promised.

"And cut down on the smoking," she wept.

"Anything in the world you say, Fan! If you'll only stop
crying."

We are settled down now. We have five lovely children.
Cherubs! I'm foreman of the works. And I can assure you I
keep a sharp eye on the young fellows. After all, I know the
ways of the world. T.J. got another job. For years I did not
lay eyes on him, until last month when I was walking down
the Marina one Sunday with Fan pushing little Sean in the
gocart, and I had Deirdre on my shoulder. Suddenly I
stopped dead. I saw the gray-haired man on the river, pulling
along at his ease. In the prow with her nose up was a red
setter, and it was that made me recognize him.

"Fan!" I said. "That's T.J."

She looked and she laughed sharplike.

"The Rule of the River," she said.

It was a lovely June morning, wind from the southwest,
and the ebb with him. Very nice. He would come back on the
tide. As late as he liked.

"Well?" Fan asked. "What are you thinking?"

"Ach! Nothing!"

"You were smiling," she said suspiciously.

"Was I?"

"Yes, you were!" she said and she gave me a dark look.

"I was just smiling sadlike. Thinking what a lonely poor divil he is."

We walked on. I watched him slowly pull away from us. I could not get the old barcarolle out of my head. *"River girls, O river girls. How we love your dancing curls"* . . .

I was very careful not to smile.

Charlie's Greek

I T was twenty-odd years before I saw Rika Prevelakis again, encouraged to visit her by, of all people Charlie, for, of all things fun, in, of all places Athens. "You will have no trouble in finding her," he assured me. "Everybody in the university knows her well."

She did not look her forty-five years, though she had grown stout, motherly and quizzical. Her hair was still black but not so oily. Her skin looked so delicately soft and pink that I at once remembered our old Dublin joke: "Charlie, does her face powder taste of Turkish Delight?" and his cheerful wink in reply. Nothing really betrayed her age except those Swiss rings she wore, too tight on her plump fingers, the faint necklace of Venus on her throat, and the hard ball of her calf. I gathered that her husband, whom I did not meet, was an exporter of fruit, and judging by her charming house, with its modern paintings and pieces of modern sculpture, he was a highly successful one. She told me that her eldest son — she had three — was nineteen, a figure that startled me by taking me back directly to the year after her famous visit to Dublin. So she had made up her mind about Charlie as rapidly as that!

She was delighted to get firsthand news of him, asked many questions about him, and although she now clearly thought of him with a certain good-humored self-mockery it was plain that she also remembered him with a warm and grateful affection.

"He made me come alive," she said so simply that the hackneyed words sounded as fresh as truth.

We chatted for nearly an hour; at the end, just as I was leaving her, I said:

"I'd be interested to know how you would sum up Charlie at the end of it all?"

She laughed and put on a stage Anglo-Greek accent:

"My husband always say, and my husband ees a wise man, that whenever he ees asked hees opinion of any man he avoids the opeenion and sketches the leetle portrait."

Wise man, indeed, I thought as I walked away from her delightful house whose garden overlooked the winking blue of the Piraeus. "Opeenions?" If I asked any dozen men who knew Charlie in his heyday I could guess the sort of juryman's anthology I would collect:

1. Charlie Carton? I'd trust him with my wife! For five minutes.

2. You know, I honestly and truly believe that he was the most outgoing, warmhearted, affectionate young fellow I ever met.

3. A cold, self-indulgent, self-centered, unprincipled hedonist!

4. A genuine lover of mankind, a born reformer and a natural revolutionary. Damn few people like him left in Ireland today.

5. What an orator! Brilliant! And so gay. A most amusing chap. A dreamer and a rebel. The essence of everything that is fine in the Irish nature.

6. Charlie Carton? That Big Mouth!

7. Would you not agree with me that he was rather a nice blend of Don Juan and Saint Francis? I mean, it was a toss of a coin which side of him would win out in the end. By the way, which has won out?

8. Had he any principles at all? I've seen him weep over a sick child in the slums one minute and the next minute deceive a woman, pitilessly.

9. No, I don't think I'd say that Charlie ever had many principles. A few? Perhaps? They certainly didn't lie too heavily on him. Do you remember what Aristide Briand said one time about principles? *"Il faut toujours s'appuyer sur les principes; ils finissent par en céder."* Always lean hard on your principles — sooner or later they will give way. One thing about Charlie, though — he was a damn good sport. A real man's man. I liked him.

10. If you want my frank opinion of him he was a flaming bloody humbug.

11. I only knew him in his college days. He'd give you the shirt off his back. You have to forgive a lot to a youngster like that.

12. Soft. To the marrow of his bones. Mush. Incapable of tenderness because incapable of fierceness. Ask any woman. The only good thing they could all say for him would be that if he deceived them he damn soon undeceived them.

There was that night he loaned me his bed-sitter in London. The telephone rang every half-hour from midnight on. Always the same woman or girl.

"No," I would reply. "Mr. Carton isn't here. I'm only a guest, occupying his room for the night." Or: "I assure you Charlie isn't here. For God's sake do you realize it's one o'clock in the morning, and I'm trying to sleep!" Each time she said the same forlorn thing: "Well, just tell him I just rang up just to say Goodbye." After half an hour, back she would come again, and again, and again, until, between fury and pity, I began to wonder whether he had not been expecting exactly this when he so generously offered me the loan of his room. In the end I appealed to the operator. In a tired, polite, English, three-o'clock-in-the-morning voice he said: "I'm very sorry, sir, I've explained to the lady that Mr. Carton isn't there. It does no good, poor thing. Besides, I'm obliged to put the calls through. And mark you, this is costing her a pretty penny — she's on long distance from Strasbourg."

A Salvador Dali would have painted him with a woman looking out of each eye. His handsome boyish face would have delighted any painter of the high Renaissance in search of the epitome of the power and prime of youth; though it would have been a Florentine painter rather than a Venetian, because of his colorless skin, his buttercup hair, his teeth so small and perfect, his heavy-lidded eyes and because in spite of his bulk he suggested surface rather than roundness, depth or solidity. Neither his face nor his body ever made you conscious of his bones. Stripped for the boxing ring his body looked so soft, almost so feminine that nobody who had not already seen him box would have taken him for a stayer. But he was a stayer, and a frequent winner, obstinate, agile as a boy, a fender rather than a fighter, winning always on points of skill. He outboxed his men and outflirted his women. His boyishness was a fake. At forty-one he was still eager, laughing, garrulous, completely indifferent to appearances, uncombed, almost unkempt, genuinely feckless — he never gave a tuppeny damn about money or possessions and he was generally broke; which may have been the main reason why, even in his schooldays, women wanted to mother him and love him. It must have come as a shock to them to discover that his fecklessness was all-embracing, in every sense of the word. Their pretty boy was as hard as nails. I thought of him the first time I saw that well-known portrait of Lodovico Capponi by Bronzino in the Frick museum — an elegant young ephebe you might think until you looked into his cool, gray X-ray eyes; they make you jump like a drop of boiling water on your hand.

One of our jurymen remembers him as a natural revolutionary; another as a rebel. He was born in the wrong place and the wrong age to be either, to the full — in Ireland after the Troubles. How happy he would have been in the thick of them! If he had been shot then (though I have the feeling that he would have outboxed them too) he would now be one of our best-loved boy heroes. He was born too soon for the war against the Nazis, and the Spanish Civil War was almost over when he was leaving school — together with the not-all-that-young schoolmistress who took him camping in a pup tent all around England for the whole of that summer.

"She completed my education," he used to say, with his usual happy grin. "What happened to her? I don't know. She got sacked, of course. Oh, yes, she wrote to me. But," with a graceful circle of his slender, strong hand, "we had completed the medallion of our love."

That was the way he always talked, romantically; and behaved, ruthlessly. He used to say:

"I'm not really all that Irish, you know! The Cartons were always Cromwellian settlers. And you know how it is with these colonials. One moves on."

"Would you," I had asked Rika Prevelakis, "say he was ruthless?"

By way of reply she recalled their last encounter. I already knew (we all knew) something about it. She frankly filled in the details.

It happened at the time of his famous Monster Public Protest Meeting in Forty-one. He was then one of Ireland's active Communists (had we twelve?), in public calling himself a member of the Irish Labour Party which, as everybody knows, was and is about as left as my right foot; calling himself a socialist in private; and (his own confession) in his bed or his bath loudly declaring himself a Marxist. The date is vital. Forty-one was a tough time anywhere in these islands for anyone to be a Communist. The Russians were still holding to their nonaggression pact with Hitler. The many thousands of Irish in the British Army felt they were there to fight Communism as well as Nazism. Dunkirk was over. So was the Battle of Britain. But when Spain invaded Tangiers, which reminded us all of the existence of General Franco, and the Germans entered Athens, which reminded Charlie of Lord Byron, it seemed the perfect moment to appeal to Ireland about the rights of small nations. Accordingly, Charlie and the Germans entered Athens, which reminded Charlie of "in honor of Greece" for the night of May fourth. The timing could not have been more awkward for all concerned. Had they waited until June, Russia would by then be fighting Germany. And four days before the meeting this old flame of Charlie's turned up in Dublin.

She was about twenty-five then; small, dark, reasonably pretty, and so enchanted to find Charlie up in arms in defense of her country that her prettiness bloomed out in a sort of fiery beauty. In every way but one she was a most appealing young woman, as all who met her agreed; and most of us did meet her because from the minute she arrived he was madly trying to fob her off on his friends. (With her, also, it appeared, he had completed the medallion of their love — anyway of his love.) Her one unappealing characteristic was that although she was highly educated — she was then teaching Greek and Greek history in London to Foreign Office chaps — and well informed about most things, shrewd, hardheaded and clear-eyed, she was pathetically unable to perceive that Charlie detested her in proportion as her pursuit of him and his flight from her made them both look ridiculous.

"It's awful!" he sweated. "It's like a blooming honeymoon! She never lets up for one minute. Can we have breakfast together? What am I doing for lunch? Where am I going for dinner? What about tonight, tomorrow night, the day after tomorrow? Listen — be a sport for God's sake; take her out to lunch for me and lose her somewhere in the mountains."

One immediate result during those days before the Meeting was that we all had her on the telephone:

"Can I speak to Mr. Carton, please?"

"Hello! Is that Rika? I'm afraid Charlie isn't here. He's never here. He doesn't live here, you know."

"But he must be there! He told me to ring this number if he didn't turn up!"

"Turn up where?"

"In Stephen's Green. At three o'clock. Beside the bust of James Clarence Mangan."

In the soft spring rain? Now four o'clock! With a drop on the tip of James Clarence Mangan's green nose? What a good idea for getting shut of a girl! But it was not good enough for Rika.

"Well, he just isn't here."

"I will ring again."

"It isn't any good. He never is here."

"I will ring again. He told me to keep on trying. When he comes please tell him to wait until I ring again."

We kept asking ourselves and asking one another why he was so devious with her. Why, if only in sheer kindness of heart didn't he give her the straight uppercut? Was this the soft streak in him? She revealed that whenever he could not avoid meeting her he would sit by her side, hold her hand, gaze into her eyes and in his rich Irish voice recite poetry to her, Byron for preference:

> *Eternal spirit of the chainless mind!*
> *Brightest in dungeons, Liberty! thou art.*
> *For there thy habitation is the heart —*
> *The heart which love of thee alone can bind*

If she raged at him he would say, soothingly and softly, "Let the doves settle, Rika! Let the doves settle on your looovely head!" Once, being still as tempestuous as (in his admiring phrase) the stormy Aegean she found him gripping her hand and asking, "Do I hold the hand of Queen Maeve?" to which she unwisely replied, "Who is Queen Maeve?" only to find herself at once bewildered, delighted, infuriated and irrecoverably lost in a golden and purple tapestry of Celtic myth and legend:

"Our past, Rika, is so old and so rich, like your great past, out of which you have come to us, so filled with wonder and mystery that it surrounds us like the murmuring night sea, crowded with the dim faces and the lost voices of our dead, whose whispering words we never cease to hear and can never hope to understand. In that dark night of the Irish memory there looms always our great goddess Queen Maeve, surrounded by the tossing heads of the eternal sea, her herd of white bulls up to their bellies in the green pastures of the ocean, her spear aloft, her great eyes roolling . . ."

She was never to know how that story ended. Dazed and mesmerized, in the very heat, heart and height of it, she saw him leap up and cry: "My comrades await me! The battle approaches. Meet me in Davy Byrne's bar in an hour's time."

And there he was pounding down the stairs with her shouting over the banisters, "But if you aren't there?" and him shouting up from the bottom of the well "Ring 707070!" She had waited for the length of four whiskeys in Davy Byrne's. She had then found that there is no such telephone number as 707070, and decided that she had misunderstood him: until she saw it the next day in a bookshop window. *I Did Penal Servitude*. By 707070.

By the morning of the Meeting she was beside herself. Up to then she had grudgingly accepted that his secret preparations for the Meeting were a reasonable explanation for his disappearances and nonappearances. But when the Meeting would be over and done with? She knew that that would be either the end or the beginning of everything. Early that morning, so early that the gulls were still screaming down on the garbage bins, she found herself awakened by a knocking on the door of her hotel bedroom. He was standing in the corridor carrying a suitcase, his collar up, his buttercup hair in his eyes, and his eyes staring. He laid the suitcase at her feet and said with a terrible earnestness:

"Rika, when, perhaps even before, the Meeting ends to-night the whole city will be a cauldron of excitement. There may be riots. Blood may flow in the streets. Unless I am in jail, or dead, I will come to this hotel at twelve o'clock to-night with a motorcar. I know the night porter. A grand young fellow from Kerry. One of us. Absolutely reliable. He will let me in by the back door. We will fly together into the mountains where a friend of mine has a lime-white cottage with a roof of golden thatch beside a dark lake where the ripples are forever washing in the reeds and the wild water forever lapping on the crags, and there at last we will be alooone."

"But," she had asked, clutching her dressing gown to her neck, "how do I really know that I can really trust you to come?"

He had glared at her.

"Trust? It is I who trust you. This case," down-pointing, "contains everything I possess — papers, books, letters, plans, maps. Enough to ruin me for life! Is this hand I grasp the hand of a weakling or the hand of Queen Maeve?"

("Idiot that I was," she sighed, "I said 'Queen Maeve.' ")

"At midnight! Be ready! Be waiting! My Grecian bride!"

(Throwing out her arms like a pope she cried: "And he was gone!")

She went to the Monster Meeting. ("I *attended* it," she said mockingly.) The evening was a trifle damp. Charlie had said that College Green would be thronged from end to end. Rika found a gathering of about three hundred people most of whom looked like evening strollers, invited by a loudspeaker — and gently shepherded by an Inspector and six guards — off the main thoroughfare of College Green into a piazzetta called Foster Place. This broad brief cul-de-sac, mainly occupied by banks, is used during the day as a parking lot, and commonly used by night for smaller public gatherings such as this. She soon observed that the organizers of the Meeting (old campaigners), having placed their decoy speaker at the farther or inner end of the cul-de-sac, then drew up a convertible motorcar at the other or open end for their main speakers, with the evident intention of leaving themselves a ready line of retreat into College Green if things turned nasty. Across the backs of the convertible's seats they had laid the kind of shallow packing case which is used for transporting such flat objects as sheets of glass, wall boards or pictures, a platform just about wide enough to support and display one speaker at a time.

The pilot speaker — a young Trinity College student named Phil Clune, who was later to become chief financial adviser to one of the new African nations — was both careful enough and lucky enough not to provoke his audience to anything more serious than a few sarcastic interruptions on the lines of "Lord Byron was a dirty scut!" or "And what did Greece do for us when we wor fightin' the Black and Tans?" or, in bland disregard for Phil's age, "And where wor you in Nineteen Sixteen?" She found it all deflating and confusing until the crowd had to turn right around to face the main speakers. Then things began to warm up a bit while still remaining confusing, especially when what she called "a butchy-looking woman with cropped gray hair like Gertrude Stein" started to speak of the Greek Church as a citadel of truth, liberty and outstanding moral courage. This produced shouts of "What Greek Church?" and "We don't recognize no Greek Church," which made her feel that it was her duty to explain to those near her what the Greek Church really was; the main effect of which was to break up the opposition into small growling groups arguing among themselves about which Greek Church recognized Rome and which recognized Constantinople. These arguments subsided when the butchy woman started talking about "the deplorable silence of the Prisoner of the Vatican," whom she referred to, rather over-familiarly, as "Papa Pacelli." The result was such angry cries as, "His Holiness the Pope to you, ma'am!" and, "Hey! Are you from Belfast?"

At this point, if Rika had known her Dublin properly she would have realized that it would only be a matter of minutes before somebody would start singing "Faith of Our Fathers," and then it would be high time for all prudent men and women to start edging off to the shelter of the nearest bank doorway. Instead she started elbowing to the front where she saw Charlie insistently plucking at the tail of Gertrude Stein's skirt and madly whispering something to her that made her quickly wind up whatever she was saying about the Red Dean of Saint Paul's and lumber down off the packing case.

Charlie at once leaped to the rostrum, his arms spread, his yellow hair blowing in the wet wind, his splendid voice ringing out:

> *Eternal spirit of the chainless mind!*
> *Brightest in dungeons, Liberty! thou art.*
> *For there thy habitation is the heart —*
> *The heart which love of thee alone can bind*

"My friends! I give you a clarion call that I believe no man or woman listening to me can fail to answer. Up the Republic!"

The crowd did not say a word in answer to this clarion call — which was probably exactly what he wanted since they at once fell silent to listen, though possibly more dominated by his fine orator's voice and his lithe boxer's body than by the actual words he said:

("Oh!" she recalled. "He looked superb. I fell in love with him all over again. Say what you like about him, he had presence. He had guts.")

"My friends!" he shouted. "We are an old and ancient race whose past is so old and so rich, so filled with wonder and mystery that it surrounds us like the murmuring night sea that defends our green shores, like the whispering Aegean whose antique memories forever ripple among the reeds and lap upon the crags of ancient Greece. That darkness of Ireland's primordial memories is crowded tonight with the dim faces and the murmuring voices of our beloved and rebellious dead, whose words we never cease to hear and every syllable of which we fully and clearly understand — whether it be Queen Maeve of Connaught among her herds of milk-white bulls, the tossing foam of the sea, her great spear aloft, her thunderous voice calling to us to remember our birthright, or the quiet, sad figure of Cathleen the daughter of Houlihan passing through the shadows like an uncrowned queen."

(Rika shrugged. "Yes! He had only been practicing on me. But I felt it made me his colleague! And I was proud of it!")

"My friends!" Charlie was bellowing. "What do those voices say to us tonight? They say to us: 'As we are free and as we will remain free, so must all mankind be free and forever so remain.' "

At which point he whipped a small tricolor from his left-hand inside pocket and waved it over his head — a gesture that actually produced a few approving cheers.

"But, my friends, I said '*all* mankind!' "

At which he whipped from his right-hand inside pocket the blue and white flag of Greece.

"This is the flag of fighting Greece! Tonight we fight under two flags in Freedom's name. Long live Liberty!"

He got a few more cheers. He now produced from his left-hand outside pocket the black swastika on a red ground.

"Does this flag stand for that liberty? For your liberty or

for the liberty of your children? What can you say, what think, what feel? I will tell you what I think of it."

And like a conjurer he produced half a dozen matches from his vest-pocket, struck them alight on the seat of his trousers, and the Nazi emblem burst into flames. ("I had it well soaked in petrol!" he explained to us afterwards.)

"A sign!" he roared, as the emblem flamed and fell. "A sign as black as treachery and as red as blood. And only in blood can all its cruelties be avenged!"

At this the Inspector and his six guards began to edge forward. After all, Ireland was officially a neutral country, even if we were more neutral against Germany than for it, and he had issued stern warnings before the meeting began that no word should be said that night contrary to Irish neutrality. But Charlie's next words made him pause, indecisively:

"I mean, my friends, the blood coursing through your veins, pulsing in your hearts with pity for the children in our slums, our unemployed wailing for bread, our aged, sick, neglected and dying all about us, the thousands of our young men, aye and our young maidens, mounting the gangways day and night to emigrate to foreign shores. Your warm Irish blood can remind you only of the triple cry of Liberty, Equality and Fraternity that led so many of our young men in every age to die for the Republic. That blood is the Rights of Man! That blood is the color of universal brotherhood!"

Reaching behind him he received, unfurled and waved, blazing in the electric light of the street lamps, the red flag.

At one and the same moment a collective howl of rage burst from the crowd, a female voice began to sing "Faith of Our Fathers," the Inspector and the guards breasted toward the car, the mob surged forwards, the car rocked, and Charlie, to prevent himself from being thrown down among the lions, grasped the lamppost beside him, and clambered up it like a monkey, still waving the red flag, still shouting 'Long live Liberty!' "

(I could see it all in Rika's eyes, immense as two colored television screens.)

"You know, those Irish policemen were marvelous! They got in a circle around the car and the lamppost. One of them climbed up and pulled Charlie down by the legs, and the Inspector said, 'Run, you bastard!' And, my God, how he ran! Some of the crowd ran after him, but he was too fast for them. I kept clawing at the Inspector and shouting, 'I am a Greek girl!' He caught me and threw me head first into the car, my legs up in the air, just as the car started and ran away with me, the butchy woman, four or five men, and the red flag streaming behind them. They stopped in a long, quiet street, pulled me out and dumped me on the pavement, and drove away off down that long street into the fog.

"My face was bleeding. My stockings were torn. I was a sight. When I got up I saw I was opposite the Abbey Theatre and I will always remember the play they were playing that night. It was called *The Whiteheaded Boy*. When I saw it I thought of Charlie. My God! I said to myself. He may want to hide in my hotel, and I ran all the way to it. I cleaned myself up to look my best for him when he would come at twelve o'clock. I packed my bags though I was shaking so much I could hardly do it, and then I threw myself on the bed and I cried for my whiteheaded boy. I cried that he knew I had seen him run, that he had been shamed into running for his life, that he was homeless and an outcast. Then suddenly I saw his suitcase and I thought, My God, the police may come here searching for him and find all his papers, and letters, and plans. I managed to lug it to the windowsill — it was very heavy — and I stood it up there outside the window and I drew the blind and the curtains, and I lay down again to cry and to wait.

"I woke up at half-past one. I ran down to consult with the night porter, Charlie's friend. He was a nice, sweet boy, about seventeen or eighteen. He told me he had never heard of

Charlie Carton. I knew then that Charlie would never come. But what was I to do with the suitcase? I decided to take this boy into my confidence. I told him that Charlie was a patriot and a hunted man. I shall never forget what he said to me. He said, 'Miss, if he's for Ireland I'll do anything for him.' I cried when he said that, it was so warm, so Greek. When I told him about the suitcase that I must protect with my life, he got a bunch of keys and a screwdriver and we went upstairs together to see what we should do with this terrible suitcase. Between us, this boy and me, we dragged it in from the windowsill — it was by this time soaked with the rain — and we laid it on the ground and we worked on it and at last we managed to open it."

(I shook my head. Not because I did not know what was in it — Charlie had told me — but in pity for her. Rika looked out of her window down at the waters of the port.)

"I suppose," she said, "in everybody's life there is one moment of shame that he never forgets. This was my moment — when that boy opened that suitcase, that nice boy who would have done anything for Ireland. It contained two bags of sand. Nothing else." She laughed merrily. "He really was a rascal! I told the boy, 'This is probably dynamite.' All he said was, 'Yes, miss.' I stayed in my room until the morning broke. Then I took the boat for London."

I think if Charlie had been with us at that moment I would have struck him. I said:

"Some people would be less kind about him than you. They would say he was a poseur, a sham, an actor."

"Oh, no! He was much more than that! Much more! He was actor, dramatist, producer and play all in one. And we were his audience. He was always trying to play out some play of life that was real to him for as long as he imagined it, though it was always only real in the way a child's soap bubble is real. A dream full of swirling colors, in the end floating away, exploding silently."

"Wasn't that a bit hard on the people who had to be his co-actors?"

"You mean people like me? Very hard. If we were foolish enough to think that any of his plays would last. Not hard if we knew that at any moment he would ring down the curtain and start another romantic play in some other theatre, in some other city, in some other country. Even then, of course, it was hard on his fellow actors whom he left behind out of a job. He was inexpressibly selfish because he was so hopelessly romantic. Always dashing away. An artist whose only art was his life."

"Some people would say he was just a Don Juan."

"I hope not! That most unhappy race of men. Always chasing shadows. Always hoping. Never sure. He is married."

Was it a statement or a question?

"How did you know?"

She smiled:

"We all marry. If it comes to that, Don Juans — and Donna Juanitas too — are of all people the most certain to marry, in order to be sure at least once before they die or become impotent. To feel sure that their search was . . . Oh, well, it's too difficult. It took me a long time to work it out. Until I did I hated him more than I have hated anyone else in my whole life. And," she grinned. "I'm very good at hating. When I realized that he just has to be what he is I no longer cared."

"Have you ever written to him?"

She looked at me coldly.

"I am a happily married woman, with three sons. I am a professor. I have an adoring husband. I have a lovely home. Why should I write to him?"

"He has not forgotten you."

She smiled a gratified smile and we shook hands.

"Give him my affectionate greetings. And all my sympathy."

I glanced at her, startled, until I saw that she did not mean it derisively. She was still smiling sadly as she closed the door.

As I walked down through the narrow streets about the port I wondered for a long time what I would say if somebody asked me for my opinion of her. Like all experienced women, sensible, practical, and absolutely without illusions? Despising above all those fantasies of which even the oldest men are never entirely free? Or would even she sometimes remember, with a tiny, secret, happy smile, certain earlier days when she had been a little otherwise?

I was amused when I told Charlie of our meeting in Athens, and he at once asked, eagerly, if she remembered him.

"Indelibly!"

"And is she still beautiful?"

"More so than ever!"

I watched his gray X-ray eyes narrow with penetration, widen with the lovely image they received, and then, ever so slowly, relinquish another dream. He had little bags under his eyes. His hair was thin as dust. Then he said, "Oh, well! We had completed the medallion of our love!" — and made a graceful circle with his hand.

Billy Billee

CHARMS, omens and dreams . . ." He came on the phrase while ruffling through some sixty-year-old papers. It was in his first penny Catechism, salmon pink, ear-crumpled, tattered. *"Question:* What else is forbidden by the first commandment? *Answer:* All dealings with the devil, all superstitious practices, such as consulting fortune-tellers or trusting in charms, omens and dreams." He grunted. He said aloud, "Oh, yes! Oh, yes, indeed!" He lit his pipe. He gazed out over the harbor. What was her name? He sniff-grinned. Presently the old man was scribbling on the back pages of the Catechism. It finally came out as and he gave it the title of "The Ballad of Billy Billee."

> *Dear Blackie, dear Lottie, Billy Billee,*
> *Star of my morning's simplicity,*
> *Whispering low that love's sorcery*
> *Is hidden in charms, omens and dreams,*
> *That love, ever true to her faithful few,*
> *Like me and like you, gives us our due*
> *Fullness of bliss, eventually.*
>
> *Did you lie? Once again, my old query!*
> *Did you really dance that night for me?*
> *That November night when I thrilled to see*
> *You leap on the stage of an earlier age*

> *To the whistles and wolf calls*
> *Of the boys in the front stalls*
> *Immediately under Box B, and me.*

Wearing his best Sunday suit, short pants with bare knees, a red bow tie in his celluloid Eton collar, fawn-edged, hot palms clung to the purple carton of Rowntree's Cream-Filled Chocolates that, to crown his night, she had put for him on the velvet ledge of Box B. His face felt underlit by the blaze of the footlights.

> *Barely fourteen, the first time I'd seen*
> *The frilly high kick, the round of a knee,*
> *The entrechat flick, splits done to a T,*
> *Full of pride as a bride till I damn near died*
> *When, tier upon tier, they started to cheer,*
> *You made it so clear, every wink, every leer,*
> *You were dancing for me, for* me, *in Box B.*

Not even barely fourteen. Thirteen and ten months. And she? Thirty-five, thirty-six? Thirty-seven? Her red, toy-soldier cheeks hopping, her breasts jumping, her shoulders powder-white, her strong legs tightly cross-gartered. Had she ever been slimmer? Or in those days did men like their women plump? They certainly did not two years later when the stalls were half-filled at every matinee by wounded soldiers in hospital cream-and-blue, smilingly lifting their crutches to the applause of the audience as they faltered to their seats. Their ideal was the teen-ager, hair-shingled, her eyes vast and unrevealing, a slim illusion of innocence.

Not that her figure was news to him. He knew all about it from certain damp afternoons when she showed him photographs of herself on her world-wide tours with the Dainty Delamare Dancers.

"That's me in Singapore, dearie. What fun that was! That's me in Toronto. Look at that snow! Seventy-two inches it was!

Me in Auckland. Here's me in Jo'burg. Me and Molly
Marples in Bombay, O how I love you! Roll on you rolling
rivah! Where the dawn comes up like thundah outa Chiner
'cross the biy."

She absently stroked his bare knee.

"Across wot biy, Mrs. Black?" (In her company he used
always to talk the way she talked.)

"The Biy o' Chiner! Doncherknow no geography, Jacky
dearie?"

She was their star lodger. She had stayed with them for
three out of the four years that Jimmy J. Black spent in Cork
as manager of the Opera House.

It was upstairs, in their sitting room, that she used to show
him those albums of her youth, one plump hand about his
shoulder and the other turning the pages, her armpits exuding
a scent that he knew was called Phul Nana because she once
bedewed his crumpled handkerchief and his hair with it.
Much to the annoyance of his mother who said that he must
have been secretly creeping into her sitting room, which was
true, or else that she was "up to no good"— a remark that
inflamed him with enchanting possibilities.

"Up to no good?" Or just that she wanted somebody to
talk to? Even if it was only a kid of thirteen, about her days
of glory.

> *So long ago yet I still want to know,*
> *After we parted where did you go,*
> *With what Jimmy or Jack, Tommy or Joe,*
> *To what house on the hill, what toff for a thrill,*
> *What military swell, tight as a kite,*
> *Laughing like hell, well out of sight —*
> *At the back, maybe, of Box A below?*

Face it! Give her thirty-seven. Hot as hell. Common as Get
Out. A lecherous, treacherous old bitch. Only a boy would
have thought her any better. English, of course. Maiden

name, Carlotta Tottle. Born in Highgate, London. Father, a barber. Mother, a dresser in the Palace Music Hall on King's Road. Pomade, patchouli and poverty.

(Across the bay the lighthouse gleamed, and was gone.)

What a throaty voice she had that day!

"You do know 'Ighget, Jacky dearie, or don't you? I mean, you must at least 'ave *'eard* of 'Ighget?"

"No! Ah, no, Mrs. Black, I don't know about 'Ighget at all, at all."

"Not even *'eard* of 'Ighget? My Gawd! Where 'ave you been all these years? 'Ighget's near 'Apmstead. Come on, Jacky! Surely you 'ave 'eard of 'Ampstead 'Eath?"

"Oh yes, Mrs. Black, I do know about 'Ampstead 'Eath. I've read *The Woman in White,* and that begins at midnight on 'Ampstead 'Eath. Remember, Mrs. Black?"

"Call me Lottie."

"As a matter of fact, Mrs. Black, Lottie, I know an awful lot about London. I've read all about Sherlock Holmes and I know all about Baker's Street, and the great detective Nelson Lee, and Sexton Blake, and Pedro and Tinker, and I've read Fergus Hume's *The Mystery of a Hansom Cab.* And I know about Paris, too, *The Three Musketeers,* and *The Hunchback of Notre Dame,* and *The Murders in the Rue Morgue,* and *The Scarlet Pimpernel.* And Rome. That's in *Fabiola* by Cardinal John Henry Nicholas Patrick Stephen Wiseman. He was called Patrick because his father was from Waterford. Lots of English cardinals were Irish, you know. That's why we always say that Ireland is the brightest jewel in the crown of Rome. I got *Fabiola* for a present at my First Communion. I read it four times."

"Fancy that now!" she had laughed — she always made two chins when she laughed. She stroked his head. Then she breathed out a deep sigh.

"See wot comes of reading books. Now, before Jimmy J.

brought me to Ireland I'd never read any book at all about this plice. If anyone had told me that one day I'd be living in Cork I wouldn't 'ave as much as known what country they meant. At your age I was dreaming of the wide, wide world."

At which she looked glumly out of the window down at the empty, Sunday afternoon square. There the only noise was a sparrow squeaking in the damp gardens of the Cork School of Art, whose tall, red railings swept around to the front of the Opera House.

It was his clearest image of her, leaning her elbows on the windowsill between the blowing lace curtains, her round, rosy face in her hands, gazing down into the square, or up the lean length of Academy Street at whose distant end she could see a trickle of traffic passing silently along Patrick Street. On fine days she used to spend hours that way. Like a wax statue. Sometimes talking, dreamily. Sometimes, then, her hand would touch his bare knee. A padded hand, not young.

> *Whenever my hand knocks out my dottle,*
> *Cowslip-freckled all over with mottle,*
> *Whenever I pluck the strings of my throttle,*
> *I understand your hand on my knee*
> *As you talked of Rio or Singapore,*
> *And why, with a sigh, more and more,*
> *As I do now, you groped for the bottle.*

When they were in their cups the rows she and Black used to have! Shouting and throwing things at one another, making so much noise that one night his father had to go upstairs and beg them to pipe down for God's sake and the honor of his house.

Black could not complain if she took to the bottle. A convivial fellow who belonged to two boozing clubs and never came home before two in the morning. A fine figure of a man, though! Tall, straight, florid. At his best standing every night in the brilliant front of the Opera House, in his white tie, tails and high choker, ready to click his fingers to an usher, wink at a club crony, bow over a city merchant and his wife, hover about a bunch of English officers down from the barracks. A solid Londoner, mounting guard, like them, over his far-flung outpost of the Empire.

That was her finest hour, too, in a feather boa and a picture hat two feet wide, in her regular place in Box B, second-up, right-hand side, drinking in the smells of canvas glue, grease paint, stale dust, old ropes, faded scent.

One night after a Rugby Final the University students started a small riot in the Pit, and Jimmy came before the curtain. (The Bay of Naples in blue, Vesuvius in scarlet eruption, acres and acres of purple bougainvillea.) They boohed him. He threatened to call in the police if they didn't stop it. They boohed louder. He retired in disdain and defeat.

"Oooh!" Lottie said afterwards. "He looked so brive. Standing up there behind the footlights. Ficing them all."

Sun-bronzed, gun in hand, topee over his left eye?

But Jimmy was smart. When the students started writing furious letters to the *Cork Examiner* he invited the whole team and their followers to be the free guests of the Opera House the next Monday night, and before the play began he came out again before the billowing Bay of Naples and made such a fine, manly, chummy speech about fair play and good-will between fellow sportsmen that they cheered him to the roof and sang "For He's a Jolly Good Fellow". . .

"I tell you straight! I nearly cried up there in my box, I was so proud of my man!"

Jimmy J. must have made lots of good friends during his four years in Cork city; not one of them ever visited her. You could see it by the bareness of her mantelpiece. Every other coming-and-going lodger, actor and actresses all, used to crowd their mantelpiece with photographs in silver frames and leather frames, smiling relatives and friends, always signed. She had only two pictures to show: one of Jimmy, in his choker; the other of herself — brief frock, bare shoulders, fat, gartered legs, standing against a photographer's woodland scene, ferns to her right, ferns to her left, her plump arms poised as if she were about to rise with a whir out of the heather.

(Directly outside his window a sea gull squawked. Alone. He listened. Not a sound.)

He had grown up in Cork, and never known until he left it how utterly alone he had been there, and how little he even still knew about what older people did there. The place was full of rich merchants. Did they have a good time? Did they entertain? Did they throw dinner parties? Did they have dinner at all? Or did they just have high tea when they returned home at night to their big houses on the hills? Did they have bridge parties? Travel? Whatever they did they would not have Lottie Black from King's Road, the barber's daughter, among their guests. She was as much outside it all as he was. Two of a kind.

They had no children. Neither of them ever read a book. They read the gray morning paper, the pink *Evening Echo,* the weekly, red-covered *Answers,* the green-covered *Tit Bits,* Horatio Bottomley's yellow-covered *John Bull,* and the black-and-white *London Life.* It was that one that lured him every week into her room to peep at its sepia Art Supplement — always a naked woman, with a figure as plump as her own. After which he might take a deep smell of her Phul Nana, with its label showing a harem girl dancing in diaphanous trousers. Their whole apartment reeked of Phul Nana. Their lavatory stank of it.

The day she came back unexpectedly to her room and caught him looking at *London Life* . . . When he saw that she saw what he had been looking at he started to bolt.

"Don't run awiy, Jacky," she ordered, going to the mirror to remove her gloves and her hat, fluff up her hair, and look at him, impaled in the glass, staring at her across the room.

"So soon?" she laughed. "You know you'll be a 'andsome fellow when you grow up. I shouldn't be surprised if."

She stopped, turned and surveyed him. Then she sat in her chintz-covered armchair by the open window and with one finger beckoned him over to her. He came and stood by her shoulder and she put her arm around his waist. Her throat whispered it, her eyes looking into his, six inches away:

"I suppose you'd like to see a real woman like that, wouldn't you?"

He hardly had the breath to breathe, let alone to answer, as she undid the top buttons of her blouse, and always looking at him led his hand firmly inside it to the hot blubber of her breast.

"Oooh!" she said. "Your hand is so bloody cold!"

And threw his hand away, buttoned her blouse and glared into the square. Then she said:

"After I first married Jimmy I used to often wonder wouldn't it be nice if . . ."

She stopped. She looked back at him for a long while. Then she said gently, "Poor little bastard!" Then she patted his bottom. Then she said furiously, "Run off to your bloody mama!" He did not dare return for weeks.

She discovered God during her second year with them, one soft, spring night when every place of entertainment in the city was as dark as her boot for Holy Week, the last in Lent. The Opera House was shut; the music hall; every cinema; our one Palais de Dance. The two clubs drew their blinds. Men slipped into the pubs by back alleys. Only the pigeons in the square dared to court openly: the male pigeon puffing himself into a muff of feather, displaying his fantail, following the female around with a piteous *luggudygoo, luggudygoo,* snubbed always by a scornful *so what, so what?* Only the black of the ash trees dared to burgeon. At night the square and streets were like a wake house until a quarter to eight when the patter of footsteps that usually hastened eastward beneath their windows to the Opera House now hastened westward to the parish church of Saints Peter and Paul.

That Wednesday night his mother and he were getting ready to go out to the chapel when they suddenly saw her standing in the doorway of the kitchen, so pale and frightened that she at once reminded him of Lady Macbeth in the sleep-walking scene. His mother, her arms hooped over her head in the act of shoving her black hatpins into her black straw hat, cried out at her:

"Lord save us, Mrs. Black, I thought you were a ghost!"

"I wish to Gawd in 'eaven I was a man!"

"But, Mrs. Black, that's flying in the face of God's holy will!"

"Then wot is God's 'oly will? I've been walking the streets of Cork until my feet are dropping off me. Everything shut tight as a tick. Jimmy in his club soaking it up. Wot about me? I awsk you, is it Gawd's 'oly will for me to become a roaring, bloody secret, soaking, stinking alcoholic?"

"Why don't you come out with us to the Devotions?"

"Wotcher mean?"

"I mean," his mother said piously, "that we must all pray for the sins of the world. For Jesus in the garden of Gethsemane. Every one of his apostles abandoning Him. And the priests praying on the two sides of the empty altar. Until only the one blessed, holy, white candle is left alight in the whole church."

"And then," he had joined in, "when that last candle is taken away behind the altar the electric lights go out and we all clap our hands in the darkness."

"For the night of Calvary," from his mother. "For the end of the world."

"The end of the world! Wot end? Wot world?"

"Every Wednesday, Thursday and Friday of Holy Week," his mother said flatly.

He sat between them in the church. His mother loaned her one of her rosaries, which, on seeing other old ladies do so, she kissed repeatedly. She went with them on the following nights. He went with her alone to the morning devotions on Holy Thursday, where she loved the flower-drowned Altar of Repose. She stood for a long while before the great statue of Calvary, which included Mary Magdalen and the Madonna, and afterwards she had long, pious talks with his mother and father about it all.

> *When you said every Magdalen everywhere*
> *Kneels at the foot of Calvary's stair*
> *Singing the song of all girls who bear*
> *The fruit of their ignorant Spring in the Fall,*
> *Whom did you see, rich with maternity,*
> *Pushing a pram for all eternity —*
> *A planet afloat in the heavenly air?*

Summer is a thin time for churches and cities. He and his mother and father went off on their usual summer holidays to the County Limerick, to watch its crops grow brown and its shallow lakes sink lower still. When they came back they found that she had pinned or pasted on the wallpaper of her apartment, pages upon pages cut from art magazines showing plump, vast-limbed nudes: naked Andromeda chained to her rock, Rubens's half-naked Sabine women, Titian's Profane Love. Every week another naked woman smiled from the wall. They curled there in the heat of an Indian summer that filled the square with boys playing football, little girls playing with skipping ropes, big girls singing, arm-in-arm, three abreast, around the Opera House, shawled women coming out from the lanes to give their babies to the cool of the night.

By September, her nudes clung like snowflakes to her mantelpiece, her washbasin, billowed from her mirrors. They pursued Black into the bedroom. A line of them hung over their double bed. They adorned the walls of the bathroom.

Every day his mother said disgustedly that her house was not that kind of a house. She announced one afternoon that either the pictures must go or the Blacks must go, and stamped upstairs to give out her ultimatum. She came down as soft as a dewdrop.

"We can only pray for her," she said. "That man," she cried, with womanly passion, "should be horsewhipped. All he thinks of from morning to night is drink. Is he a man at all? Ah," she sighed, looking across at the statue of the Virgin in the kitchen corner, "may the mother of sorrows look down on the poor mothers of the world."

Day after day he used to spy on her from a far corner of the square, gazing up at her window where she sat gazing glumly down at the mothers with their babies, and the children playing; or, at dusk, listening to the arm-in-arm girls singing their love songs from one lamppost to the next. Then, in the damp of October, the pictures began to slide to the floor, where their slavey, Bridie McCarthy, used to collect them and bring them, with much lewd smirking and winking, to his mother, who would at once seize them and poke them into the red fires of the kitchen range. Not until they were all gone did he dare to start revisiting her in her room. She let him hold her hand.

Then she discovered Magic. One morning, just after breakfast, she appeared in the kitchen, radiant, gurgling with laughter, to tell his mother what had happened the night before. That week there was a conjurer in the Opera House called Chung Ling Soo. He did all the usual tricks, including the Lady Sawn in Half — a shapely, blonde young woman who also stayed with them and who always laughed merrily when his mother said to her each morning, between relief and disappointment, "So ye're alive still?" Chung Ling Soo also threw cards, magically produced out of the air, down to the people in the stalls, entitling them to have their fortunes told during the interval by a chiromancer sitting in oriental robes in a little colored tent in the foyer. Billy had got one of these cards, and had her fortune told.

"I let down my veil and I took off my ring so he wouldn't know anything about me. The things he said to me! Oh, very clever, you know! Oh, very clever, those orientals! He said, 'You've got bed trouble! The third finger of your left hand is lonely. You will cross deep water in the space of Three. You will meet a fair man under the Crown. You will walk with him under the Star between Trees and Water. He will have great Hearts for you. You will touch Gold. You will have three children.' "

She burst into peals of laughter.

That was when she first began to show him those albums of her tours, her arm about his shoulder, her plump fingers touching his knee, her eyes wandering down over the square or up the lean street. It was then, too, that she started going to the Turkish Baths on the South Mall to get her weight down; and to Professor Angiolini's Dancing Studio in Cook Street. She was less and less often in the house, especially on weekends, when, so she said, she was able to use the stage of the Opera House for rehearsing. Finally she announced that, for a charity concert, she was going to dance again.

(The foghorn grunted like a pig across the misting water of the bay. He laid down his pipe and began to scribble some more figures on the pink cover of the Catechism. She danced on the night of November 10, 1912.)

> *You danced for a dream, for a gleam in your eye*
> *That no one could spy, not even I,*
> *Perched so close, perched so high*
> *That I once saw you spit in the wings.*

At the end I raced down the long corridor,
You winked one eye through your dressing-room door,
And laughed. I turned. I wished I could die.

The next day when he came hurrying home from school she was gone. The only sign of her was one small, lace-edged handkerchief in the fireplace. It smelled of Phul Nana and whiskey. He kept it a long time. Then he stuffed it into a mousehole in his attic bedroom where — he presumed he might now suppose — the mice dreamed on it and had lots of fat little babies.

Come the next July, just as they were all about to go off again on their holidays, Jimmy Black told his father that she had died and was buried in Bombay.

"Very hot," he said stiffly. "Very hot in Bombiy!"

It was rumored later around the town that she had died in childbirth. Then he remembered how she had said, "Bombiy! O how I love you!" and had whistled seductively. And he had wondered if any of it was true.

(Across the bay the foghorn moaned as softly as a dove. He rose, threw his papers back into their cardboard box, stretched his arms, and groaned. Old men's bones are so dry. He went out to the doorstep. Distant gulls squawked. He could hear the wavelets whispering. It was not the foghorn. It was a homing ship, its portholes bright as candlelight. The winter evening dark and still.

"Whispering to me now? As once to you?")

Two gulls. Our fullness due?
Not even a child to dandle.
I wouldn't care if I only knew
Just what, just who you saw that night
You sailed away by candlelight
Into a sea as dark and still
As this that whispers now to me, of you.

Charms, Omens and Dreams?
That's a game no man can handle,
Though — say it, say it —
You who led me on to play it,
Always worth the candle.

Before the Daystar

WHEN you come out into the Place Pigalle from its dark side streets your first impression is of its brightness, then crowds, then noise, and then you become one more aimless wanderer around the jammed pavements. Tonight there was a sharp sense of liveliness, even gaiety, almost like the end of a feastday, although the streets were cold and damp and a cobweb of pink mist hung suspended over the roofs. It was Christmas Eve, about ten minutes short of midnight.

In a corner of the overcrowded terrace of Le Rêve five young people, three young men and two young women, sat crushed about a small table behind the fogged glass partitions, talking loudly to make themselves heard above the gabble. The youth who was doing most of the talking looked like a lightweight boxer. He wore a black polo-necked sweater; his blueblack hair, harsh as metal, peaked over his forehead like a wound-up watch spring; his smile was a lighthouse flash. The others interrupted him only to spur him on. Their Shahrazade? Their pet liar? Indulged. Bantered. Approved.

In a pause in his flow of talk the fair-mousy, pretty girl at his side tilted her scarlet tarboosh so as to tickle his cheek with its blue silk tassel, and said, "Happy now, Andy? This is better than Dublin, isn't it? Or isn't it?"

He gave her his white grin, gripped her frail arm and squeezed it.

"As happy, Jenny, as a lamb with two mothers."

He turned swiftly to the fat youth at his other side. "Jaysus, Fatso, I wonder what'd we be all doing this minit if we were back in Dublin?"

Fatso raised a finger for silence, groped inside his mustard-and-cress overcoat and slowly, very slowly, drew a vast, silver half hunter from the well of his fob-pocket. He clicked it open with the air of an ancient out of an ancient world, considered its convex face, smooth, shiny and milkwhite as his own, and pronounced in a slow Abbey Theatre brogue, "I would be afther thinking, dearly beloved, that at this minit we would all be up in the Lamb Doyle's, or in The Goat, or The Cross Guns, or The Purty Kitchen, where George the Fourth had his first glass of Guinness, being thrun out on our ears for the fourth time in succession. Althernatively, Andy, you would be snoring in your little white cot in your little white home in Templeogue."

"Would I now? Well, then, let me tell you, Mister Laurence-O-bloody-well-Toole, I'd be doing no such a thing. I'd be being hauled off by my ma by the short hairs to Midnight Mass. That is, after the usual couple of preliminary breast-wallopings with the Dominican fathers up in Blackhorse Lane."

He paused to turn to Biddy.

"Our privileged heathen," he mocked.

Champagne-blond, older than Jenny, not pretty, her splendid pigeon's bust straining her white sweater. "Yes?" she queried, in an English voice so tiny that the first time they met her they had asked her if she had the pip.

"I mean Confession," he explained, politely flicking two imaginary crumbs, one-two, from her bosoms. "The annual clear-out. Old Father Berengarius. A mile of hardy sinners queuing up before me. The ould chapel as cold as a vault, and the wind under the slates moaning like a hundred banshees. He's as deaf as a post. Very convenient for your's truly. Doesn't hear a blooming word you say. Did I ever tell ye the night he disgraced me ma?"

He received their quizzical attention.

"There she was, late one Saturday night, inside in the confession box, asking him, if you please, was it a sin for her to believe in spirits and ghosts, and the mile of hardy boys outside all grumbling, and growling and rearing to get in and get out before the pubs closed on them. 'Having commerce with ghosts,' was what she called it. 'What are ye saying to me?' says he, and his hand to his ear. 'Is it a sin, father,' says she at the top of her voice, 'to have commerce with ghosts?' 'Speak up,' says he in a roar that you could hear down at O'Connell Bridge. 'To have commerce with ghosts, father,' she squawks, and the buckos outside all leaning sideways to hear the pair of them. 'You have been having commerce with goats!' he roars at her. 'At your age?' "

Once more they gave him the soft accolade of their laughter. Modestly rejecting the honor he turned aside and as suddenly turned back. Crook-necked he gestured to the dark street behind their corner café.

"Will yez look, boys! The foxy-headed whore is back again. Trying to click a G.I. she is this time. They're brazen tonight. Out in the open. He's twice her height. He'll make pancakes of her."

They all swayed. The nearest of them to the glass partition was Mackinnon. He peered out under his black homburg hat, low over the boils on his forehead. She was a small, skinny woman in a sheepskin jacket, a white beret, a white satin bottom as taut as two mushrooms.

"She must be frozen," said Jenny pityingly.

"Behold the fruits of French logic," Biddy piped. "They

close the brothels and every woman in Paris gets pneumonia. That foolish man will be streaming at the nose tomorrow morning."

"I consider it most unseemly," said Mackinnon. "On Christmas Eve!"

Andy pointed his index finger at him, pulled the trigger, said, "Bang, you're dead!" They laughed. They knew their Mac. A tongue of gall. He had never said an original word in his life. He worked at the Irish embassy. He would go far. They called him Mac the Knife.

"Mac!" Andy said. "I wish you to understand that I am on the side of all rebels, exiles, outcasts and sinners. What Genet called the Saints of the Underworld."

Biddy calmed his clenched fist with one scarlet-netted palm. "Easy, Andy! And it was not Genet. Pasolini. And I do trust, dear boy, that you are not going to go all romantic on me tonight. I mean, talking about Dublin. And your mamma. And Midnight Mass. And Confession. And Dominican fathers. And, now, French hoahs."

He was too fascinated by the comedy in the street to heed her. She enlisted Jenny's help.

"Jenny, is our broth of a boy about to get plawstered on us yet once again?"

"Haven't you observed," Jenny sniffed, "whenever he takes to the bottle in a big way it always means the one thing? Some new crisis with his precious Deirdre."

"Deirdre?" she whispered. "But that little Irish fool doesn't mean a thing to him. Deirdre is merely the girl he sleeps with."

At this Jenny laughed so bitterly that Biddy peered one-eyed at her.

"I trust, my dear, that you are not getting soft on him? I mean, as one old harridan to another, you must be hitting twenty. And," she whispered out of the side of her mouth, "he is only a poo-o-oodle!"

Jenny considered him seriously. In Paris less than six months, as Dubliny as the first day they met him, light-headed, light-hearted, feckless, a liar, much too fond of his liquor. Nobody was ever going to travel very far on his roundabout. Certainly not Deirdre. As if he felt her looking at him he grinned at her, and turned back to the street. She said loftily to Biddy, "I assure you!"

Biddy grinned.

"There is no need to protest, dawrling. We're all gone about Andy. That irresistible Irish charm. He's even gone about himself. It's his disease."

Under the table Jenny felt his hand creeping slowly over her knee.

"Andy, why didn't you bring Deirdre tonight?"

His hand withdrew. He sighed, "Poor little Deirdre." He burst into a sudden passion. "Jenny! Do you know what I am? I'm a sink!"

"Tell us, Andy," she said sympathetically, "why are you a sink?"

"No! You tell me! Examine me! Have no mercy on me! Tell me what's wrong with me."

Mac the Knife tapped his arm. His speckled forehead became suffused with venom. He assumed a stage-Cockney's wheeze.

"I'll tell you, chum, wot's wrong with you. You're 'omesick for dear, old, dirty Dublin. Your wrists long for the chains. Your back aches for the lash. Cheer up, chum, this time next year you'll be back there for keeps, with no Pigalle, and no cafés, and no nightclubs, and you'll have your eye on a good job, and be wearing more holy medals than a Lourdes veteran, and you'll be running off like a good little boy to Midnight Mass, and Aurora Mass, and Third Mass, and Fourth Mass, and . . ."

Andy leaped up. His chair fell. All over the terrace heads turned lazily towards them. A waiter paused in his stride.

"Do you want a sock in the kisser?" Andy roared.

The two girls dragged him down.

"Andy!" Jenny chided and stroked his arm as if he was a cross dog. "Aa-a-ndy!"

He retrieved his chair. He sat down glowering. Then he leaned over, seized Mac's hand and shook it warmly, rapidly, hurtingly.

"Mac! My old pal from schoolboys' happy days! As one unconverted and thoroughly corrupted Irish crook to another leave us be honest for one brief moment of our all too long and useless lives. Leave us admit that we've both been emancipated by La Belle France. We've killed Mother Ireland! We're free!" His grin fell dead on the table. His visor sank slowly over his toddy. "We're emancipated. And disbloody-wellillusioned."

"I knew it," Biddy piped to the striped awning. "The Celtic Goat of Pure Romance. I saw it coming. I felt it in my bones. And I warn everybody present that I shall not be able to bear much more of it."

Andy's head shot up.

"Anyway I gave up all that Holy Joe stuff years ago. I was a converted atheist at the age of seven. I was thrown out of school at fourteen for denying the existence of God. I proved it by logarithms."

"You don't say so?" Mac jeered.

Andy shot him again on a quick draw, turned to Jenny, put his arm about her narrow waist and confided into her ear for all to hear.

"Jenny, my love, I'll tell you why I'm a sink. This morning Deirdre said to me, 'Don't go out from me tonight, love! Don't leave me on Christmas Eve,' says she. 'Okay,' says I, 'come along with me.' 'You'll only get tight again, chéri,' says she. 'Don't abandon your own loving, little Deirdre,' says she. 'Spend it alone with me,' says she. But I did leave her! And I *am* going to get tight! And to hell with her! God Almighty, does she want to turn me into a monk? Imagine a fellow not having a couple of jars with his pals on a Christmas Eve! The trouble with Deirdre is she's not emancipated. There's one for you, Mac, who'll be back in Dublin in six months. In five years she'll have a squawl of kids around her saying the Rosary every night. Still and all I did ditch her. And there's no getting away from it. I'm a lousy sink!"

Jenny stroked his cheek with one long finger.

"I don't think you're a lousy sink, Andy. I think you're a sweet sink. You just can't hold your liquor, any more than you can hold your conscience."

He tightened his arm about her waist.

"Jenny! You understand me better than anybody else in the entire, global world. You're the grandest girl in all creation!"

"Better than Deirdre?"

He banged the table and shouted.

"I'm worse than a sink. I'm a flamin', flittherin', filthy, finished-off sink!"

"Jesus help me," Biddy moaned, and began wearily to powder her nose.

Jenny whispered something into the whorls of his ear, he let his head sink on her shoulder, her blue tassel fell over his eye, he put his arm around her again. Mackinnon twirled a palm of antique boredom at Larry Doyle, who beamed pleadingly at him as if begging indulgence for all young lovers. Suddenly Andy flung up his head with a wild jerk.

"Boys and girls! I have a smashing idea! Why don't we all tumble into a taxi and go off to Midnight Mass in the Irish Church?"

"Here it comes," said Biddy, brightly snapping her compact. "Back to our vomit. Cassandra the daughter of Priam, that's me. Often heard, rarely heeded, always right. Never let it be said that I am a spoilsport," she begged them all, gathering up her handbag and a four-foot-long, peacock-blue umbrella. "Which is this church you mentioned, Charlie? Church of Ireland? Papish? Celtic synagogue? I'm with you all the way even to the Mosque. Or would it do if I led you to some good, old, solid ten-by-twenty Noncomformist tin chapel somewhere?"

Mackinnon rose, took off his black hat, held it to his chest and spoke with Castilian pride.

"Mademoiselle, vous oubliez que je suis Catholique."

She made a soft noise like a duck getting sick, they all laughed, and while Andy was paying the bill they scrambled out onto the pavement. It was jammed by the crowd outside Le Jardin d'Ève looking at lighted photographs of naked women with breasts like udders. Biddy said in annoyance to Jenny, "I notice they always leave him to pay the bill."

"The boy is a fool. He loves to play the milord."

"Tell me, does he always get religion when he starts thinking of Deirdre?"

"You've known him as long as I have. Are you getting soft on him now?"

Biddy shrugged.

"I wouldn't mind having a bash at old Andy."

"He's not your sort. He is what you said. A poodle. A puppy. He's just a kid. Let him alone."

The kid rushed out and hooked the pair of them into the crowd. They saw the redheaded whore, her eyes circling slowly about her like a slow waltz, glance at and dismiss Mac and Larry. Andy laughed, "Business bad tonight." It occurred miserably to Jenny that her eyeballs would be circling under her green eyelids even in her sleep. Larry called out, "The Irish Church is miles away, can't we go somewhere else?" The crowd bumped them. The doorman of Le Jardin d'Ève barked at them to come and see the most nude women in the whole world. "Ask him," Andy suggested, and Larry approached him. While Larry and he were comparing silver half hunter with gold half hunter Biddy said he was like

George Brassens's daddy. Jenny said he was like her own daddy. The barker closed his watch, directed them to the Rue des Martyrs, called after them, "Vite, mes enfants! C'est tard!" Then, behind them his voice soared, "Les plus nues du monde . . ."

They turned from the lights, and the crowds, and the rumbling beat of Pigalle's heart into the narrow street whose prolonged silence gleamed distantly with colored windows. By the time they were filing into the church the congregation was shuffling erect for the Gospel. Biddy halted inside the door. Mac and Larry stayed with her. Andy probed along the aisle and found two empty places in the front row directly facing a small Christmas manger with the Infant, the Virgin, Saint Joseph, the cow, the ass, the shepherds and the colored kings huddled about a crib under an amber light and a bald electric star. Whoever had arranged the crèche had perched a stuffed robin-redbreast on the edge of the cot. Andy nudged her, nodded at it, and winked conspiratorially.

She was back, one frosty morning, four years ago, at home, awakened by a thud on her bedroom window: it was a robin lying stunned on the windowsill. In her nightgown by the open window she had held it, throbbing between her palms, staring at the one big eye staring up at her, and for that one sleepy moment all life was as simple as a captured bird. She opened her palms, the robin flew off into the frosty air, and the morning star gleamed above the hills and the murmuring beach. *In splendoribus sanctorum.* The priest was intoning the psalm. In the brightness of the saints, she remembered from other midnight masses. *Ex utero ante luciferam . . .* From the womb before the day star, I begot Thee. Did he remember? She touched the hand beside her and they looked at one another. Thereafter, silently from her white shore her bright moment ebbed. It fell as softly as a leaf from a book, a rose petal. Her window empty, her beach dry, she saw, leaning against a pillar beside them, the woman in the sheepskin coat. When the sanctus tinkled everybody else but she knelt. When everyone raised their heads she was still standing there, staring blankly in front of her. Andy was gone. There was no sign of him back down the aisle, nor could she see the other three.

Crossly, she made her way back to the doorway, and out to the street. It was so dark that at first she saw nothing; then she made out the four figures on the opposite side of the street clumped like a bunch of gangsters, smoking cigarettes. She crossed over.

"Why did you come out?"

Biddy slowly smoothened her netted fingers and said sullenly, "It wasn't my show, dawrling." Larry Doyle looked uncomfortably at Mac the Knife who made a half-moon with his hangdog mouth, performed a high, dissociating shrug, and looked at Andy who let out a zany guffaw and then said sulkily, angrily, "We should never have gone!"

"It was you who proposed it!"

"We shouldn't have done it!"

"I thought they were doing it very nicely?"

He appealed to them, boxer-crouched.

"When you don't believe in a thing what is it but tomfoolery?" He stood back, his claws to his chest. "I don't believe in anything. It's all kid stuff. I felt indecent inside there." He shot out his left. "And that bloody redhead in there finished me off. God Almighty, people have to be honest, don't they? They have to come clean, don't they? When I saw that wan in there I felt, Jaysus, what am I but another dirty bloody hypocrite?"

Jenny slapped his face, stepped back in dread, ran a few yards downhill, he after her, turned, a lean hare, ran faster and faster until he caught her, whirling her against a black wall under a streetlamp, gasping, her palms spread against him. They panted.

"What's wrong, girleen?"

"What's wrong is that you *are* a hypocrite. First Deirdre. Then that streetwalker. Who are you going to blame yourself on next? Me? Biddy? Why don't you go back to Dublin and rot there? It's what you want, isn't it?"

She turned to the wall and burst into tears. He waited while she sobbed. When she was quiet she turned and asked him for his handkerchief, wiped her eyes, said, "May I blow?" and blew.

"Why should I want to go back to Dublin? I'm happy here, with you, and Biddy, and all the gang."

"Are you?" she challenged. She gave him back his handkerchief. "I think, Andy," she said quietly, "you'd better go back now to Deirdre. You know she'll be waiting up for you all night."

He made a noise of disgust.

"She's not the answer."

"And what is?"

He took her arm and led her back to the group. Sacerdotally, Larry blessed them with a sweeping arm. *"Benedicat vos. Pax vobiscum."* Mackinnon said, with immense bonhomie, "A Happy Christmas to the happy pair!" Biddy said, coldly, "And what does one do now?" Larry threw his arms around Jenny, and intoned:

> *My beloved, drink the cup that cheers*
> *Today of past regrets and future fears,*
> *For, ah, tomorrow we may be*
> *With yesterday's seven thousand years.*

Nobody commented. The woman was standing alone on the step of the porch looking across at them. As they looked at her Andy walked over and spoke with her. Then the two walked off slowly, out of sight.

Mac gave a beck of his head to Larry, said to the girls, "Le Rève," and the two of them went off, hunched together, nose to nose, back to Pigalle. Jenny whirled and stared downhill towards the pink glow over Paris. For a while, Biddy considered her rigid back. Then she contemplated her long slim legs. Then she regarded her left thumb, wiggling it double-jointedly. Then she looked up at the sky and said, "Andy once told me he spent an entire night discussing the works of Guy de Maupassant with a hoah in Marseille. He said they were still at it when the sun rose behind the Chateau d'If. Odd! Even in Marseille the sun does not rise in the west. I shouldn't worry about him if I were you, Jenny. He will be back in Le Rève in half an hour as chaste as the dawn and without as much as a franc in his pocket. He'll tell us that she has a grandmother in Provence, or a child in hospital, or that she reads Pascal every night. The party's over. The night is bitter cold. And I am sick at heart. We'll get a taxi and I'll drop you at your door."

"I want to walk," Jenny said sourly.

Biddy's fledgling's voice took on an edge.

"In this cold? To Saint Germain? Do you want to die for him, like Mimi?"

"What is he up to? Always expiating for something or other? What's the point of it? Why doesn't he grow up? If he does give that woman all his money he'll only leave Deirdre penniless for a month, and borrow from us, and then borrow from his mamma to pay us back."

"Unlike us he is young and innocent. It is what makes him so appealing. In his bothered way he's different."

"Or is it just that all Irish men are different? Look at the other two. My God! What are we *doing* with them?"

Biddy hooted.

"Dear child, you obviously have no idea what Englishmen are like. I know! I've put dozens of them through my little white hands. Full to the gullet of guilt, black silences, sudden glooms, damp despairs, floods of tears and then that awful, manny, British laughter and 'Let's have another one old girl.'

Paris has been absolute bliss after London. Every Frenchman a swine. It's been such a relief. It's his only trouble — he thinks he's a sink and he isn't. It takes centuries to produce a really first-class sink. Still he shows promise. The right woman could do a lot for him. Not Deirdre, a silly little Dublin chit, just as stupid as himself. Let's get a cab. I'll pay for it and drop you right at your door."

"I still want to walk," Jenny said stolidly.

"It's savage. My ears are dangling by a thread. A cab, for God's sake!"

"Are you trying to get rid of me?"

Biddy regarded her with admiration, and shrugged.

"Biddy! What do we see in him?"

"Ignorance? Hopelessness? Eagerness? Terror? Charm?"

"But he is such a fraud!"

"And as you said, such a fool!"

"But, you say, innocent?"

"As a rose!" Biddy sighed.

"Let's go back to Le Rêve and see if he does come back."

"He will come back. His type always comes back. One of the lads."

He came, wildly excited, bustling in, penniless, full to the gullet of lies and boastings — or, if they were not lies, of fantasies, and if they were not boastings, of his dreams.

"All our lives," he pronounced, "we dream of love, and love eludes us. We have fled, Mac, from the sow that eats its own farrow. And all the time we dream of our childhood and are never free of it. O exiles of Erin, love ye one another. My bloody foot! Two single tickets to Dublin, that's the right ticket. But where shall we find her? Every mismatch Irishman a born matchmaker, and good at it. Saving others who cannot save himself. Sitting in a Dublin pool of drink and dreaming of the Arc de Triomphe. I told her I'd follow any woman to the ends of the earth but not to the end of the world. Nobody would take a fellow up on that! Gimme the Queensberry

Rules and begod I'll not complain. I want a loving, lovely, innocent wife!"

"With squads of babies?" Jenny asked and felt his hand start to rove over her knee.

"Squads and squads of them!"

"All chawnting the Rosary?" Biddy piped mockingly, and pressed his other hand.

Their mockery could not halt him. The girls looked at one another with big eyes, shook their heads and made wry mouths of self-astonishment. Mac's eyes kept closing and half-opening from sleep and drink. "What are we waiting for?" he asked dully. Larry Doyle looked at his turnip watch and sighed, "It's gone two'clock." The terrace was empty. The pink haze fell as glistening rain on the street. Nobody stirred. Even their talker was silent.

After a while he spoke, looking around at them sullenly.

"I'm going to take a plane to Dublin in the morning. Who'll lend me the money?"

£1000 for Rosebud

ROSEBUD met him one summer afternoon in London while she was lying flat on her face on the pavement of St. James's Street outside Prunier's restaurant during an air raid. "Suited him down to the ground," she used to say long afterwards, with a laugh, "I didn't stand a chance." When the bomb fell somewhere in Green Park she looked sideways and saw a handsome young fellow in the R.A.F. lying beside her, head on elbow, pensively admiring her. He might well admire her — hair like a wheat field in September, two big frightened eyes of cornflower blue, aged, he rightly guessed, about nineteen, and nicely fat. Plump girls were at a premium in London during those years of food rationing. She was happy to let him lead her off to the Ritz for a drink, downstairs in the crowded bar; all present, he assured her, being either spies or counterspies, heroines or whores. He told her that he was in Intelligence, with the effective rank of Wing Commander, and that his father owned a racing stables in Ireland. His name was Mick Donnelly. He had the mouth of a boy, the jaw of a man, and wicked brown eyes. She told him she was Rose Powis, straight off a farm in Wiltshire. Within an hour they were madly in love, within a week she had slept with him, a month later he married her, and the next day he left her, for Sicily and the Italian campaign, promising that when the war was over he would transplant his Rosebud to the finest house in Mayfair where they would live like a king and a queen.

She believed every word he said, and she knew that nothing he could ever do or say all her life long could hurt or surprise her. Within two months of his return, demobbed and jobless he had surprised her so often and so variously — even though she was by then twenty-two, and those three years in London had taught her a lot — that she never mentioned him afterwards to any old, wartime chum without ending up, "Say what you like about Clarence, life is never dull with him."

The "Clarence" had been her lightest shock.

"You see, Rosebud," he explained to her, "it was all Mummy's fault. She christened me Clarence Michael, after the Duke of Clarence, and then, God knows why, always called me Mikey. I hated it but it stuck. Furthermore, the proper spelling of our name is not Donnelly but Dunally. So, from this on I am Captain Clarence Dunally. Much better style! More dash to it! And much more in keeping with the kind of appointment I want, and," sternly, "mean to get."

She had been Mrs. Mick Donnelly. Now she was Mrs. Clarence Dunally. She thought it great fun. She was game for anything — so long as it was not mean, or calculating, or nasty. Reared on a farm, educated by a war, total and timeless at every moment, she had the simple appetites of a kid goat and was as innocent of morals as a child. In other circumstances, depending on what wind blew into her eager sails she could have been anybody, done anything, died in the swamps of Ravenna wearing a red shirt, stabbed Marat in his bath, been a Manon or a Margherita, Lady Macbeth or Lucy Lockit, Judith or Saint Joan.

"Fine!" she said. "Clarence! And what's my name?" she asked with fond assurance.

"You," he said throatily, "will always be my Rosebud, let's go to bed."

It also surprised her a little, but it did not trouble her as long as the funds lasted, that he showed no sign either of getting a job or of much wanting to get one. She was merely sad for him when he broke the news to her that his dad's racing stables had gone bankrupt during the war so that, as he put it, he had "no very large prospects for the future." She was further surprised, but more angered, for his sake, when he explained that owing to certain low army intrigues, too complicated for her to follow, he would not enjoy the pension due to a Wing Commander. Only one thing he did really shook her — the place where he took her to live.

On his return to London and civilian life they had gone straight into Claridge's for three gloriously spendthrift nights, and then into a lodging house in Paddington. They were still there two months later. What with the bombing, and no houses being built, and mobs of extra people in London, they soon found that they would be lucky to get house room anywhere. At last, nagged just a tiny bit by her, Clarence solved the problem overnight. He rented a small houseboat, called *Evangeline,* permanently moored to the towpath above Walton-on-Thames.

"Do us for a few months," he said. "Just to get over a bad patch. Just long enough to give me time to explore the ground at my ease."

One glance at *Evangeline* made her eyebrows soar and her heart sink. She felt her first hint of fear. She saw an ancient, waterlogged wreck; everything metal on it was rusty; the glass in the tiny portholes was broken; its woodwork had fed generations of woodlice. It had, obviously, stood, lain or leaned there for so many years that nothing now kept it from keeling over in the mud but its gangplank, its hawsers and its long-settled condition. She foresaw fog, smelled rats, noted that it was a mile from the nearest shop, guessed that it must be twenty from Mayfair, and on dark nights every step of that overgrown towpath would be a menace. She threw her arms about his neck and said, "Clarence, how clever of you! We'll make it simply lovely. Let's get cracking at it right away!"

It was October and raining. They worked on *Evangeline* like galley slaves all through that autumn and into the fogs of winter. They caulked the yawning timbers, replaced what they could afford of the rotted woodwork, painted the super-structure in pink and every inch inside in white. Rosebud lined the scuppers with Henry Jacoby geraniums in toffee tins and hopefully set an Albertine rose in a tub to grow across a trellis above the companionway.

One afternoon in November, when they had almost fin-ished the job, that is, done about as much to the junk as they could do, a lone passerby along the towpath paused to watch them, said, "Looking ahead to the summer? It will be fun," and winked. They thanked him and said yes, it would be nice for weekends in the summer. When he had passed on they looked at one another shamefacedly. They had come to know from various words dropped by tradesmen and others that that was about what the river had always rated in those parts — a raffish wink. Clarence said nothing. He had al-ready noted that Rosebud could never mention the name *Evangeline* without an embarrassed flutter of her eyelids. She had already observed that whenever he gave his address to a stranger he let his hands rise and fall feebly like a dying duck, though if the man said encouragingly, as he usually did (with or without a wink), "Lucky to have anything these days!" Clarence would always gallantly agree, and always add, "It's not exactly Mayfair, of course."

That night — they were below, finishing their dinner of sausages and mash, and their one bottle of beer — she said, probing him, "Clarence, if this isn't exactly Mayfair, what *is* it?"

"It's County," he said bravely, and then hit his fist a wallop on the deckbeam two feet over his head. "Rosebud, we've got to get out of it. We're mad to be living in this Chinese sampan. Into the Rialto! Into Mecca! I said Mayfair, and I mean Mayfair! Some people might even settle for a mews off Pont Street, or a mews in Kinnerton Street. They might even settle for N.W. 1 — all those super Nash terraces. But not me! If I could only lay my hand on a thousand quid, if I . . ."

"Here, here, hold on! What's a 'supernash' terrace?"

"Nash? Great English architect. Don't you know? Haven't you heard? Sir Henry Nash. Wonderful houses. Pure seventeenth century."

"Seventeenth century? That was the time of Queen Elizabeth. They must be as rotten as this junk. And what's wrong with a nice little house in Hampton, or Kingston, or Richmond, or even in Walton-on-Thames?"

He looked at her as coldly as if she were a stranger.

"Did you say Walton-on- . . . ? Rosebud, I see I've got to take your education in hand."

He had placed, she had seen them but never looked into them, three books on a small bulkhead shelf. He shoved aside the plates, the beer bottle and the bits of holly branches she had stuck in a milk bottle, took down the three books and lobbed them on the table. Then he stared at her, like a dentist gazing speculatively at a really hopeless tooth.

"Where can I begin? This is *Who's Who*. Observe! A plain statement. No question mark. Everybody, I mean everybody, is there — who counts. This one is *The Home Lawyer*. I've won a dozen court-martials out of that."

She ruffled it. It was, in due course, to become her favorite book of the three, so much so that whenever she laid it on the table it opened of its own accord, as softly as a sea anemone, at the chapter headed "Divorce." "This one is the map of the known world. *The A.1 Atlas of London and Outer Suburbs*. Latest, revised edition. Three and six. This tells us where everybody out of *Who's Who,* who lives in London, lives. Now!"

He opened it. Like a field marshal he spread his hands
above the web of black streets and began.

"Operation Rosebud! Here," drawing a swift line about
Mayfair, "is our objective. The heart of W.1. But don't let
that fox you. Soho is also W.1. And a damned shame it was
to put it there. Good Lord, if it comes to that, Tottenham
Court Road — and we all know what that means — is W.1.
But this," finger on the M of Mayfair, "is the citadel we shall
enter and conquer."

"I see."

"Where are there any alternatives? N.W.1? You've got
some really posh places up there. Clarence Gate. Or York
Gate. Down here, S.W.1. Pretty good. Backs on Belgravia.
Which, you observe, backs on Buck Palace itself. S.W.3?
Tricky, but not bad. I've been tempted in my time by Cheyne
Walk, even Brompton Square. Time was when I wouldn't
have sniffed even at Egerton Gardens. Though, God knows,
the way the world is going nowadays you never know who
might be cowering in some godawful square off dim places
like the Fulham Road. Would you believe it, Rosebud, I know
a depressed peer who's actually reduced to a boardinghouse in
Bayswater. And a pal of mine told me the other day, it made
my hair stand on end, that he knows a retired general who is
actually living on a barge beside the gasworks on the Grand
Union Canal at Hanwell! Could you ever believe such a thing
would happen in England?"

"If you say so, Clarence!"

"The moral is plain!" he snapped. "Never give up a major
objective for a lesser. I have set my face against that pitfall.
Because if you once let yourself think that you might put up
with less than the best you'll end up by taking less than the
less. And in the end, less than the less than the less! No! A
garret in Mayfair, Rosebud, even a simple garret will do us
for a first foothold. I know so much. I can teach you so much.

If we could only lay our mittens on a thousand quid and a garret in Mayfair I know, I simply know, that with your beauty and my brains we'd be on top of the social tree in six months."

"But, tell me, Clarence, supposing we did get a garret in Mayfair, what would we do there?"

"Ha ha! Second stage of Operation Rosebud. It wouldn't really matter a damn what we did, ye know! Infiltrate. First get in. Once in — spread. I could start by making leather belts for Fortnum and Mason like that fellow Roskolski who began with five quid in a back lane off Burton Street and now has a swank shop in Bond Street. And how did he do it? He got to know the right people! You could sew old school ties for Burlington Arcade like that Polish Countess who came there as a kitchen maid and now has that posh boutique in Pont Street. Clients, friends, backers! That's the ticket. I could even be a taxi driver and some day pick up Lord Who's Who, the fellow that started Marks and Spencers on a borrowed five hundred quid. 'Where do you live?' he'd say. 'Oh,' I'd say, casually like, bowling him over on the spot, 'I've got a little hole in Mayfair. Why don't you drop around some night, my lord, and have a good Russian vodka? I could tell you things about London that not even you know.' Into my lap in the click of a finger! But supposing I said, 'I've got a little hole in Pimlico?' do you think he'd bite? See what I mean? Be around. Have your ear to the ground. Be in the way of luck. Be where the pickings are. Plant your knowledge where it's going to bear juicy fruit. But how in hell can we possibly hope to get to know anybody from a base like this? I tell you, Rosebud, I'd commit the most foul, fiendish, hellborn, stygian, diabolical, unforgivable crime this minute for even a coal hole on the uttermost edge of Mayfair."

She laughed fondly at him, patted his head, told him he wouldn't hurt a flea, and went off with the dishes to the galley.

"Little do you know me, my lass!" he called after her. "Little do you know!"

Rubbing the greasy dishes with her rosy fingers and throwing the scraps out of the porthole into the flowing river she wondered. Three months on that houseboat as a wife had taught her more than her three years in London as a grass widow. She had foreseen the rats frisking under the floorboards, the fog lying thick as wool on the river. She had not foreseen the savage damp, or how lonely the drip off the poplars could sound on the deck when he was in town, the discreet pawnshops of Kingston and Richmond, or that Clarence was full as a honeycomb of secret places where no woman would ever go. She was often reminded of him by their cat, Rodolphe, squatting by the stove with eyes half-closed in veiled aloofness. On such lonely days and dripping nights she had sometimes got the feeling that *Evangeline,* stuck in the mud, moored by the edge of the flowing river, was an image of her own life in those three years since she left the farm at Tisbury for the blackout, the bombs, the excitement of London. Which was why, on many such nights, silent except for more instructions about Operation Rosebud, more nervy plottings and wonderings about how could they get to Mayfair and where the hell could they get a thousand quid, and the life they were going to have when they got out of this junk on the Upper Amazon, she would silence him with, "Darling, do you really love me?" and he would simply utter her rosy name from the depths of his throat and she would say, from the depths of hers, "Let's go to bed," and, for a while they would hear only the water muttering past their ears, and, for a long, wild, heavenly while nothing at all. (She was not a girl to make any bones about that. "He was *marvelous* in bed!") Then, after he had fallen into a contented sleep she would lie awake gazing fondly sideways at him who, for all his boastings about all he knew, looked then as helpless as a boy.

All he knew . . . They were such odd things, and so interesting, and always so mixed up with "our future," and with "maintaining us in the manner to which we are accustomed" — not "his" future, or the manner "to which 'I' am accustomed" — that she could listen to him happily for hours of it.

One night it would be all about food and drink.

"Drink is very important. Vodka, for example, must always be served in paper-thin, ice-cold glasses. And whatever the hell it is always call it Soviet vodka. No real gentleman would drink anything else. Major Grey's Chutney? Sound stuff — but never ask for it, too many people know about it. Gentlemen's Relish is definitely eaten by gentlemen. But Riley's Royal Fishpaste is most certainly not eaten by royalty. Then there's sauces. Very tricky. I once heard about a fellow at a bank luncheon who asked the headwaiter in a loud voice for some stuff called Kutie Katie's Curry. I believe you could have heard a pin drop. Draw a veil! Painful story! Poor slob had to emigrate to Australia."

Another night it would be clothes.

"A law of life! No matter what depths a fellow may be driven to he must never, simply never, wear a made-up tie. If you're rich you can dress in rags. If you're hard-up — best tailor in Savile Row. Last button of the weskit left undone? No, madam! Only grammar-school boys, Africans, Abyssinians — poor old Haile Selassie always does it — Indians and Americans trying to be English do that any more. No weskit! Weskits are gone! Absolutely out of date. So are watches with chains. Better have no watch at all. Or a signet fob on a black ribbon. Did you know that Edward the Seventh creased his pants down the sides?"

Conversation.

"I suppose you think good chat drips from the tongue? No, madam! You make it up the night before. Little casual odds and ends. Such as, 'I wonder how many of Edward the Seventh's bastards could I name offhand?' Or, 'How many people

know that if Oscar Wilde hadn't rejected the filthy advances
of the Marquis of Queensberry he'd never have been hounded
by that old sod?' Or somebody happens to say 'Trilby.' Ha,
ha! That's my cue. 'Did you know that her real name was
Billy O'Farrell? Father a parson in Trinity College, Dublin.
Had her by a barmaid in Paris.' Oh, we'll keep them gaping,
Rosebud! We'll dazzle 'em!"

"We?" Love would gush in her. "Do you really love me,
Clarence?" And the sleeping boyish face on the unwashed pillow slip of the double-berth, and she, as the winter dragged
on, and he still jobless, feeling fear for him or, as the first
signs of spring came, jealousy, of certain unknowns, creeping
slowly over her love like the lichen scaling the tree trunks on
the bank.

Her mamma's letters from Tisbury always ended, "What's
Clarence doing these days?" She never answered the question.
She could only have said, "He goes to town every morning" — having kissed her tenderly, taken his bowler hat, and
his rolled umbrella, said "Into the breach once more dear
friends," stalking then across the gangway, back erect, gamp
on shoulder like a gun, along the towpath for the train to
Mecca. If she asked him on his return — she soon ceased to
ask — what he had done during the day, he would talk vol-
ubly about it.

He had met an old pal at the Army and Navy Club. "A
grand chap! He swears he's got a real opening for me. It appears that the latest idea in textiles is plastic lavatory basins.
Let me tell you all about them. You see, the great thing about
these gadgets is that if you wanted to you could roll 'em up
and put them in your pocket. They're made in . . . ."

Or he had run into Tommy Lancing at the Union Jack
Club.

"Let me tell you, Rosebud, about Tommy Lancing. My
bosom friend. Saved his life once outside Catania. He's sitting

pretty now, importing furs. He's mad about racing. He persuaded me to put ten bob, ten whole bob, on a horse running at Kempton Park, an absolutely wizard tip he got at the Cavalry Club."

And that would be a day when he would then either plank down on the table ten single pound notes, or sadly produce Tommy Lancing's carbon copy — careful man — of an I.O.U. for ten shillings. She never asked him how he got entry into those clubs. She was too eager to know what it was like inside such grand places.

On bad days he might have just dropped into the Distressed Gentlefolks' Aid Association, or visited an old chum in the Star and Garter Home for Disabled Soldiers and Sailors, on Richmond Hill. Once — they were at rock bottom that week — he had called in, "just for idle curiosity," to the Army and Navy Labor and Window Cleaning Corps. Her heart leaked for him that night. Now and again, through his "contacts" he would get a real job, never held for long. ("Bum lot! Pointless! Leads nowhere.") Once it was with the Society for Improving the Condition of the Laboring Classes; once with the Junior Imperial League; once with the Irish Church Missions and Scripture Readers Society, a job he held for two whole weeks. She always asked him what he had for lunch, to which he would always say, "Beer and a sandwich," and he would ask what was there for dinner. She would reply, "The usual — mash and bangers," or, "There's a bit of cold meat left," and produce an excuse for a meal, with branches of wild flowers from the towpath stuck into the milk bottle. After it they would always go down to The Bunch of Grapes for a half-pint of mild-and-bitter apiece — if they had the money.

The jealousy began over what he called his art gallery, five framed photographs of female nudes fastened to the wall of the cabin. She had never bothered her head about them until the night she heard him hail her from the deck with a joyous cry of "Lolly!" and come clattering below to throw fifty quid in tenners on the table under her widening eyes.

"Who?" she asked in excitement.

"Ha ha! I have friends."

An old chum! Spike Halloran of the Royal Irish. "Let me tell you about good old Spike . . ."

They had drinks in The Bunch of Grapes that night, and went out the next night to celebrate in style. "As befits our station in life." They went into Richmond for steaks and wine at Shortt's, and afterwards around to The Three Crows on the Green to booze up. There they ran into a young fellow named Milo Doyle — blue eyes, a complexion like a girl's, a creamy brogue, a customs officer somewhere — a simple chap who enchanted Rosebud by seriously believing Clarence's joke that he was Sir Clarence Dunally, and gave Clarence even greater delight by being so obviously taken by Rosebud who, as he well knew, would not have given the trout's eye to a duke. Afterwards when he teased her about the lad, in their double-bunk, she had just laughed and said, "Nice boys like him shouldn't be left out alone in London."

"Nicer than me?" he had asked throatily.

"Lots of men are nicer than you, darling. But nobody is so attractive."

After that they heard no noises in the boat for a long while. Then, as he slept and she lay awake, jealousy burst in her like an aneurysm of rage. Her eyes, wandering around the cabin, had halted where there had always been those five photographs. Now there were only four. For a long time she again heard nothing, neither the occasional rat awake, nor the gurgle of the water, nor the distant sound of the railway. She waited until he left the next morning, unscrewed two of the photographs and carefully took them apart. On the back of the first she read the inscription, "Belinda — altogether yours"; and on the back of the second, "Coco to Clarence, with luff." The other two pictures were also of Belinda and Coco. Staring at their bare haunches she remembered that during their very earliest days together he had a camera and had coaxed her into letting him photograph her in the nude. She also remembered certain coy references to a Lady Belinda. She had laughed — she had never taken men's boastings about women seriously. She knew now that a picture like that would be easily worth fifty quid to a real Lady Belinda.

She held her fire — she had too often heard her mamma say, "I'm not going to dig my grave with my teeth, or my tongue" — until a month later when they were broke again. Coco disappeared and another fifty quid came — he came back with it quite late that night. She had been simmering all day and now she let him have it. She called him names and words she had never known she knew. She finally leaped on him and scrawled his face with her nails.

"What am I married to? A pimp, or a blackmailer, or both? How long has this been going on? How long have you known these women?"

"Hi! Hi! Hi!" was all he could shout, fighting her off, pursued by her from saloon to cabin and back again. "What's all this about? You gone daft?"

She hit him on the head with the beer bottle, she threw *Who's Who* at him, she tore his *A.1 Atlas* down the spine, flung it on the floor and kicked it. To his horror she grabbed his ten fivers, tore them across and showered them at him. Then, glaring and panting, she was sitting on the berth, spitting at him when she had the spit, he standing in the farthest corner of the saloon by the companionway, ready to dash for the deck, dabbing his bleeding face with his handkerchief.

"You second lieutenant! You were never a captain, you were never a wing commander, you were never anything, you ground-force garbage emptier, with your bowler hat, and your rolled gamp, and your two splits behind over your duck's bottom! You toy drum major! You vain, vapid, muttonheaded, silly, bone lazy, bloody ass!"

"But, Rosebud," he said gently, "I did it for you. Honestly!"

At which appalling statement, patently true, she had to bustle out to the W.C. and sit there weeping on the can for sheer love of him. When she came back all she said was, "You do it again, Clarence, and I'm quitting. And for keeps." She asked no more questions. Unasked, he told her that he took all those silly pictures for fun, during the war, when everybody was a bit crazy, and kept them for fun, and for memories, and, anyway, it all happened before he met his own, his only, his dear. "My darling, loved Rosebud." Bit by bit he melted her. Then he got throaty, she forgave him, and locked in one another's arms, they did not hear a sound until the morning.

The next night he made her come out to dinner on, his own words, "the wicked lolly." She only went because he had run into that young Irish fellow Milo Doyle and, for her sake, asked him to join them. They had by then met him several times and become quite friendly with him. He had visited them on the boat, they had met him for drinks at Hammersmith, he had taken them to supper in a little Italian place off the Brompton Road. She liked him, Clarence's pal, a pleasant young fellow, neither handsome nor unhandsome, quiet, a bit dull really, the son of an Irish farmer, always sighing for "Ioreland." This night he was in high fettle — he was about to be transferred from Dover to Holyhead. He even sang them an Irish song called "One step nearer home!" Clarence was at his deludering best as the fellow exile. "Go on," Clarence kept prodding him, "tell us more about good old County Roscommon." She liked him a lot then, talking excitedly about County Roscommon and his boyhood there. She exchanged Wiltshire and her childhood. She even pretended to flirt with him because he blushed so easily. It was a good night.

"All the same, Clarence, it wasn't worth it. Poor but honest — that's me."

The next morning, as he was sitting up in their berth drinking his morning cuppa, she sitting sideways on it, leaning across his legs, drinking hers, she knew by the way his eyes were half-closed that he was moving around inside his own secret mind. Presently he said:

"Wasn't that interesting, what Milo was saying last night about gold watches?"

"What about them?" she asked, and felt her heart going bang-bang.

"Silly! Or were you too busy flirting with him to notice? Gold watches smuggled out of Ireland. Every one of 'em worth in London, depending on its value, anything from five to ten quid in sheer profit?"

"Clarence! Stop it! For God's sake, if you're thinking . . ."

"Somebody's got to think or we'll never get out of this madhouse!"

From there the argument began. It went on hammer and tongs for an hour. He must have known he had won when she said, "And anyway, where would you get the money to buy them?" He leaped from the bunk, in his red-and-white spotted pajamas, seized his striped trousers, emptied the pockets on the blankets and counted his cash. There were forty-five pounds odd, in coins and in notes — now mended across with stamp selvage.

"See! We've got forty-five. Another fifty-five and we've a hundred quid in capital!"

He began to wash, shave and dress, whistling, fresh as a daisy, pursued by more hopeless pleadings and warnings, even while he was stalking across the gangplank, and vanishing, rolled gamp on shoulder, his bowler hat on his ear, two splits behind, down the towpath for the Rialto.

It came as no surprise to her when he returned that evening triumphant. ("If he had put only one-tenth of the persistence . . .")

"Got it! Fifty-five quid! Tommy Lancing! And it's God's truth this time. The three bottoms are still there on the wall. And there's his carbon of my I.O.U."

"You will do this once, Clarence."

"I'll try it once."

"If it works you will try it twice."

"Possibly."

"You will try it three times, and then you will either be caught or I won't be able to stand it one second longer. But whether you're caught or whether you're not you'll give me whatever rotten money you make, every single penny of it and I'll open a bank account for it in my name. Not that I want to be associated with this swindle, but I can at least try to protect myself and you, and I can stop you from wasting your precious lolly on your usual swank and nonsense."

He agreed, sulkily. He made his haul. And it was a wash-out. There had been no hitch in Dublin — no country is much interested in what goes out of it. There had been no hitch in Holyhead. In the Customs hall he had easily picked out Milo along the line of counters, planked his hide suitcase in front of him, said, "What cheer, Milo!" and opened it with a frank sweep of his honest arm.

"Hello, Clarence! You've been over?"

"Just been vetting a horse for a hunting friend," Sir Clarence said. "No dice. Spavined brute. Hoho! Can't trust these Irish. What, what?"

Milo had patted his shirts perfunctorily, chalked his bag, said "Give my regards to herself," and Clarence had walked onto the train with his five watches — all he had been able to afford — strapped around his waist under his shirt. It took him a week to sell them, and, when he had deducted his expenses, about ten pounds, he found that all he made was twenty-three quid odd. For half a day he was filled with gloom. At this rate it would take him years to achieve a coal hole in Pimlico. She did not tease him — she was too happy that it was all over. She even felt sorry for him. But that night he had rallied. The answer was simple: they must go into this thing in a much bigger way. He had about one hundred and thirteen pounds. Where would he get another hundred quid?

"What can we sell, Rosebud?"

She laughed at him affectionately. He jumped up.

"I've got it! We'll sell *Evangeline*."

"Are you out of your mind? It's not ours to sell. We only rent the junk."

"We can sell it to somebody who wants a houseboat for the summer. Offer them an option for a hundred quid down and the rest on possession. Three months to go until June, they'll never cop on. In June we pay them back the option and if the worst came to the worst we'd be no worse off than we are already. Hoopla! Bob's-your-uncle!"

She closed her eyes in agony and gave him up.

"Surely," Milo said to her afterwards, "at that moment you should have known."

"Known? Known what? Known Clarence? I knew him from the first day he led me to that houseboat. Our home. You saw her after we'd worked at her. Hoo, hoo! If you'd seen her that day! It was October, and raining. That night! Don't remind me of it. I looked around me and I said to myself, 'So this is the sort of bloke I'm married to.' Oh, I knew Clarence! You never did. He'd charm the birds off the trees. He'd sell radiators in hell. And aren't you forgetting something? That love is perfect and the loved one can do no wrong."

"I meant, 'known yourself.' "

"And who does, smartie? But there was something I did get to know. Going away like that he left me alone for the first time in my life. Really alone, for days at a time locked up in that bloody submarine."

She had been alone in London when he was off with the Eighth Army, but she was working then and had friends. The dank towpath, the locked-down houseboat, the fogs, the total silence, the rain, the jet-black nights relieved only by the distant glow of London on the underbelly of the sky were very different. Forcing herself to go alone one night into Walton-on-Thames, wandering alone in her white mackintosh around its streets, she saw it for the first time as it really was. The pub lights appealed, the Palais de Danse was neon-red, the cinema lights blazing white, she felt that in every other little villa house — red roof, tiny garden, bow windows, empty garage — people were playing bridge or listening to the Light Programme. To hell with Mayfair! She wanted a home, and kids, a pram, going shopping, hearing the *Daily Mail* flop on the hall every morning, the milkman jangle the bottles, Clarence yawning and saying, "I better get up, I suppose, and get off to the office." She knew what she wanted.

On his second visit to Ireland he took with him a round two hundred quid. On the resale he made fifty. His third haul, she noted with satisfaction, brought her bank total up to three hundred ten pounds. A couple of days after his return he got a letter, one sentence: "The chief officer here asked me on Monday after you left were you a pal of mine." There was no signature and no address but the postmark said Holyhead. He did not hesitate a second. Tommy Lancing was clamoring for the repayment of his loan. That morning Rosie had put pussy willows in the milk bottle. April.

"Rosie! I've been warned. Milo has copped onto me. But not to *you*! Now *you* must go."

"No!"

"Rosebud!" — appealingly.

"No! And that's flat."

"Rosebud!" — threateningly.

"No! And now I've said no three times and that's three times too many. I won't do it. I like the money just as much as you do but this I won't do. I won't deceive that kid! He is honest as the daylight, he'd hate me if he found out."

"Rosebud, you damned fool, do you realize that on two more runs, just two more runs, we'll have five hundred of that thousand quid we've been wanting all our lives. We'll be within sight of a home where we always wanted to have a home."

"Lives? A home? What do you know about lives? I want a decent home, kids, a pram, a . . ."

"I *want* you to have a real life."

"And I want it! I'd do a lot for it. But not this. I won't do it. You know damn well either one of us will get caught or that poor boy Milo will get into trouble. He'll get the sack. Do you want that to happen? I couldn't live with it."

"For me, Rosebud? For us? Say just one, just one more run!"

Once more the hammer and tongs began again. She gave in. She had her own dream now.

The evening she came back from Dublin and Holyhead she threw the watches on the bed and sat down and stared at him like death.

"For Christ's sake, Rosebud! What happened?"

"Nothing."

"Then what's wrong?"

"When he chalked my bag he looked at me and he blushed."

Clarence snatched up the watches. He held them over her head. He clutched them to his chest. He laughed triumphantly.

"Splendid! Perfect! It's in the bag. He'd do anything for you."

She said quietly that he well might, and that was precisely why this (she screamed it) was the bloody end.

He approached her, hooped, white, trembling, his eyes peering, his hands shaking.

"Then I'm going to do it the next time. And this time if I'm going to chance it I'm going to chance it big. I must get another hundred quid. Another two hundred quid! We'd be over the line, we'd be in the big push. It's your life that's at stake, our lives."

She caught his glance over her head at the three photographs. She said, "No!"

They squabbled for two days. Then it was she who got the letter this time, from Dublin.

> Dear Mrs. Dunally,
>
> I am so happy in myself that I must tell you my great news. I've done it at last. I'm back in Ireland. A while ago there I applied for a post with the Irish Customs. Last week they called me for an interview, and the Wednesday you passed through Holyhead, you brought me luck, I went home and there was the letter waiting for me telling me I had been successful. I am in Dublin now stationed at Dunleary Pier. I had to tell you because I knew you would be particularly pleased by my news. Please give my regards to Clarence. I remembered you both at Mass this morning.
>
> Yours sincerely,
> Milo Doyle

She gave the letter to him and went to the porthole. A swallow skimmed the water. She heard him utter a deep and fervent "Damnation!" After that he was silent for so long that she turned to look at him. His eyes half-closed, he was slowly winding the letter about his forefinger. She sat down, and watched him and waited. He tossed the paper tube on the table and glanced over at her. His voice was very soft and very slow.

"So there is a Customs in Dublin . . . Does that suggest something to you? No? It does to me. It means there must be things worth smuggling *in* there. Eh?"

She did not stir. She sat looking at him like a brass idol. He did not say anything until, bowler-hatted, his rolled umbrella in his fist, he was ready to leave the boat. She had not stirred.

"I have to do it. Within a month that fellow will be coming around about the boat."

She did not answer. He went to the bulkhead, ripped the three photographs from it, slipped them into his pocket and clattered up the companionway.

She spent the morning and early afternoon cleaning and polishing the boat. She took the brown-paper coverings from her geraniums and pruned them down — there could hardly be any more frosts. She let the Albertine look after itself. She washed herself from head to foot, packed a suitcase, ate a sandwich, drank a beer, wrote "Goodbye" on the back of Milo's letter and propped it against the bottle of beer. Then she looked about her carefully for the last time, and left. She put the key where they always did under a stone on the bank.

At the ticket office of the Southern Railway she bought her ticket for London. She was turning around to pick up her suitcase when she found him beside her holding it. He took her by the arm and led her firmly to the waiting room, sat her down, sat beside her and laid the three photographs on her lap.

"I couldn't do it. I did better. I spilled the whole thing to Tommy Lancing. God, what a rocket I got from him! Why the hell hadn't I told him before? Was I a pal or was I not? He rumbled it in one second. Fur coats! That's the real Mc-Coy for Ireland. As you know, he imports them. He's putting five hundred quid into it. He takes a third and we take the rest." He laid a fat envelope on top of the pictures in her lap.

"There's five hundred Johnny-O-Goblins in that. Now, are you with us?"

She took the lot from her lap and gave them back to him.

"I'm going home to Mum and Dad."

"Don't do that! Believe me or not, God's truth, I'd be lost without you. I want you. I couldn't live without you." Furious, she made to get up; he held her down. "Why don't you just go to London for a couple of days and think it over? Get away from me. We've been too much on top of one another. Go to Bournemouth. Forget me for a while. You could go to Dublin."

She looked at him.

"Why Dublin?"

"Anywhere, but, for God's sake, not home. Give me a break, lass. Just two or three days. If you come back I'll never raise the question again. We'll go on just as we did before all this began," and he lobbed the pictures and the five hundred pounds back into her lap and strode out the door. By the time she had thrown the stuff after him he was gone.

She sat beside her suitcase for as long as it took two trains to pull in and out. Then she got up, took the package, and went out on the platform to wait for the next train. She spent the night in a cheap hotel near Waterloo. If there had been a telephone on the boat she would have phoned him. She even thought of going straight back to him. The next day, not thinking, not planning, not deciding, just going, she found herself on a plane for Dublin.

That night, sitting among the Saturday night crowd in Mooney's in Dunleary, over a couple of Guinnesses, she told Milo about the watches. She had heard of Catholics going to Confession. Now she knew what they felt like. In the shame in his eyes she saw her own shame.

"I know I shouldn't have done it, Milo, but I had no one to talk to about it all. Now I have. Should I leave him?"

He pondered on it, or on something.

"Does he love you, Rosie?"

"He says he loves me, he says he's doing it all for me. He calls it Operation Rosebud. He doesn't call it Operation Clarence. But I wonder."

"That's the crux. After all, a fellow has to give proof of his love. Show a woman what he'd do for her. I don't mean he has to go out and kill tigers, or, like the old knights long ago, go out carrying his lady's handkerchief and come back with the Golden Fleece or something. That old houseboat he put you into! I suppose you might think my ideas about love are very dull, and ordinary and, as you might say, homespun. But from the first day I started earning money I started putting a bit aside every week against the day when I might meet a girl and want to marry her. I could see it — the red roof, and the bit of a garden, and how we'd have a television." He laughed at himself. "And we'd have a washing machine. And a pram in the garage. *Very* dull!"

"You're making fun of me. You're mocking me."

"*Me? Mocking you?*"

She could not stop herself; she put her hand across the formica table, clasped his hand and pressed it.

She wrote to Clarence that she was not going back to the *Evangeline* ever again, she did not know if they could ever make a life together, but if they ever did it would have to be in a real home, and she described to him how nice Walton-on-Thames was. If he sent her the address of the man who had taken the option on the boat she would send him a check for a hundred pounds. And he must get a job. She signed it, "Love, Rosebud," and enclosed a five pound note. He recognized the address of Milo's lodgings. He wired: "Send me a tenner. Leaving junk. Will write soon. Have a lovely time. Longing for you. Clarence." When his letter came, a week later, it was headed "13A Antrobus Street, S.W.1, Near Buckingham Palace." It ran:

"My Rosebud! I've done it! S.W.1 . . ."

(It was, indeed, technically in S.W.1, although the street turned out to be in Pimlico, and on the wrong side of the railway lines radiating out from Victoria Station.)

. . . And I've got a job. It's not much but it will do for a while. I've left the junk for keeps and as nobody but you knows where I am we needn't pay back that option money . . . London is absolute heaven, people, people, people. I'm dying for you to see it, and to touch you and give you a thousand smacking kisses and great hugs. Your own, wicked old Clarence.

The next morning she was outside 13A Antrobus Street, and there was Clarence at the door going off to work in his dungarees, jacket, neckerchief and cap — he was window cleaning — with a grin as wide as a church door and a hug like a bear.

The room was terrible. She worked on it in a frenzy all day to astonish him when he came back, with half-a-dozen bottles of beer in a bag, and a mouthful of jokes, and then she was sitting beside him in a pub, or arm-in-arm out in the streets, with the crowds, and the traffic and the good old smells of London, until the cozy night opened its arms to them both, and she was utterly certain of him and herself as the noises gradually vanished into their own breathing and his words of love.

On the third day, at lunchtime, he said,

"Rosebud! I'm really on to something good at last! I met a man today . . ."

"Clarence! If you could only get a decent job!"

His brows sank. His rage soared.

"What do you mean decent job? Do you mean five quid a week? What do you want to do with me? Make me a commissionaire outside Harrod's in a guardsman's coat, with a bandsman's epaulettes, and big brass buttons, tipping me cap to nobs in swank cars? A car salesman selling dud cars in

Paddington? An auctioneer's assistant in a green apron holding up antique chamberpots? Let's face it! I'm not trained for anything. I'm thirty. I can't start at the bottom at thirty. I'm making for the top!"

"But before the war . . ."

"Before the frigging war I lived in Ireland, I was a young fellow about town, I lived off my people, I hung around Dublin. The only job I ever had was for six months before the war and do you know what that was? In a drapery store selling yards of flowered muslin for women's frocks. Do you expect me to go back to that?"

"But other men . . ."

"Rosebud! One run. Just one run with two fur coats, another two hundred quid, within yards of the winning post. One more . . ."

"One more, and one more! I won't do it. I'd be caught. You don't care if I'm caught."

"You can't be caught, not with Milo there."

"He wouldn't know. I couldn't tell him. He'd kill me if he found out."

Clarence peered at her.

"You soft on Milo?" he asked gently.

She stared at him sullenly.

"So what?"

"Nothing. I was just thinking. An idea. Look! Just one more little run, Rosebud? And this time I mean it. Honest to God, just this once and it's in the bag."

"Clarence, don't send me back. I beg and implore you, don't send me back." She said sadly, "Or do you think more of your thousand frigging quid than you do of me?"

And she snatched up her mac and her headscarf and went out alone to the pictures.

It may have been then that she made her decision, or later, wandering about stuffy, smelly streets that had suddenly become hateful to her, thinking of the cool rain of Dublin, a shadow of a mist, so light that the earth was dry under every bush, so faint that you saw it only against dark tree caves or in hollow archways, or on the windows of Rosita's Fish and Chip Shop where she had eaten with Milo, hearing the evening bells, looking out and up at the long, gray, tented daylight. In early May she went back to Dublin, laden.

All the way across she had wondered, What will I feel? Will he suspect? Will I blush when he chalks my bags? She stood tense on the deck as the morning light slowly touched the mountains, the green hills, the wet houses, the town's church spires and, at last, they were bumping the black pier with its fenders made of hairy ropes. When she saw him, pink, fresh, young, absorbed in his job, she was so far from feeling anything but pleasure in his sudden flash of delight — "Three bags? I see you brought everything!" — that it was she who blushed, forgot all about her contraband and was about to open up her suitcases when he chalked them with a cheerful grin and a "See you later!" Within hours she was wondering what on earth she had ever seen in Pimlico or why she had ever left Dublin.

They were together all day, and still together late that night at the pier's end, looking at the late Irish sunset — it was nearly eleven o'clock — still red and low over distant Dublin.

"Milo," she said suddenly, "I'm not going back to London."

For a second she thought he was going to kiss her: then she realized that he was the sort of fellow to whom a kiss is as good as a promise. Without intent, or the desire that waits on it, she leaned her head on his shoulder in a posture that obliged him to put an arm about her waist.

"You're married to him."

Slowly she released his arm and stood erect. She turned from the last red-black line over the city and looked eastward across the sea. As she looked creeping horror entered her. Only last week, in that crowded pub outside Victoria Station, talking over their beer with some fellows about marriage and divorce, Clarence had said, "Funny thing, there's no divorce in Ireland. But any man or woman who was married in a registry office in England can remarry in Ireland. Catholics don't count that as a real marriage. So, Rosebud here," he laughed, "could chuck me any day she liked and marry an Irish Catholic!" And he had looked at her, smiling softly, with half-closing eyes.

"Let's go back," she said somberly to Milo, and all the way along the slim lamp-lit pier she was silent. She halted and gripped Milo's arm, staring at nothing.

"Are you all right, Rosie?"

Was the bastard thinking that if she married him it would be awfully convenient . . .

"Sit down here. You've been having a hard time of it."

She sat on the bench, still holding his arm.

"What you need, Rosie, is a long, long rest."

"With you around I mean to take a long rest." She leaned towards him. "Milo, for Christ's sake, kiss me!"

He did so, chastely, on her cheek. She did not press him farther.

The furs were locked in her wardrobe. Every morning, after Milo went out to work, she took a cab at the pier and drove into Dublin with them. Within a week her bankbook showed a total touching the last quarter of the thousand. After that she dawdled on happily, blind to thought — every day Milo and she seemed to have so much to do, to see, to talk about. She mentioned to him this strange idea that an Irish Catholic could, if he wanted to, marry a woman who was already married legally in England. He had never heard of such a thing. She said, "It must be a crazy idea I picked up all wrong." When she wrote to Clarence about the furs he wrote back, "Wonderful woman! Have a nice time, ducks! I can wait. But don't keep me hanging too long. I'm only human. And I'm mad about my Rosebud. Every day I clean a window I say, 'Soon one day I'll be watching some other poor bugger cleaning ours.' "

She heard no more from him until, as if he was inside her head, as if he knew every movement of her body, she got a letter headed Tisbury, Wiltshire, in his handwriting. "Dad is ill. The doctor talks about heart. Do come and see us, even if it's only for a day . . ." Wavering, she kept it for two days. Then she tore it up, savagely. That night, in Rosita's, she said:

"I've made up my mind, Milo. It's not very ladylike of me to say it, but it's say it or go back. If I stay will you marry me?"

He whispered his answer:

"As a matter of fact I found that I can. I remembered what you said and I inquired about it. There is nothing against it in principle. There have been several cases like it. Only . . ."

"Well?"

"There's only one thing I'm not sure of."

"Which is?"

"I'm not sure that you love me."

She made him sure that night. She was astonished by his wild passion, of which afterwards he was both touchingly ashamed and youthfully proud.

She delayed writing to Clarence. Then she invented an illness and sent him a tenner. When his letters became impatient she replied to them lovingly, sending more money, and telling him that she was now all in favor of his scheme, exploring everywhere for better markets. By late June he was getting angry. She tried to pacify him by telling him that since it would be far better to sell the coats to private customers she had already fixed one and nearly fixed another, that she wanted to bring three or even four coats, that he would be wise to wait. She sent him twenty pounds. When June ended he ordered her to return within three days or he would come over himself. She did not reply. He wired her: "Am crossing by tomorrow's mailboat." When she wired back she wrote at first only, "You may come," then, with a last vestige of old feeling, chiefly pity, she added, "But take no chances," signing it, "Rose Powis."

Her time was up. The next morning she went to a doctor; that afternoon she told Milo. He was so tender with her, so wildly full of love that she told him everything else as well. If she had been confessing to one of his priests she could not have bared herself more completely. When she told him about the naked photographs the disgust on his face terrified her. At the furs his rage was as wild as his love had been. From Clarence she would not have minded the words he spat at her; from his mouth they were horrible because from him they were just. Liar. Thief. Deceiver. Trollop. Slut. Whore. When at last he had exhausted himself and was sitting, sobbing into his hands, on the edge of the old, velvet armchair of the sitting room of their lodging house, she sat in the farthest corner of the room and stared at him hopelessly. The rest was as quiet as mice talking.

"I did it only for you, Milo. Honestly!"

He raised his head.

"Honestly? That! From you?"

"I loved you. I still love you. I want you always. I wanted your baby."

"How do I know it is mine?"

"I know! I'm four weeks gone, and I'm as regular as clockwork."

"I don't believe you."

"All right! If you won't have me, I will just have to go back to Clarence. I'll palm it off on him. Is that what you want?"

"You mean if you could fool me you could fool him. If you could fool him you could fool me. You think you could fool everybody."

"I wouldn't. There's just that difference, Milo. I love *you.*"

"Love!"

There was a long silence during which they sat and stared at one another.

"Why don't you chance it, Milo? We could be very happy. We could make a go of it."

He kept staring at her. She got up.

"It's not such a big chance to take," she said sullenly. "Well? Finish me off! Say it, blast you! Do I stay with you? Or do I go back to him?"

"You could do that? Maybe you love him, too!"

"Milo! I don't think that any more."

"Think! Do you *know?* Do you know anything? Which of us do you love?"

"Isn't that up to you?"

That was their longest silence. The room darkened slowly. She saw seagulls wheeling against a blue-black sky above the mailboat's masts. She went to the door. He stood up.

"Will you swear to God in heaven that it is my child?"

"No! I don't hold with that lark. And I'm not going on my knees to you. If you don't believe me, you don't love me, and I don't want you if you don't love me, and if you don't love me it wouldn't make any bloody difference to you anyway. Let it go, Milo! You've had your fun. Besides, it's not your baby! Or mine! It's ours!"

She opened the door. He banged it to. He gripped her arms.

"Suppose I did chance it?"

"Why should you?" she raged. "Why chance anything? Why don't you go on being Careful Paddy?"

"I suppose I'd chance it because I once thought you loved me."

"Why am I in no doubt? Why is it always the man who can't trust?"

He fell, weeping, on her chest.

"I believe you, Rosie!"

She threw her arms about him and gave out a deep triumphant sigh, like a ship sloping into harbor with furling sails.

"Milo, I'll never let you down. You'll see. We will make a go of it! Oh, Milo!" she laughed, and he with her. "Isn't it just like that picture we saw last week at the Pav!"

She rummaged in the bag on her arm, found the bankbook and gave it to him. The thunder crashed. He threw it on the floor as if it was a snake.

"Why do you give me that thing?"

"Throw it into the sea. Do what you like with it. All I'm worth now is what I'm standing up in."

"It's the way I want you," he laughed. "Or in less."

They stood clasped together, her heel grinding the bankbook, their eyes closed, their mouths one, indifferent to the sudden downpour of rain and the rumble of the thunderstorm as it wandered away to sea, where, miles out, under the vast, blue storm stretched across the horizon, a small brush of smoke indicated the mailboat beating its way into the wind towards their sheltering shore.

"My darling!" he muttered throatily through her lips, and seized her hand and fled with her through the dusky corridor to her room. There they were so lost in love for so long that they did not hear the soft hoot of the mailboat making its dark entry to the pier.

A Sweet Colleen

THE stink and smell and dust of this bloody station! And the rudeness of that fellow in the ticket office! What a fool to come by bus, and an hour too early. She was exhausted from lugging this old leather suitcase of Aunt Edie's. She let a parcel fall. A porter came over to her.

"Can I help you, miss?"

"Oh, please do! The Irish Mail."

"Got a seat reserved?"

"O Lord, I forgot!"

Nice voice, nice kid, nice legs and the real Rossetti neck.

"This way, Miss."

When he had lobbed her case up on the rack of an empty carriage and she was fumbling for a coin in her purse, he said:

"Forget it."

She looked up at him. He had the most beautiful eyes she ever saw, pure cerulean, with long lashes. His temples were gray. Plump apple cheeks like an old lady.

"I'm Irish, too," he smiled. "That's a heavy bag."

He removed his porter's cap to pad his forehead with a blue handkerchief. He could be forty. He chucked down his waistcoat, put away the handkerchief in his back pocket. But she noted that he still held his peaked cap in his hand. He was so tall that he was able to lean on one foot with his other hand grasping the rack above him.

"Been on a holiday?" he asked.

"I work in London."

"Over long?"

"Three months."

"First time?"

"Yes."

"I could guess. Like it?"

Was this a bit unusual? But the platform was empty, there was no rush yet and Daddy used always to say that once you got on the Irish Mail you were in the friendly climate already.

"I have a nice, quiet job. It's all right. I work in the National Gallery."

"I'll be blowed!" he laughed, but quietly. "I worked there for three and a half years. I used to be one of the warders."

She could imagine him in the Gallery uniform, and knew at once that he had been in the war, and she would take a small bet that he had been a sergeant.

"And what do you do in the Gallery?"

"I work in the bookstall."

He laughed happily, as if recalling the good old bookstall.

"I'd better drop into the Gallery one of these days and count the pictures. There were a couple there I used to like. The Rokeby Venus."

She smiled discreetly. He said:

"Actually my favorite painter is Dante Gabriel Rossetti."

She saw that he would have liked to go on chatting and gave him full marks for not doing it. He stepped back onto the platform, put on his cap, half an inch sideways, swept the gray wing of his hair back over his ear, closed the door and said through the window:

"Give my love to O'Connell Street. And take good care of yourself. You ought to. A girl as pretty as you."

He went off laughing. Funny little fluting voice she has. He suddenly wheeled and came back to the window.

"Tell old Rutchie I was asking for him. My name is Tom Dalton." He laughed back mockingly over his shoulder. "Tell him give my love to Pom Pom."

Rutchie? She wondered a bit at a Gallery warder becoming a railway porter. Maybe there was more money in railways. The journey sent him out of her head: the sleepless discomfort, the changing to the mailboat at Holyhead in the small hours, meeting her sisters, Dublin, everything.

Then one afternoon about a month later she heard herself being asked for the postcard of the Rossetti *Damozel,* looked up and saw the beautiful blue eyes smiling at her.

"Hello," he said politely. "Forgotten me? Tom Dalton. Euston Station. The Irish Mail. Did you have a pleasant holiday?"

"I remember you," she said, and caught herself blushing and glancing along the counter out of the corner of her eye to see if Lorna Alleyn was listening.

"How is Dublin?"

"Just the same old Dublin," she laughed, responding to his genial smile. His own teeth; staining; he smoked too much; and a pipe, the way Daddy used to. "Have you been home this summer?"

"Why, girl, it's fifteen years since I saw Dublin. I wish you'd tell me some time what it's like nowadays. You wouldn't care to join me for lunch? No harm in asking, I hope?"

Her eye wandered to a waiting customer and she excused herself. When she came back to his end of the counter he was still there, leafing through the cards. He was wearing a well-cut, gray suit and a soft, brown hat with a snap brim. She wondered what his story might be.

"No?" he asked lightly, yet with such a note of pleading also that she hated to refuse him.

"I'm sorry, I'm not free for lunch."

"Why not come out and have a bit of dinner with me to-night at a nice little Greek café?"

In her embarrassment she laughed.

"Aren't you working now?"

"I can get a pal to stand in for me. Give him five bob. We often do it on night shifts."

"Oh, all right! Thank you. It is very kind of you."

"Fine! I'll see you outside when you knock off. Now I'm going in to see my favorite picture." He held up the postcard. "She's very like you."

During the afternoon she went into the Gallery herself to have a look at that picture. She was standing on one leg looking at it, searching for some mirror-likeness when she became aware that two men who had been talking quietly in a corner of the room were parting, and that one of them was approaching her. He was sallow, middle-aged, very dark-eyed, soldierly, not bad-looking. He said amiably:

"Excuse me, you are at the bookstall, aren't you?"

He spoke as softly as befitted the place and the heavy, June afternoon.

"Yes."

"I noticed you a couple of times. It is pleasant to find that one can go from postcards to pictures as well as from pictures to postcards. I'm in the curator's office. My name is Rucellai. Guido Rucellai."

"What name did you say?"

"Rucellai."

"Oh? Did you know a warder named Tom Dalton who used to work here?"

"The mad Irishman?"

"In what way was he mad? By the way I am Irish."

He raised an apologetic hand and eyebrow. His teeth were white as paper. A strong, hooked nose.

"There is no real harm in being considered a little mad,

you know. My English friends consider me a mad Italian. I have several Polish friends and I think them all quite mad. Only the English are never mad. Do you like Rossetti? Of course he was not really English. His father was an Italian. Very nice drawing there."

"Somebody said that she appears to be a little like me."

He looked to and fro between her and the picture, so often that she felt herself blushing.

"Nonsense. You are High Renaissance. Parmigianino?" he suggested, looked her all over. "No, it must be a Florentine. Domenico called Veneziano? No! Pollaiuolo? Or why not Botticelli? The sloping shoulders, the distant look, the firm legs. That's it. As a matter of fact there is a girl very like you in the Villa Lemmi frescoes."

"Why was Tom Dalton considered mad?"

"Do you know him very well?"

"I do not know him at all. I just met him by chance last month at Euston Station. He is a railway porter now."

"Hm! He may be more suited to a railway station than an art gallery. I think I may have said that he is mad because he got so excited and cross with me one day. He told me, an Italian — consider my position here — that he hates all Italians. I had to reprimand him. I found out later that he married an Italian girl during or just after the war, and it turned out badly."

"Oh, well! I must go."

"Come again, Miss Plunkett."

"You know my name?"

"I inquired," he smiled. "I don't know your first name."

"Barbara."

"Come again, Barbara," — and he bowed from the neck sedately. A bit superior? Or was he soapy?

Dalton took her first to a pub called The Cat and Cage off Oxford Street, at the Marble Arch end. It was a quiet street, among flats, mews, office buildings and the backs of hotels. Evening sparrows chirruped in the runnels. One might expect to find near at hand a flower shop, small but elegant houses, a church, an expensive boutique.

"This is a nobby district," he told her. Watching her looking around at the mahogany and the cut-glass mirrors, he could tell that she had never been in a pub before. There were less than a dozen customers there. "Anyway it once was a nobby district. We are in what Sydney Smith called the parallelogram — that is the whole district between Oxford Street south to Piccadilly, and from Park Lane over to Regent Street. Cream of the cream when England was an empire and Ireland was her pup."

"Who is Sydney Smith? A friend of yours?"

"He's dead long ago, a famous English writer."

"Do you read a lot?"

"It passes the time. What's your poison?"

She did not know what he could afford so she asked him to decide. He brought her a dry sherry and a pint of mild-and-bitter for himself.

"Sherry is always safe," he advised her gently. "It is a ladylike drink. And take it dryish, never sweet. Never take martinis. Two of them could knock you out so you wouldn't know what you were saying or doing. Besides, they are expensive and no lady feels happy if she feels she is drinking beyond the means of her consort. I hope you don't mind my bringing you here for an aperitif. I thought it might interest you. Nowadays it is quite a respectable thing to do. Of course, there are some pubs I wouldn't bring you into."

"It is a lovely pub. It is the nicest pub I have ever been in. Thank you for bringing me to this pub."

He asked her what he might call her; and if he might call her Barbara; and would she call him Tom; he felt as if she were his own daughter; and did she mind if he smoked his pipe?

"I love a pipe. Daddy always smoked a pipe. It makes me feel quite at home."

He laughed, a little mockingly, but she plainly did not see his joke. She was as slim as a sapling in the moon of March, with the Damozel's waving hair, and eyes blue as speedwell. *"The wonder was not yet quite gone from that still look of hers."* No lipstick yet. A bit on the skinny side, in spite of the strong legs.

"How old are you, Barbara?"

"Nineteen and a bit more," — adding one to her eighteen.

"I've got an idea. The next time you go to Dublin I'll get you a 'P' Ticket. 'P' stands for Privileged. If I say you're my daughter I can get you a ticket for next to nothing."

"You are awfully kind, Tom," she said, considering him. "Are you sure that would be all right? I mean wouldn't they want me to prove my identity and so on? I would not want to get you into trouble."

He looked hard at her.

"You're not being snobby, are you? Not wanting to say you are a porter's daughter? There are no questions asked, you know. You just present your ticket like everybody else. We're all one in this on the railways. Each for all and all for each as you might say." He patted her knee paternally a couple of times. "It's all right, I've upset you now I can see. You're not a bit snobby. What was the journey like this time?"

"Fine. Except for having to change for the mailboat; get out at two in the morning just when you are almost beginning to fall asleep."

"How I know these night trains! During the war — ooh!"

As he talked on she was pleased to find that he had, indeed, been a sergeant, fought in the desert and right up through Italy. And, as Rucellai said, he had married an Italian girl and it had not worked; in fact he had only lived with her for a year and then sent her back with her child to her people in Italy. He told her this quite calmly, as if it was something he had put well behind him.

"Last time I saw her she was a little bit of a thing. She'll be fifteen now. I've seen her photograph, quite pretty. It was a pity, but what's the use? I couldn't bring up a child on my own in London, and her mother was a washout. Her old *nonna* will look after her. If I could have married again . . . But being a Catholic!"

She said he must be lonely, but he waved it away.

"Tell me about dear, old dirty Dublin," he said, with one eye over the rim of his tankard. "Where do you live there?"

Well . . . She lived with her mamma and her three sisters up in the hills behind Rathfarnham. It was a dear old house, supposed to be eighteenth century, all curls, and corners, and humpty-dumpty roofs. Daddy was dead. He had been a re- tired army captain. She did not specify British Army, but he knew it. He asked her where exactly in Rathfarnham, or be- yond it, she lived; he wanted to know; he really would like to know.

"Up near Rockbrook. It's lovely there. We can see Dublin miles away below us, on the bay. At night you can see the line of yellow lights strung out along the edge of the water beyond Clontarf. And all the little lights of the city. It's really lovely, Tom! It's like a stage, with footlights. We've always lived there. It's a bit far out, but Donna and Lulu and I went in every day for two years to Alexandra College. Of course since Daddy died we've been hard-up and I knew that, sooner or later, I'd have to take a job. I wanted to be an air hostess with Aer Lingus but Mamma was dead against it. She always said, 'It's no use, Babs, our sort never earned their living.' She thinks what I am doing now is not work, not real work. She lives in a dream. I think she always hoped I'd marry an earl or something."

She laughed gaily at the folly of their lives. He chuckled.

"All Ireland lives in a dream, bless its heart. I believe I

know your house. I often used to go up around Rockbrook on Sundays when I was in the cycling club with a lot of boys and girls out of the factory — Jacobs. We'd cycle all around through Glencree, on up the Old Long Hill or up the Sally Gap. And so that's where you always lived?"

"Always and always."

From Oxford Street they could hear, through the open doors, the swishing of tires. That night below Monte Cassino, looking out of that cantina, the bombing up in the hills, he had a letch for Oxford Street: a pipe-dream Oxford Street, with no blitz or blackout and the girls all wearing light cotton frocks.

"What did you used to do all day up in Rockbrook?"

"I used to love drawing horses. I could sit drawing horses all day long. I'm really quite good at drawing horses. I think that's why I looked for a job in the Gallery. When they asked me what was I good at I said, 'Horses,' so they gave me the job. You see, it did help. We used to ride a bit when we were able to afford it. Played tennis a bit. The old tennis lawn was full of bumps. We went to a dance once or twice. Nothing much, really. Or went down to town to meet somebody for a coffee. Really, the time just passed. But I did like drawing horses. Bears, too, but I was not so good at bears."

He put down his tankard. He felt his heart beating. Smoking too much? He looked around the pub. In one corner a small man in a bowler hat was feeling a fat woman's knee and she was shaking in her fat with laughter at whatever he was saying to her.

"Barbara! Have you got any friends here?"

"Not real friends. I have Aunt Edie, of course, but she lives in Hampton Court. She is one of those State widows or whatever they call them. Her husband was governor of the Bahamas. She has arthritis, so she never comes out."

"Where do you live?"

"In Oakley Street. I have a room there."

"Are you sure you're able to look after yourself in London?"

She opened her speedwell eyes.

"What on earth can you mean? I've been looking after myself all my life. Mamma is sweet but she does not know whether she is coming or going. I've often cooked for the five of us. So there!"

"What can you cook?"

"I can cook a steak. I can cook bacon and eggs. I used to be good at cooking a ragout, but I'm forgetting recently what I used to put into it. I was thinking of it only the other day when I saw onions selling in a shop. Tom! What does go into a stew? Do you put onions in yours? Oh, I can cook when I put my mind to it, I do assure you. You must come to my place one night and I will show you!"

He laid down his pipe. His hand fondled his heart side.

"I am going to have another beer. Another sherry?"

"Will it make me tight?"

"I don't think so."

He had intended to take her to a Greek place he knew between Oxford Street and Soho Square; instead he took her to Bertorelli's in Charlotte Street. He ordered for them both, including a half of Chianti.

"It is Italian but it is good. Now and again, for a blowout on payday, I come down here from my hill fortress."

She felt sad that he lived on the Harrow Road because she had passed that way once and got an impression of an Irishy quarter with flats over cafés, a bit toughy: he probably could not afford anything better, supporting his wife and daughter in Italy. For no reason she saw him in his room on a Sunday evening, when London can be rather dreary, sitting in his room reading his Sydney Smith, looking out at the noisy street. Oakley Street, anyway, was at least quiet. Maybe this was what made him become a railway porter? He could make friends that way.

"Don't you ever want to go back to Ireland, Tom?"

"You ask me that? You know how it is being a misfit in Ireland."

"True, I do know, don't I?"

They considered one another silently in the noisy, cheerful, crowded hither-and-thither of the restaurant until he wandered out of that island of silence into a winding, wandering discussion about what it is to be an exile and about friendship as an island in an island — "You know, like Robinson Crusoe and the footprint."

"The Irish are like the Jews. It's in our blood. We never belong, not really. Being Catholics, too, cuts us off. We are exiles in the bloody world. Shaw said somewhere, I think it's in *John Bull's Other Island,* that the Irish are hardheaded and realistic. I don't believe a word of it. What makes us get on in the world, whenever we do, is the outcast feeling, never knowing when some blow is going to fall. You and me, though, we don't give a damn about the world, do we? Do you?"

"Not really. No! I don't think I do."

"All we ever want is a couple of drinks and a friend to pass the night."

That, she was to find, was always his style of talk.

He was on now to love and marriage, talking nonstop, even when they went out into the summer-lit evening and took a bus to the Park and were strolling across it, threading their way through the last couples strewn like forgotten dolls on the grass, enjoying the coolness after the hot day. He was telling her about the odd characters he had met in the army, and out of it; "opening your blue eyes," as he said with his little mocking smile, "to the ways of the world"; just to show her the queer, dark things that are in men, especially men you would never suspect, and how all but a few confuse their lives in love and marriage. All she said was, "Yes!" or "Oh, yes, indeed." Nobody had ever talked to her like this ever before.

She saw his big hands, pallid in the evening light, and wondered mildly, though only for a second, and for the last time, if she was wise to be with him, alone. They sat, and he talked now about Italy, while the sky over the farther roofs became masked with silver-gray, the grass grew dusky, the trees grew heavy and dark, and the water darkened, and then, across the park, lights came out in the streets and the booming traffic dulled.

"You loved Italy, really, didn't you, Tom?"

"But not Italians. I don't trust them. And I advise you, if you ever run into any of them here, don't you trust them either. We never trusted them in the army. All the men ever think about is their looks. Combing their hair all day long. Pfu! And all the girls think about is men. I knew lots of men besides me who fell for Italian girls, and it never worked for any of them that I knew."

She was on the point of mentioning Rucellai. She shied off it.

"Tom, tell me about your wife."

"She was pretty. I met her in 'forty-three one night in a village called San Vittore. Just below Monte Cassino. Oh, maybe she wasn't all that pretty, maybe I was like a lot of other chaps who fell for Italian girls, maybe we weren't so much in love with the girls as dying for a taste of home. Besides, I was only twenty-two when I went into the army, straight from Ireland where twenty-two is equal to about seventeen or eighteen here. I'd had four years of the war. I saw her only twice, then we pushed on to join up with the Yanks from Anzio. It was months before we entered Rome. You know what I mean — absence. I got three days' leave to meet her in Naples. A girl like you couldn't even imagine what Naples was like that time. God! It was filth! She was young, and sweet, and lovely, and O Lord God, innocent as the moon, and I asked her to marry me. I had to wait until 'forty-six. I was thirty and that was the first time I slept with a girl, believe it or not. She gave me a baby and syphilis."

Her white throat was the only thing he could see clearly. Like the whisper of leaves, that was her voice. She would have breasts like little white apples. He jumped up.

"I'll see you home," he said, and led her, arm in arm, through the Park, talking incessantly, as if he had not talked to anybody for months, walking the whole way to her door. She politely invited him in for a cup of coffee. He did not seem to hear. There were five bell-pushes on the doorjamb and he was examining them. He laid his finger on one of the tabs and, in a dark, heavy voice, he asked, "Antonelli. Who is he?"

"I believe he is a musician." She opened the door. "He plays the oboe. Listen, I think he is playing now. My landlord says he is a nice man."

"How do you know he is nice?" he said angrily. "You think every man you meet is nice. Is he young?"

"Oh, no! About your age, I should think. He is quite an elderly man."

He gave a sharp laugh, looked abruptly at his watch, said: "I'll give you a ring some time."

"Thank you for a delightful evening. I enjoyed it immensely. You were really very kind to ask me, and nobody has ever talked to me before like you. Not even Daddy. And we were great pals."

He jerked out another laugh, and ran down the steps, waving backwards. She watched him almost race across the street. He seemed a little put out. Perhaps she should have pressed him to come in for a coffee. She closed the door. The hall was stuffy. No letter. Upstairs the oboe had stopped. She regretted the end of the day. The Irish are so nice.

He did ring her again about a week later, and they met again at The Cat and Cage; but not for dinner, because — or so he said — he was on a night shift. She hoped it was not because he was short of money, and she noted that he was not smoking. She happened to utter the wish that she were going home for the long August weekend, now a month away.

"Go!" he said. "I'll get you the ticket. Cost you hardly anything."

He did get her the 'P' ticket, then met her, all smiles, at Euston Station and put her into a First Class carriage, to which — she already felt him an old friend — she did not demur.

"You've squared this up, too, Tom?"

"All the way," he grinned. "It gives you a better chance to snatch a sleep before they turf you out at two in the morning in Holyhead."

Of unkindness she had no experience, though she knew indifference, yet his attentions made her think, when she was home, that he must be one of the kindest men alive. She had done nothing for him to deserve his kindness; merely met him, twice, at a pub, brought him twice to her room for coffee and a chat, sent him two postcards to cheer him up; so that she was furious when her mamma laughed over the railway porter who got her daughter free travel on British Railways, saying, hootingly, "There you are! It shows you the depths to which the Socialists have dragged poor old England. Corruption from top to bottom."

She was so furious at this mean-spirited way of looking at his kindness that she did not bother to explain. All she said even to her sisters was that she had a secret man in her life, but they refused to take it as a joke, probing and probing until they got it out of her that she was talking about a railway porter, at which they said:

"You and your jokes! Now, if you said a Member of Parliament, or a movie actor, or a stockbroker . . ."

Bored, she listened to them babbling by the hour on the telephone to their boys. She was ashamed for them when she

heard them telling Mamma cover-up lies about their meetings
with boys in town. (As she said, afterwards, to Tom, "They
seemed such kids to me. And dreadful snobs.")

She never mentioned Rucellai, whom she had now met several times, in the Gallery restaurant, over elevenses, and at
tea, and who had twice taken her to lunch outside. She loved
listening to him talking about Italy and his experiences during
the war when he had known and worked with all the famous
partisan leaders, Ada Gobetti in Torino, Dante Livio Bianco
in Piedmont, Filippo Beltraine in Val d'Ossola, Bisagno in
Liguria — at first mere names to her, then growing, as he
talked of them, into real men. What she most liked to hear
him talk about was his boyhood and youth outside Turin —
the hill villages, the vineyards, the small fields, the screens of
reeds, the river in its deep valley, the tiny, faraway passing
train, small things that glowed in his mind like bits of an old
world slipping away into a legend that had once been his life.

"It is my myth," he once said, between a smile and a sigh.

Lying on the dandelions of the ragged lawn on her stom-
ach, with one of her daddy's war histories between her elbows, open at *The Italian Campaign, 1944,* she looked out
over Dublin at the clouds moving in a white mass slowly towards England. She sent a postcard to Signor Rucellai, at the
Gallery; and another to Mr. Thomas Dalton, at his address in
the Harrow Road. Apart from their first meeting, that day in
the Gallery looking at the Rossetti drawing, she had not mentioned Tom to him. But he had spoken of him.

"Odd your meeting Dalton. Oh, I have no doubt he is a
decent chap, as the English say, but he wouldn't know anything about Italy or the Italians because he never knew any of
these things. He only saw the war from the sergeant's view-
point. It is all over now and I am a kind of clerk, if you like,
and he is a railway porter, but we are made by our experiences. Twenty-two years ago when I came over here first to

help Don Sturzo to explain these things to the stupid British all this was high politics. The things we do pass but the lessons of the things — that is the important matter, that is the real experience."

Twenty-two years ago? He looks so young, with his dark hair, and his straight back, and his clear eyes. If there was a war tomorrow he could be in the thick of it again. But not poor, nice old Tom!

When she stepped down to the platform off the Irish Mail in the early morning she saw him in his porter's cap and vest. He was limping. He saw her and waved to her. She looked like a child, tousled after her sleepless night. Passengers off night trains always reminded him of soldiers or children, waking up like puppets coming alive.

"I knew you'd be on it," he said gleefully, "I got your postcard."

"Tom, you're limping!"

"Pfu! Just a touch of sciatica."

"Oh, Tom, you've not been taking care of yourself."

"Now you're here I will" — taking her bag. "Have a nice holiday?"

"Not really. It was a failure, really. Really and truly. I must be getting old. Or losing touch. I'm very glad to be back. That is the real truth."

He chuckled down in his throat.

"Come back to England, mavourneen, mavourneen. I'll tell you this — I'm damn glad to have you back, Barbara."

It touched her that one person more or less in London could make any difference to such a lonely man. His limp was bad as he led her to a taxi — she had to be at her post in the Gallery that morning. As he closed the door of the taxi he said, "Tonight we'll have a drink at The Cat and Cage and you must tell me all about it. But right afterwards you go right to bed, my dear, and make up for your lost sleep. Tomorrow night I'll show you a new restaurant I've found. Spanish. Tops. Have a good breakfast."

She wiggled her fingers to him as she drove out into the morning sunlight of the station yard. A red milk-car by the curb on Euston Road welcomed her home.

As he watched her go a mate said to him, "Oye, Paddy! You're picking 'em young!"

"That," he said with dignity, "is my little girl, Barbara."

"Sorry, chum. Didn't know you had a daughter. Got any more as pretty as her?"

"My one and only," he said, and limped away.

For economy's sake she let breakfast wait until elevenses in the Gallery. Rucellai was there.

"Welcome," he said. "I am glad to see you."

"Do you really mean that?"

"I never say things I do not mean. London has been making *la festa,* and making me feel a stranger. I stayed in my lodgings all Sunday, reading. I felt a little jealous of you, able to go home and be happy. But all my life I have been unhappy."

"But you know, Rucellai, I wasn't happy." (Neither then nor at any time did she call him Guido. He preferred to be called Rucellai because it was not his real name: it was his partisan name. He had, he said, bade farewell to his youthful reality, and he once startled her by saying that she would, soon, bid farewell to hers.) "I was miserable. Is that awful of me? I ought not to feel that way about my own home."

At once he lit up, both excited and pleased.

"Exactly the same thing happened to me after the war when I went back to Turin. For years I'd been dreaming of going back home. It was no longer my Torino. All my friends were either scattered, or killed, or married, or interested only in making money. Heroes had become men. I was an exile in my own country. I am also an exile here. You are experiencing the same thing now. And here you, too, you are also an exile, in this Anglo-Saxon city with its queen, and its court, and its rich clubs. What does one do about it? We must talk of this," he urged. "Will you dine with me tonight?"

Alas! She was exhausted by the journey, already half-asleep on her feet. He need not be surprised if she were found curled up under the counter of the bookstall, snoring.

"Very well," he ordered, "tomorrow night we dine. We will go to La Speranza. One of the best Italian restaurants in London."

He rose, bowed, left her. She would have to tell Tom that she had forgotten that tomorrow night she must go and visit Aunt Edie in Hampton Court, with messages from Mamma. And so she did, fixing to eat with him two nights after. Later, looking at herself in the washroom mirror, she remembered Lulu and Donna deceiving Mamma about their meetings with boys because they thought they were in love.

"Am I," she asked her mirror, her comb suspended, "in love?"

She laughed it away. How old was he? Forty? More? It was just that he was interesting to talk to; as she again found him the next night, sitting beside him in the expensive-looking pale cream and green restaurant, with all the waiters dressed like gentlemen at a dance, and all the other diners obviously rotten with money. She said, "I hope this is not too expensive a restaurant, Rucellai? No lady feels happy, you know, if she is dining beyond the means of her consort."

He had some profound thoughts (his words) about this.

"Money," he said, "does not necessarily make people happy. Happiness comes from the heart. Happiness is freedom. Freedom, to me, is not having bonds. You have no bonds. I have no bonds. This is one of the great merits of being an exile. No ties of relatives. Here I am just me. You are just you. It is a great thing to be oneself. I have never been attracted by any Englishwoman because I could not feel that I possessed her completely. Only the beloved should exist for the beloved. This country which you and I inhabit is a good place for us because it is the land of loneliness."

Trying to understand his strange and interesting philosophy she asked:

"Are you lonely, Rucellai?"

"I," he said proudly, "am always lonely. I am a dreamer of dreams. I am a sad, bad man. *Tristuccio.*"

"But you have been a man who did great things too. A man of action. Those days of the partisans were not just dreams."

"My dreams came true — briefly. I was in love those great days with my country. The land of loneliness — and this is a profound thought — is the land of love where love is unrequited."

"Poor Rucellai!"

"Do you not," he asked her seriously, "ever feel this loneliness?"

"Oh, yes!" she agreed. "I am often lonely on Sunday afternoons."

"Tonight," he smiled at her, "I will not be lonely. Nor you. Tonight our country of dreams will have a population of two."

"Will you never go back to Italy?" she asked hastily, fearing that she understood him.

"What should I do in Torino at my age? One day I will go back, as all Italians do, but only when they can *far figura,* cut a dash, as you say, with a lemon-colored car and a pretty wife. If I went back now I would be competing with men twenty years younger than me, men who have been keeping their eyes on jobs ever since they went up to the university, flattering their professor, carrying his briefcase, opening the door of his car for him, taking his daughter out, with discretion, agreeing with all his rotten political ideas. No! *Sta bene qui.*"

"What does that mean?"

"I'm fine here."

"You must help me to learn Italian. Whatever else you lose you cannot lose that."

"I should not want to. I love Italy, there is no country like Italy, but I do not admire her as I used to. I have seen her naked and ashamed. You must come to my flat for lessons. I will give you a lesson every night. But now we must hurry."

Every night?

He had tickets for a concert of Italian music, mostly of the seventeenth and eighteenth century, Cimarosa, Lully and Tartini. During the largo of the Cimarosa Concerto in G, he laid his hand on hers and they smiled at one another over the dreamy flutes and the muted strings humming like bees. "All the tears and gaiety of the south," he whispered. During the Lully he laid his hand tenderly on her knee. In an interval she delicately pointed to his temple and dared to say that she saw one gray hair.

"Do you mind?" he asked. "I could dye it if you wish."

"No. I think, really and truly, I prefer older men. They are more interesting. Usually."

He made her blush by asking her if she had had great experience of older men. During the Tartini she held his hand, tightly. After the concert she invited him to have coffee with her in her room. As he helped her to doff her coat he kissed her, and asked her if she were a Catholic. When she said, "No! Daddy was a Presbyterian," he said that he would instruct her, and began to unbutton her blouse, and her heart began to go wallop.

"There! The sloping Botticelli shoulders. The wide-eyed look of the air and the sea and the earth."

"Rucellai," she whispered, while he was removing her blouse, "I never let anybody do this before."

He laughed, "You prefer to do it yourself?" His arms were around her, groping for the fasteners of her brassiere. She grabbed it to her bosom.

"Rucellai! I'm, really and truly, not that sort of girl. Really and truly I'm not!"

"You have not had lovers?" he demanded, glaring at her.

"Lots!" she said, terrified. "Dozens!"

"Tell me the truth!" be bullied.

"No!" she squeaked. "Never!" She paled. "I mean not really and truly."

"Which is it in the name of Jesu?" he shouted.

She clasped her arms in front of her and burst into tears of misery and shame.

"None!"

"Donna e madonna!" he shouted, fell on his knees, clasped her about her thighs and gazed up at her in joy. "A virgin!" Rising, he gently slipped down one strap, kissed the slope of her breast with reverence, and replaced her blouse. "We shall be married in the New Year. And we shall live in a flat in Wigmore Street. And drive a yellow MG. It has been my dream for years."

He gazed at her voraciously, threw his hands up in the air, and moaned, "See what England has done to me! I am behaving like a milord. Italian and religion tomorrow night," and dashed for the door.

O gosh! Tom!

"Not tomorrow night! I have to go to my dear Aunt Edie to Hampton Court Palace with a pair of chickens from Mamma."

He paused at the door. He said in the cool lofty voice of an old Wykhamist, "Hampton Court Palace? Really? You have an aunt in the Palace? Can you find your own way to the Palace? Will you be returning late from the Palace? After dark? I'm sure Aunt Edie would disapprove strongly. As do I!"

"I've done it a dozen times. And it will not be late, nor after dark."

He shook his head dolefully.

"You don't know how attractive you are, or how innocent you are. All those coloreds! I have often thought that young ladies in London should all carry police whistles. I shall buy you one."

He looked as if he was about to hurl himself on her. Instead he hurled himself down the stairs, thump-thump. Just as it was beginning to soak into her mind, which felt like a flowerbed after a Newfoundland had lolloped over it, that he had talked about marriage, her doorbell rang. Her white blouse flying she ran to the window, lifted it and looked down at the pavement. He started waving, and using his palms as a megaphone he shouted up:

"Cover yourself! No bra! Button up!"

"What is it?" she shouted down, clutching her collar to her neck.

"Those chickens!" he shouted. "They'll go bad. The heat."

"The what? I can't hear."

"The chickens!" he boomed.

"What chickens?" she shouted down.

"For Aunt Edie!" he shouted back.

A window lifted across the street and a man shouted:

"Would you please be quiet, you silly oaf!"

"They are waiting for me at Fortnum and Mason's," she shouted, astounded at her powers of invention.

He waved and sent her up an immense shrug, threw one arm into the air to the man across the street, uttering some Italian vocable which may have been meaningless but which sounded insulting, and to which the man in the window replied with two uplifted fingers and an English vocable which she knew had no meaning but sounded just as rude, and so — he replying to the man, the man to him, he back to the man, the man to his back — he went away. Then the man, who she observed was young and stark naked, waved to her, whereupon she slapped down the window, flicked the curtains together, and threw herself on the bed staring at the mottled ceiling.

"But I couldn't," she said, and on her fingers started to make calculations.

If he is now twenty years older than his competitors who would be, say, twenty-one, he is forty-one, in which case — forty-one from 1962, one from two, four from six, leaves 1921, and that means when the war broke out, 1939, one from nine leaves eight, two from three leaves one — he was only eighteen then and could not have taken part in high politics with Don Furso and is A Liar! No! He said he came here twenty-two years ago, which is 1940, and was only nineteen, and is still A Liar! Or else he is much older. My God! How old is he? He could be forty-five! Twenty-seven years older than me. Oh! If I had only somebody to talk to he could have a wife in Italy, too, if only old Tom didn't hate all Italians, I could trust Tom if he knows anything really about anything but I know all he would say is that Rucellai is a treacherous Italian. Oh Gosh!

At which she thought how awfully awkward it would be if the two of them ever met, and got up and looked with wide eyes in her mirror at her Botticelli shoulders.

Tom took her to his Spanish restaurant and talked about Socialism, and an American philosopher named George Henry, and loaned her a slightly worn paperback copy of Shaw's *Intelligent Woman's Guide to Socialism and Capitalism,* which had the mark of a tea cup on the cover. She took him to Oakley Street for coffee. There, in the hall, she found waiting for her a portable Gramophone and a record of the Cimarosa Concerto in G. She deftly hid the card accompanying them — it bore the message, "Music, Religion, Language and Love, this is Our Lonely Land"— and said to Tom, "Oh, look at what I bought at lunchtime. I wanted you to hear a record that might remind you of happier days. It contains all the sorrow and gaiety of the south."

As she played it for him she sat curled on the floor, thinking, while he tapped his foot to the rondo and the allegro, that he was very like old Sullivan who used to help Daddy in the garden, and to whom she often confided her troubles; which, in turn, reminded her of old Sulky the white Persian into whose belly she used to cry whenever she was sad. When it was over she said, "Are you a Catholic still, Tom?"

"Yes."

"Are all Catholics very strict?"

"Some of them are. In Ireland most of 'em are. In Italy they take it in their stride."

"Are *you* strict?"

The way she was sitting . . . He looked out the window. "Not as much as I ought to be."

"Tom, what do Catholic girls in Ireland do about men?"

He chuckled his throat smile.

"They do their best. Why are you asking?"

"What does 'do their best' mean?"

He shuffled in his chair, and coughed a bit, and rubbed his heart, and said, "Ye're wearing yeer skirts very short this year." She pulled her skirt over her knees. "Listen! Didn't you ever have any boy friends? You know what I mean."

He got up and went over to sit on the edge of the bed. She slewed around after him. He looked out of the window again.

"Oh, yes!" she said scornfully. "I have had lots of boys, of course, and am quite familiar with what is known as the facts of life if that is what *you* mean. I know all about babies and what they call sleeping together. What I am interested in is if Catholics are all that strict what do they do when they fall in love?"

"They marry. Why are you asking me these questions?" He

got up and went back to his chair. "Sit on the bed, you'll get cold on that floor. What are you after?"

"It is Lorna Alleyn. She works at the bookstall. She is in love with a Catholic and she is not sure that he is not married. She does not know what to do about him. You would condemn her, wouldn't you, for going on with him?"

"I condemn nobody," he said glumly. "Everybody's case is different. We're all human."

She sighed. They were silent for so long that she got up and said, "I will put on that lovely largo again."

It floated softly over them, part-dance, part-dream, part-dirge. She stood by the window looking up at the ashen and pink sky. Suddenly she found him by her side, his arm around her shoulder.

"Barbara! I want to be honest with you. I want you to know why I left the Gallery. I got mixed up with a loose woman. She used to come after me at all sorts of times. She followed me into the Gallery. You know that fellow Rutchie in the Gallery? You must have seen him. He came over here during the war. He was down and out, like all those refugees. He got a job as a clerk in the railways, then he got a job as a clerk in the Gallery. He was over us warders. He caught her bothering me one day, and he threw her out. I had to leave. She follows me still. I'm terrified she'll find out I'm at Euston and come after me there. Every night going home I never dare get off the bus at my own door for fear she'd be waiting for me, wanting money."

The pulse of the largo burst into the race of the rondo, into dancers, blue sea, blazing sun. They stood back from one another.

"Poor Tom! You never did have any luck with women, did you!"

"Not until I met you."

"Oh, me? I'm only a girl. I'm only a kid. Why do you let

yourself be persecuted like this, Tom? Why don't you clear out of London? Get a job somewhere else?"

He looked at her. He looked down into the street. He tapped the window with his forefinger. So sweet, so good, so innocent, so beautiful.

"So that is what you would advise. Is it?"

"You would be so much happier. It is better than staying here and being tormented."

He looked at her. So cruel.

"You would advise that?"

"Yes, I would," she said in a firm, practical tone. "Have peace, Tom. Have peace."

"In Birmingham? Liverpool?" He gave his sour, throaty chuckle. "I'll think about it."

"Poor Tom!"

"Don't give me pity!" he said furiously.

The music stopped. He grabbed his hat from the table and went out so fast that she could only wave to him over the banisters and, for fear of disturbing the house, whisper, "Give me a ring, Tom, won't you, some time?"

She returned to her room and her window. Across the street the young man of last night was leaning on his elbows on the windowsill, smoking a big, crooked pipe, looking idly into the empty street, his shirt off — perhaps more.

She leaned her left temple against the windowpane and glared at the darkening sky over the chimney pots. If Rucellai were here now she would lever the truth out of him. But, first, she would praise him for not betraying Tom Dalton's secret to her. She would certainly ask him, please, really and truly, how old he was. But she could not mention Tom — he would never understand. He was sweet to give her the Gramophone. She put on the largo again, first swathing the black box in her bath towel so that the music could be barely heard in her room. She undressed, and lay down to sleep, letting the record play itself out. Was this the real Rucellai? Dreaming of Italy, and yellow MG's. He would never go back. He would never have a flat in Wigmore Street. And I am never going to ask him any questions, ever, about anything at all.

In October he gave her an engagement ring (telling her never to wear it at the Gallery: their secret for another while) and put her into a tiny top-story flat in Wigmore Street: two tiny rooms, with a bed in one and a table and a chair in the other. Nothing else. Her heart went wallop and her eyes grew big as she looked at the size of him and thought that now at last her hour was come.

"It is all yours," he said. "I shall not intrude. Not very much."

"Am I," she thought as she looked about the almost bare room, "a kept woman?"

"Now," he said happily, "you can tell Mamma that we are engaged to marry."

"But she will never allow it. I am only twenty!"

"You mean I am too old?" he asked angrily. "Or is it too poor? I have always been poor. Because I fought for my country. Do you know that when the war ended I had to take a job as a clerk in the railways? Me! A Rucellai! Are you ashamed of me?"

"I will tell her at Christmas when I go home! Really and truly!"

Every week after that they went shopping for furniture; this week an armchair, next a rug, then a picture, then he could not resist a set of six Regency silver dessert spoons, then he persuaded her that they would need this small silver salver "for visiting cards when our friends call on us!" She had to rebel to get a mirror. "I am your mirror," he throated like a wood pigeon. "Besides we have so little money." They met every evening, for dinner, or a film, or a concert, and afterwards there was a little Italian lesson, and a little religion, and a little love, never going beyond, or stopping short of, a lowered strap and a kiss on the slope of her breast, usually followed by a roar from him like a lion from whom a joint of beef has been snatched, a rush, and a banged door.

One night she moaned to him, "But, Rucellai, why do you insist on tormenting yourself?"

"I am a man of deep feelings!"

"I have deep feelings, too!"

"Am I a brute?"

"I want to give you peace," she whispered, sad for him. "Besides you get me all upset! I don't know what you want from me!"

"Innocence," he said, drawing himself upright, "is a precious jewel. I never knew," he groaned, just before he banged the door, "how expensive it could be."

He fled, and with a sigh she slowly unzipped her skirt and removed her blouse. The door crashed open and his eyeballs stared at her.

"I do not understand you," she wailed. "Don't you want to go to bed with me?"

His whole frame seemed to dissolve like a polar bear sitting down.

"I have sought you too long," he said feebly, "to lose you now," and very slowly, and quietly, he closed the door, and flung it open again to growl, "Lock it! Tight!"

She got a postcard from Tom Dalton, forwarded from Oakley Street. It was a colored picture of Rossetti's *Annunciation* in the Tate Gallery. It was from Cardiff. "I am among the dark Celts. I do this for you. One step nearer home? Tom." She burned it. Then she got another, a postcard, in color, of a railway engine. "You do not reply. Where are you? I need you. Pray for me." She burned this in the tiny grate, knelt and said an *Ave Maria* for him in Italian. That was November. The first week in December she got a telegram, at the Gallery, from Naples. "PLEASE MEET ME IN THE GREEN

LION AT EUSTON TONIGHT AT EIGHT NEED YOU BADLY LOVE TOM."

She had arranged to go with Rucellai to a concert that night, and went to his office to explain about Tom. She said, blushing to the roots of her hair, "An old gentleman friend of Mamma's is suddenly come to town. I really must meet him tonight. Do you mind if I don't go to the concert?"

"Who is this man?" he asked irritably.

"A friend of Mamma's. Old General Butterly."

"Why didn't she write beforehand?"

"She thinks I have nothing to do at night, any night."

"If you had told her about us months ago this deception need never have happened."

"What deception? Whose deception?"

"Yours, ours, mine, to everybody, about everything, about me. How old is this man?"

"He is as old as a general."

"I don't like old men taking you out. I know all about old men."

"I'll be back after the concert. I'll be back by ten o'clock. I will tell Mamma at Christmas. Really and truly."

"I wish we had got married last summer. You are too simple, too innocent, too beautiful, too attractive, too sweet, too good! What are you going to talk to this general about?"

"I don't know, the war I suppose, he's always talking about the Dardanelles."

"But that was the 1914 war! He must be ninety."

"He's awfully old, very, very old, really and truly. He is much older than you."

"I shall expect you," he said severely, "at ten-thirty. We have to do the Conjunctive Pronouns and the Tenth Commandment. You will then be ready to go for final instruction to my dear friend Father De La Poer at Farm Street. And not a minute too soon! For either of us!"

He took up his pen. She almost said: "Yes, Daddy."

It was a dripping night. From beside the door of the Green Lion he saw her approach under the hazy light of a street lamp and knew her at once by the slim neck and the strong legs. She was wearing a tight-belted white raincoat and a little red beret on the back of her poll, her hands dug into the two big patch pockets of her coat, her head bent against the rain. She knew him by the slouch of his back. He was wearing an old army raincape and a cap. When he took her two hands she saw that he was gray-faced, worn, tired and lined.

"The same old Barbara!" he said warmly.

"The same old Tom," and she laughed to make it sound true.

"I've a surprise for you," he said quickly, "I'm just back from Naples. My wife . . ."

"Your wife?"

It came out in a rush:

"My wife was killed last week when a house collapsed in Naples. I'm not married any longer! I'm free! In the summer I'm going to bring back my little Gemma. She's about your age. You'd get on fine with her. I've got lots of plans. I have it all worked out in my head. You and everything."

He led her into the pub; very different to The Cat and Cage — crowded, noisy, damp, smelly. No sooner had he set her on a bench by a plastic table than he jumped up and limped over to the counter for drinks. She got a disturbing feeling that he was glad to move away from her. She hoped he was not returning to live in London. As he moved back slowly, cap on poll, still in his waterproof cape, his head down, watching the glasses in his shaky hands, she saw that he was drinking whiskey and realized that he had been drinking before they met. When he sat down he clutched her hand. By the way his eyes kept sliding away from her as he talked she felt afraid that he was afraid of saying something.

"It's this way, Barbara — I've been thinking about security. We all need security. I've thought it all out, all the way from Naples. I've never had a home. Gemma needs a home. I'm going over to Dublin tonight to look for a —"

He stopped dead and stared at her.

"You look terribly tired, Tom. Tell me everything."

"I'm worn out. All this week in Naples — discussions, arguments, fighting day and night, the priest and the lawyer, her father and mother, brothers and sisters, grandmothers and grandfathers, uncles, cousins, aunts, all of them rubbing together in that coal hole in a wall in a lane that they call a house, crushing around me like a lot of bloody damp dogs yapping at me, it was them, seeing them all together there, one family, all in a bunch, that made me see how much I need a home and a wife."

She laughed. "A wife? Good for you, Tom! Never say die!"

He waved her laughter away from him, roughly.

"I didn't know what they were saying, and all I could say — I was saying it all the time — was 'I want a *mollyeh*,' that's Italian for a wife, 'I want a *casa*.' Did you know the Italians have no word for a home? Only a *casa*. Like a bloody packing case, and that's about all they have. I can marry! I'm free! And I want that little girl of mine, to bring her up like you. That's where you're going to be so marvelous, Barbara. Look at you! Exactly the way I thought of you, the way I was dreaming of you there in the middle of them all, and all the way home in the train and the boat. Good, and lovely, and pure and innocent. No stinking Italian scent about *you*, no paint, no powder, no gewgaws. You will, won't you, Barbara? You'll be my little Barbara always? Say it, Barbara, say it!"

Inside in her she felt a big, choking breath that she could not breathe out. She heard her mamma saying it, and Donna and Lulu: "My dear! How utterly squaliferous!" And, to her horror, she heard the words go ballooning out of her mouth, just the way Mamma would say it, "I am afraid, Tom, we are a trifle intoxicated, aren't we? Don't you think it would be advisable for us to continue our chat on a more propitious occasion?"

"Stop that! Don't be snotty with me! I've had a rotten time. All those bastards fighting me! But I'll get my rights. I'll get what I want, everything I've been dreaming of for months and months. I'll best them!"

"Sssh! Tom!"

His voice had risen. Two men at the near counter were looking over at them. He clutched her hand more tightly.

"Bloody Italians, they'd sell their souls to best you. But not me! Not me, thinking of you, Barbara! To Dublin, tonight! I have the 'P' tickets. First-class. Once we get to Dublin and get a nice little house . . ."

She dragged her hand away, she half rose, he grabbed at her and knocked over his glass so that it spilled over the table, and his knees, and broke on the floor. She looked around for help. More people were looking at them now. A barman in a white apron was approaching.

"I must telephone," she said.

She slipped into the booth and dialed the first letters of Rucellai's lodgings, and stopped. He wouldn't be in. And if she told him he would never trust her again. Through the misty glass she saw him feebly wiping the table, with his hands, and mopping his knees, and the barman upbraiding him. She dialed the complete number. A foreign woman's voice replied, "No, Signor Rucellai is gone out." She came back to the table and sat down helplessly.

"He isn't in."

"Who?"

"I was trying to get Rucellai."

He all but shouted the name: "Rucellai?"

"I thought he might help."

"Help who?"

"You, me, all of us."

He was really shouting now, "Why should you call that bloody skirt-chaser? What's he got to do with it? Is he butting in on me again? If that bastard butts in on me again . . ."

"Don't you dare talk about Rucellai like that."

"Why the hell shouldn't I talk about him like that?"

"Rucellai is a gentleman."

"Oh? So Mr. Bloody Rucellai is a frigging gentleman? How long have you known Mr. Bloody Gentleman Rucellai?"

"It's none of your damn business!"

(I'm arguing with a drunk. In a common pub.)

"It's very much my business. I found you first." He sobbed it. He shouted again, "If he's buttin' in again on me . . ." His gray face went white, completely white. "What's between you and him?"

Like a woman putting down a trump card, she slapped her splayed fingers on the wet table, staring at him, waiting for him. He stared at her. Then slowly he lowered his eyes, and saw the ring.

He looked up slowly and whispered it, evilly, "You cheap little bitch!"

"And you!" she cried, getting up, shaking all over. "You dirty old ram!"

He scrambled up, his chair fell, this time her glass. The barman came back and grabbed his arm. "Now then, out with you, both of you!" He struck at the barman. The whole pub was watching them, their glasses held immobile. The other barman rushed out and the two concentrated on hauling him, cursing at them, his heels dragging on the tiles, out through the cut-glass doors. One of them returned for his old suitcase and a brown-paper parcel and threw them out after him on the wet pavement.

With her palms to her cheeks she stood for a moment looking around at the indifferent crowd, and then she ran. She halted at the glass doors looking between the two barmen at the street where, through the hazy rain, he staggered from one lamplit pool to the next, dragging his suitcase. One of the barmen glanced at her, and said coldly, "Hop it!" She went out and stood with her back to the window of a closed shop and watched him move slowly toward the station. He would be all right in there. His old station. The friendly climate.

She followed him at a careful distance, hanging back under the porticos, now bustling with passengers. She watched him pass through the railings where an engine stood in a cloud of hissing steam, and pass out of sight behind it to the Irish Mail. She bought a platform ticket from the machine and went as far as the train's hither end, watching him move slowly along it, his cap falling, his paper parcel, and at last clamber into a carriage. She waited there for a long time, against the brick wall, out of the way of the travelers filing noisily into the train. She kept her eyes fixed on that one carriage until, at last, the porters slammed the last door, the guard lifted and waved his lamp, and all the lighted windows began to curve away, flickering like falling cards, out into the wet dark. Then her head sank, and she wept for him. She walked all the way down to the Strand and westward as far as Charing Cross. Her hair was a tangle, her shoes and stockings were sopping. She got a bus to Oxford Circus and walked home. When she got into the little flat she leaned her back against the door, and it seemed as if it was only then that she let out that pent-up breath of terror. She felt safe, cruel and bitchy, and filled with a deep longing for love.

She was still trembling as she lit the fire and drew a hot bath. She put her Femme Fatale oil in the bath. In her old blue dressing gown, that she had had ever since she left Dublin, tied about her neck, she made coffee and sandwiches and squatted with them before the fire. Under her dressing gown she wore nothing at all. Full of guilt she heard her mamma's voice, "London, my dear Babs, I warn you, is no place for little girls." Resolutely she shook her head. "I am not a little girl!" Feeling the warmth of the fire and the food steal over her she began to paint her toenails; made up her lips with a pale lipstick; tried on a pair of coral earrings that Rucellai had given her, turning her head now to the right, now to the left, straightening her Rosetti neck, holding back her Botticelli shoulders.

Maybe all he had meant was that she should cross with him to Dublin to ease the way for him? As he had done for her? But how long did he think . . . ? He must be crazy to think . . . The rain glistened in the streetlights on the window. She looked at her watch where she had laid it on the mantelpiece. He would have a bad crossing. She put on the Cimarosa record and squatted again before the fire, and with the little gold scent-spray that Rucellai had given her she lightly dewed her hair, her shoulders and above her knees, which, Lorna Alleyn had said with an unlikable covert smile, was the way you should do it. The wind sweeping down Wigmore Street rattled the windows. She saw the old *Hibernia,* all its lights ringed with mist, waiting at its moorings in Holyhead Harbour. She put on her Italian slippers and curled up in the armchair to do her fingernails. An hour later she was awakened by his insistent rapping on her door.

His black raincoat was shining, his black umbrella trickled, his black homburg hat dripped on the mat. He looked big, grave, and — his pet word whenever he felt melancholy — *tristuzzo.* She took his things and as she was stacking the umbrella upright in the kitchen sink, with his hat on top of it, she called out, "Rucellai! I hope you aren't cross with me? I came back early specially for you."

He was standing with one hand on the mantelpiece, one leg, held to the fire, already steaming, staring into the fire.

"Oh, my poor Rucellai! Your shoes are wet. Let me take them off. Sit down, darling." As she untied them she said again, "You're not cross with me? You don't think I am a naughty girl? Did you have a lovely night? You are sure you are not cross with me?"

"I did not think of you at all," he said somberly to the fire.

"Your socks are damp too! Let me take them off."

She got a cushion and laid it near the fire, and laid a towel on it and tenderly laid each bare foot on the towel near the heat. She sat back on her hunkers and stroked his instep.

"I felt quite lonely," she said to him as he looked down at her, looking up at him.

"I have never seen you look so beautiful, and so innocent."

She laughed, "You said that last night."

"But you don't know how beautiful, and how good you are!"

"Let me make you some coffee."

"Play me some music. It will calm my soul."

She put on a Lully ballet suite that he often asked for and sat with her arm across his thigh looking at the fire.

"Nymphs and shepherdesses," he murmured and stroked her hair. "Enchantress. Wafted on a seashell as a gift from the spring."

"You said that last night, too."

He clasped her to his side.

"Barbara! Promise me you will always be my little Barbara. Promise me you will never change. Say it!"

"I will always be me. And you, Rucellai? Promise you will never change."

"I shall never change!"

She felt his fingers gently undo the silk knot of her dressing gown for his usual ritual kiss. Drawing back her head to see better, she waited for the look in his eyes. The dressing gown fell to her knees. She saw his eyes widen and then close with what, afterwards, she could only think was despair. Three wild and rushing minutes later, during which he dragged on his socks and shoes, and ran for his coat, hat and umbrella, she found herself staring, defeated, bewildered and ashamed, into the fire.

He was not at the Gallery the next day, nor the next after. On the third day she rang his lodgings and was told that he had left. On the fourth day she went to his office in the Gallery where she found a strange young man. "I was looking for Mr. Rucellai," she said, wild-eyed.

"He has gone to Italy, I believe. Perhaps," he said, smiling agreeably, "I can be of service?" She said, "Oh!" and, not taking in his question, she added, "thank you." He said, "Not at all. Do come again." She went away. Two days later she found a letter from him in her letterbox. The postmark said Torino.

Dear beautiful, good, sweet, innocent, lovely Barbara,
  I have fled from you because I am unworthy of you. I have betrayed you too often in the grossest ways. I am torn asunder by the hounds of Artemis for gazing at her beauty. My Hercules has been too strong for me. (Pollaiuolo. Formerly in the Uffizi Gallery, Florence.) Do not try to seek me out. I am a monster. The flat is all yours. The rent is paid to December 31st. I shall never live in Wigmore Street. I shall never have an MG. I shall never see your loveliness again.
                                          Your despairing,
                                                Rucellai

Proscritto. Corrupt as I may be your innocence has corrupted me more than ever before. As the great Lord Acton said — All innocence corrupts, but absolute innocence corrupts absolutely. You are like Eve. You will strew ruin everywhere you go.

Over and over she said aloud, "It is extraordinary!" For days she kept saying it. Sometimes she said, "It is really and truly extraordinary." Once she found herself saying it standing in Trafalgar Square, and said to herself, "I must stop it, I'm talking like old Aunt Edie!" An hour later she found herself holding a postcard out to a customer, her eyes on the window, thinking that it was really and truly the most extraordinary thing that had ever happened to her in her whole life. Only the customer saying with a smile, "Please, may I have my card?" brought her back to where she was.

In the end she had to talk to somebody about it all, so she confided one day in Lorna Alleyn at the bookstall. She even showed her Rucellai's letter. Lorna, a dark, goat-toothed wench of whom it would be kind to say that she was largely endowed in every way, and frank to say that she was fat, read the letter in wide-eyed glee. When she had read it she hooted with wicked laughter.

"Oh, Gosh! 'Dear, beautiful, good, sweet, innocent . . .' That's a tall order! To be beautiful is good, Babs. To be good is, I suppose, good too. But to be beautiful and good? Fatal! You will always attract the wrong kind of man." Then her black eyes narrowed and she said angrily, "You kept all this to yourself very cleverly! You never uttered a word about Rucellai. You *are* a minx. And a silly, bloody little fool. I could have told you!"

"I did not want to hear!" she said proudly. "In love the beloved has no faults."

Lorna lifted dismayed paws.

"Beautiful. Good. Innocent."

"But," Barbara wailed, coming at last to the point, "I am just like any other girl."

"Of that, my dear, I have no least doubt, only you don't look it!"

"Then, what's wrong with me?"

Lorna went back to her postcards, banging and boxing them from Antonio da Messina to Zurbaran.

"Men!" she said, furiously; then, she added with a sour laugh, "And women!"

Passion

DEAREST LOVE. When will we meet again? It is only a few hours since I left you, and I am already full of melancholy thoughts.

Why on earth did I think tonight, after I had left you, of Conny Hourigan, and of that soft, wet night when the lights of Cork down in the valley were weeping through the haze, and everything as still as before dawn; and not a sound but the jolt of an old tram over the worn points, or the drip of the rain on the old tin shed in the backyard?

I think it was because I went to my window and saw the faraway lights of Dublin, and at once I was again listening to that silence of twenty years ago drumming in my ears. I was waiting for my aunt to play the next card, and looking across the cozy eye of the fire in the kitchen range at Conny breathing contentedly over his evening paper and stroking his Moses beard.

He suddenly lifts his eyes to look over his spectacles at the tiny window, and he says — "Them bastards of slugs will be out in their marching orders tonight." And he is just about to heave himself up and go out to his beloved patch of a garden to kill some of them when we hear a rat-a-tat-tat at the hall door. With a look over his glasses at my auntie, and a look at the clock, and a "Who on earth can that be?" he goes shuffling out along the little hall. My aunt suspends her card.

We turn our heads when we hear the voices rising sharply and
Conny shouting, "No!" And again, "I tell you, no!"— and
then more loud voices and the slam of the door.

He came back, flushed; gave a hitch to his belly, sat down,
growled, "Bloody cheek!" and tried to resume his reading.

"Who's that, Conny?" said the auntie, still holding up her
card.

"Three buckos from Blarney Lane. Asking me to give 'um
me six Easter lilies."

"Oh, law! And why so?"

"Some kid that's dead up in Barrett's Buildings. Name of
Delurey. Molly Delurey. Died up in the Fever Hospital. The
best I ever heard. God Almighty! Asking me to cut me six
Easter lilies for some wan I never heard of in me life before.
Did you ever hear the beat of that?"

His sister, of course, wanted to know all about it. Cork
may call itself a city, but it is really a big town made up of a
lot of little villages, and in each "village" everybody wants to
know everything about everybody else.

"Delurey?" she says. "I don't know any wan now of that
name. To be sure, we had a little apple woman used to come
here . . . Ah, but she was a Minny Delaney. And how did
they come to know that you have the lilies?"

"You may ask. Your brave milkman. Spotted 'um every
morning coming in with the milk. I knew that fellow had his
eye on me garden. I always said that fellow's too sweet to be
wholesome. 'Oh, Mister Hourigan, haven't you the grand geraniums! Oh, isn't the verbena massive, Mister Hourigan!'
Making a big man out of himself. 'Flowers? I'll get ye the
flowers. Go up to Mister Hourigan and tell him I sent you.
Ask him for his lilies.' The cheek of him! The cool, bloody
pig's cheek of him!"

My auntie played her card without looking at it. She forgot to take her trick. I suppose she was seeing the little deal
coffin, or the child laid out on the bed in the back bedroom.

The rain played its harp strings in the yard. The fire purred.

"What they usually do," she ventured, "is to make up a collection to buy the flowers."

"That's what I said to 'um."— Over his spectacles. "They wanted to blind me that there's none in the shops. I don't believe wan word of it. And if there isn't," his voice kept rising and rising, "why did they come up to *me* for *my* poor little flowers? How fair they wouldn't go down to Bolster has a glasshouse full of 'um? Oh, no! Up to the foola! Me poor little six Easter lilies that I reared, that I looked after as if they were me own children, that I . . . But these buckos have no consideration. 'Go up to Mister Hourigan and tell him I sent you.' The . . . But what . . . Me poor little lilies. Who ever . . . God Almighty, I . . ."

He choked off into incoherence.

I said, "Your trick, auntie?"

She gently swept the cards aside with her hand and breathed rather than whispered, "The poor child."

Down with his paper, off with his specs.

"That's all very fine, woman, but am I going to give me six Easter lilies because . . . And aren't they me own property? Or aren't they? Amn't I entitled to do what I like with 'um? Or amn't I? And if I don't want to give 'um to 'um what right have them cafflers to be coming up to me own hall door giving me lip?"

"Conny, I hope you didn't have *words*."

"And am I going to let a pack of Blarney Lane cafflers tell me up to me puss that there won't be luck nor grace about the house if I don't give me flowers to 'um?"

"Conny! Conny! Conny! You refused the dead."

He dashed down the paper and tore out of the kitchen. We heard the front door opening. I could imagine the dark and the haze and the smudgy lights down in the valley. He shuffled into the bedroom and struck a match. That was for the candle. I saw how the lilies outside the window would be pale against the smudgy lights of the city.

The wind wailed down from the convent grounds behind the backyard. My auntie was slowly putting the cards back into the old cigar box. The candle clattered against the basin and ewer and then he came shuffling in along the linoleum of the hall. He blew out the candle, took up his paper firmly, and began to read it. The aunt closed the cigar box and folded her arms about her and turning to the fire was lost in the little fluttering puffs coming out of the coal.

"The loveliest funeral I ever seen was the time of Lord Mayor MacSwiney. All the bands of the city. And the pipers. And the boys marching. And the Dead marching Saul. And the flag on the coffin. And all the flowers. And people in every window crying down salt tears." Conversationally she inquired of him: "Isn't Packey Cassidy buried up there with the Lord Mayor?"

"How do I know where he's buried?"

"Sure aren't they all together up in the one plot?"

"I dunno who you're talking about, let me read me paper, woman."

"Yerrah is it pretending you don't know Packey Cassidy from the Glen worked with you down in the gas house? Oh then many the night he brought you home when you had a sup taken. Didn't the two of us stand outside there in the garden and the pipers playing him up the Western Road to the cemetery?"

Conny pretended to read. The wind brought us the soft tolling of the nuns' bell. Conny looked over his specs again at the window and gave a poke to the cozy fire.

"That's a nor'wester. There'll be a flood in the river tomorrow."

"Ah, God look down on us. 'Tis no harm to say it — once we're dead we're soon forgotten."

"You'd betther be beatin' your way home, boy, the last tram is gone."

I hated to leave the warm kitchen. Somehow this talk of processions and bands and floods in the river and the nuns' bell and the squeaks of the last tram had wrapped me into a cozy nest of Time and Memory, and I remembered with pleasure how somebody had said that "All Cork is out of the wan eggshell," and I understood for the first time what that meant. I wanted desperately that Conny should give the lilies to the dead child, and I felt bitter of him that he wouldn't do it. Timidly I said, "Wouldn't you give her three of them, Uncle Conny?" He roared at me, "No, nor wan nor half a wan." The aunt's face got pale and venomous and miserable and she stabbed at him:

"No, nor I don't think you'd give them to meself if it was a thing that I was stretched in the next room!"

After a moment he said, quietly: "Go home, boy."

As I left his patch of a garden — it was about as big as a table — I saw the six lovely lilies, calm as sleep, by the pale light of the hall. The child's face would be just as pale. Down in its hollow the little city seemed to have locked every door and window against the storm and the rain. There were few lights.

That was twenty years ago. Why did that wet night flash on me when I walked into my bedroom tonight and saw the land under the full moon?

The sky is bleached, the fields are white, the lights of Dublin are bright as youth. They drained me so that I had to lean on the windowsill and let it all pour over me as if I were a stone under a river. It was like hearing an old, old tune on a brass band; or the sound of church bells on a wet Sunday morning; or the hoot of a ship's siren on Christmas Day. Frightening shadows under everything — under the gooseberry bushes, under the cabbages, under an old ash can. And nothing between those shadows and that high moon but those lights of the city, low down, and poised over them, one long narrow cloud stretched from east to west like a scythe about to sweep the sky. It is the sort of night that might make a man ache for love, but I was suffused with you, dear heart, and should have been full of joy and content. I ached not for love but because of it.

That night, so long ago, was very different to this serene moon. All through that stormy night the drums of the rain beat on the roofs of the city. In the morning the river was in flood. Rafts of branches and wrack and reeds torn up by the storm sailed on the muddy water through the city. And Conny's lovely white lilies were battered into the mud. When he saw them he just went back to bed and he stayed there for three days. The aunt didn't say one word to him. But outside his window he could hear everybody who came into the little garden — including the milkman — loud in commiseration. After that I no longer envied him his hobby, as I once used to. I began vaguely to understand that his garden was a sort of torment to him.

Or is it, dearest one, that all passion is an unhappiness? Are we always looking forward to our joy, or thinking back on it, or so drunk with it that we cannot realize it?

The night is nearly finished. The moon is going down. The lights of Dublin are still bright. The shadows are long and pale. You are asleep, with your dear black hair spread on your pillow. Your body is as pale as a lily. Do I hear a wind creeping up from the northwest?

Dear Love, when will we meet again? Let it be soon, Dear Love. Let it be soon!